Loren Piper Strikes Again

BY JENNY FYFE

Published by Jennifer Fyfe

www.jennyhickman.com

Loren Piper Strikes Again / Jenny Hickman - 1st ed.

eBook ISBN: 9781962278270

Paperback ISBN: 9781962278232

Cover Design by: Lils @lilitherie__

AUTHOR'S NOTE

This book briefly touches on the topic of pregnancy loss (mentioned). I have done my best to handle this element sensitively, but if this issue could be considered triggering for you, please take note.

CHAPTER 1
LOREN

EVERYONE HAS HEARD THE SAYING: *Love conquers all.*

Well, that's a load of bull if you ask me.

I'd love to know why the folks who came up with it didn't write more helpful proverbs. Something like: "Don't fall for someone at a funeral."

I know what you're thinking: *But Loren. That's obvious. Funeral homes aren't for falling in love; they're for mourning and grief and death.*

Normally, I would agree with you. However, when you spend ninety-five percent of your free time stuck in the funeral home your parents own, you don't have a lot of spare hours to troll the bars or dating apps or wherever the rest of the world's twenty-somethings meet other twenty-somethings. Or thirty-somethings.

Or forty-somethings if they're hot.

But let's get back to the falling in love part.

Here I am, offering tissues to a bunch of related strangers mourning the crochety old woman who lived right next to us for as long as I can remember. Guess what I don't remember? Any of these people coming by to help mow her lawn or bring her meals when she couldn't leave the house anymore.

Makes me wonder how genuine these tears really are.

I actually knew Hazel VanMeter and, I'm sorry for saying this considering she's stretched out in a pine box at the front of the room, but she was awful.

When I was twelve, she called the police because I accidentally left the back tire of my bike on her lawn. As I got older, she constantly ratted me out for sneaking out after curfew. I'm still not sure how she knew because I was pretty damn stealthy slipping from my bedroom window and down the drainpipe.

Most recently, she told my parents I was smoking in the shrubs at the back of our house.

That one, I can honestly say wasn't true. I haven't smoked a cigarette a day in my life except that one time back in college when my friend Erin and I were drinking out the back of a frat house and I thought I'd try it.

Disgusting, by the way. Would not recommend.

The fact that I'm a twenty-five-year-old woman and can make my own choices didn't stop my mother from texting me picture after picture of grayish-brown lungs that became riddled with disease after their owners had fallen victim to their vices.

Needless to say, I'm not shedding a tear for poor old Hazel VanMeter.

These tear-free eyes have a decent view of the whole funeral home as those who've gathered "celebrate" the life of the Wicked Witch of Westmorland Street. They all bow their heads for *Amazing Grace* performed by my mother on the organ in the far corner next to two arrangements overflowing with lilies and baby's breath—the world's worst flower name, in my opinion.

How did someone come up with it, anyway? *Baby's breath.*

Makes me think of blended peas and sour milk.

As I'm scanning the crowd, my gaze snags on a guy toward the back. Taller than the older blonde woman and the silver-haired man next to him, he doesn't seem that put out by the loss of my old neighbor. His head isn't even bowed.

This should probably be some sort of red flag.

He could be a psychopath who feels no emotions.

Then again, maybe Hazel called the cops on him when he was twelve too.

Although that would mean he would've had to stop by her house at some point, and I have never seen this guy in my life.

That square jaw and those shoulders are two things I would definitely remember. Thirteen-year-old Loren would've tried sculpting his features out of clay during her artist phase. Fifteen-year-old Loren would've found out his full name and deep-dived his social media profiles so she could learn everything there was to know about him and then drop hints about all the things we "have in common" during a completely "impromptu" run-in at his favorite place to hang out.

Yeah, teenage Loren was weirdly obsessive.

I blame it on this one-stoplight town where nothing interesting ever happens.

Thankfully, quarter-of-a-century Loren is much, much smoother.

I'll casually sidle up to him after the committal and say something witty and charming that will endear him to me. In no time at all, we'll be walking down the aisle hand-in-hand, me in an ivory gown and him in a sexy black tux.

Call me an optimist, but this feels like fate finally coming through for me after Sean Malloy and I broke up.

Who is Sean Malloy, you ask?

The other undertaker here.

Tall. Dark. Pale as a vampire.

A product of my Paranormal Romance phase.

Everyone says not to date a colleague, but for a hot minute I thought, why not? Might as well find someone interested in taking over the family business because I sure as heck don't want to.

Sean was *fine*.

But I'm not looking for fine. I want fizzy tingles and flapping butterflies and shortness of breath.

Enter: The tall mourner with a great head of thick, golden hair.

If the older man next to him is any relation, this one might even get to keep all that hair when he gets older.

Unlike poor Sean who has aged at least ten years since our breakup.

My ex smiles at me from where he stands next to my father, the light above them reflecting off what's left of Sean's dark hair, their hands clasped in front of them like they're ready for caskets of their own.

I love my father, but I do *not* want to end up with someone exactly like him.

Tried it. Hated it. Not for me.

The service ends, and the family and friends shuffle out, waiting for the pallbearers to carry the casket to the hearse. Guess who gets to drive that sex machine?

This girl.

Did I mention how much I hate my job?

Thankfully, the graveyard isn't far away, and once Hazel VanMeter is in the ground where she can't haunt me anymore, everyone is free to head back to the church for a dinner catered by the local diner where Hazel had a corner table reserved in her honor.

I use the term "reserved" in the loosest sense of the word. Basically, everyone was too scared to sit there in case she came in and ripped them a new one.

The crisp autumn air rattles the browning leaves still clinging to the branches as I lean against the hearse and wait for everyone to pile into their cars so I can maneuver this gigantic black metal cockroach out of here.

"Hey."

I turn toward the deep voice and *holy hell*, the golden god with shoulders of stone has found me.

Is this real life?

"Hey." Not exactly the smoothest start to a meet cute. Good thing there's nowhere to go from here but up.

I can see my own reflection in his aviator sunglasses, and while my hair is on point, my smile looks tight as hell.

Oh no...

Words are starting to bubble from my throat and—

"How do you know the Wicked—I mean, the deceased?"

Tell me I didn't nearly call this man's poor relative the

Wicked Witch of Westmorland Street! Those are inside thoughts, Loren.

The bridal march playing in my mind has morphed into the out-of-tune chorus of *Amazing Grace* because this is now my funeral.

He mustn't have caught my slip, because his lips tug into a smile. "Hazel was my great aunt, but I didn't know her very well. She and my grandmother didn't exactly get along."

That voice. Think Clooney crossed with Damon.

Perfect. Just perfect.

If he can look past my terrible introduction, we're destined to be together. I just know it.

Okay, maybe I don't know. But a girl can hope, right?

He pushes his sunglasses onto his forehead, revealing a pair of deep-brown, puppy-dog eyes that look a little sad. Like a young Richard Gere or John Cusack. You know the eyes I'm talking about. When they meet mine, my stomach doesn't just drop. It completely bottoms out.

When he holds out his hand and says, "My name is Josh," my knees go weak.

"Loren. Loren Piper. Of Piper Funeral Homes." Why did my mouth think it was necessary to add anything after Loren?

"Nice to meet you. Are you going to the dinner after this?"

"Oh, yes. We're a full-service funeral home. Taking care of everything from start to finish."

Thank goodness the beautiful man takes pity on me and chuckles.

Flashing me another perfect smile, he slides his glasses back into place. "I'll see you there, Loren Piper of Piper Funeral Homes."

The golden god blessing our tiny town with his presence is named Josh Bosnick.

I learned his last name over a plate of crispy fried chicken and green bean casserole in the church social hall. For reasons I cannot fathom, Josh stayed by my side the entire dinner, and then asked me out to dinner the next night.

Dinner led to a movie which led to the most glorious goodnight kiss a girl could have ever asked for which led to coffee the next morning and lunch after he finished helping his father prepare old Hazel's home for an estate sale.

He's charming and smart and handsome and everything I've ever wanted in a partner. The only downside is that he happens to live in Nashville.

That's right.

Nashville Tenne-freaking-see. A short ten-hour commute from where we currently stand on his great aunt's front porch.

Now there's nothing to do but say our goodbyes.

It's funny how someone you barely know can become so important in such a short amount of time. The thought of him leaving brings tears to my eyes.

Surely that has to mean something, considering Sean and I dated for almost two years, and when we broke up my eyes were as dry as the grass on a sunny July afternoon.

Josh hugs me tight and presses the sweetest of kisses to my lips, saying, "I wish we had more time."

It's like the end of one of those terrible movies I watched as a kid that you thought was a romance but ends up being a depressing drama. My heart feels like it's being shattered into a billion pieces by one of those comically large sledgehammers at the county fair.

I kiss Josh one last time and wave goodbye as I watch him drive away.

My mother calls from our porch, telling me someone needs to collect the lilies from the florist for tomorrow's funeral.

Is this how I want my life to play out? An endless wheel of death and sickeningly sweet flowers and hearses?

Hell no.

When you find love, you chase after it, no questions asked.

If you don't, you'll be living in a perpetual third act break up instead of finding the happily-ever-after you deserve. At least that's what all those classic nineties romcoms have taught me.

And I'm desperate for a HEA of my own.

I race over to my house, telling my mother as I pass that there's somewhere else I want to be (hint: it rhymes with Crashville Spennessee).

As I stuff all my worldly possessions into suitcases, my dad threatens to disown me, reminding me that, as their only child, it's my responsibility to take over the funeral home that has been in our family for three generations. They spend the rest of the night trying to talk me out of leaving.

When I wake up the next morning to get an early start, my mom cries on the stoop, sobbing loudly enough for the neighbor we have left to hear.

But I'm following what could be true love.

And when you follow your heart, nothing can go wrong.

CHAPTER 2
LOREN

MOM

You're making a terrible mistake.

Come back home.

EVERYTHING IS GOING WRONG.

Not only did my poor car break down on the side of the highway an hour outside Nashville, it's going to cost an arm and a leg—and probably a lung or two—to fix the freaking thing. I thought my day couldn't get worse, but every time I try to get ahold of Josh, the call goes straight to voicemail.

This is where impulsiveness gets you. Leaking sweat on a curb outside a Waffle House, questioning your life choices and being dive-bombed by gnats.

I know what you're thinking: Things can't get worse. This is as bad as it gets. Rock bottom. Nowhere to go but up.

You're wrong.

My heartbroken mother keeps leaving tearful voice notes filled with all her bitter disappointments.

I can't take much more of her wailing, begging me to come back home "where I belong."

I may have told myself that this move was for a guy I barely know, but spontaneously relocating to "Music City" was for me too. I have lived in the same town since I turned four. Went to high school there and attended community college thirty minutes away while still living with my parents to save money. After that, I went straight into full-time employment at Piper's Funeral Home.

Even I'm putting myself to sleep thinking about my life.

I was a twenty-five-year-old woman facing a future of dead bodies and grieving relatives.

Don't get me wrong, the world needs people to run funeral homes. Helping folks say goodbye to their loved ones is an important role in society. I'm not knocking the job, but it's not for me.

That's part of the reason I got a degree in marketing. Not to work for my parents, but to work somewhere else. *Anywhere* else.

I got this degree to do more with my life.

To prove to my parents and to myself that I can make it on my own.

Instead, I'm going to melt into a puddle on this curb.

It's almost November. Doesn't Tennessee recognize autumn as a season?

When I press the button on the side of my phone, the little battery icon in the top right-hand corner flashes an alarming shade of red.

This is what I get for forgetting to grab my charger before the tow truck took my car.

My phone rings, and I nearly burst into tears when

Josh's smiling face flashes on the screen. I took that picture of him in his sunglasses the day before he left.

Man, he's good-looking.

I answer the call with a smile of my own. Even rock bottom looks brighter when there's someone wonderful in your life. "Boy, am I glad to hear from you."

Josh's deep laugh rumbles through the speaker, warming me all over like gooey toffee. "Hey, girl. I didn't expect your call until tonight. How are you?"

"Great." I'd be better if this damn fly buzzing around my head would find someone else to annoy. I swat at the thing, but it keeps on coming. "So, fun fact: I'm almost to Nashville."

"You're kidding! Where are you staying? If you don't have any plans tonight, we should grab dinner. There's a great place that just opened in the Gulch that I've been dying to try."

"I'd really love that." So, *so* much. "The thing is, I don't have a place to stay yet. I'm sorta winging it."

"How about I get you a room at the Hilton? It's right downtown and our company has an account with them, so we get a discount."

That sounds a bit out of my price range, and letting the man who may one day be the father of my children know I'm not exactly flush with cash feels more like a one-month-anniversary conversation. "That's sweet of you, but I was actually thinking of staying for a while so a hotel may not cut it." I tug on the white fringes along the hem of my jean shorts, which are unravelling one frayed thread at a time.

What keeps them from falling apart completely?

"No way. How long are you going to be in town?"

"I don't know. A year? Maybe two?" Or forever and

always depending on how things go with my potential soulmate.

There's a pause.

The longer it lasts, the more I start to freak out and wonder if this really was all a colossal mistake.

As if on cue, my phone buzzes with another message from my mom. "I told you so" is going to be the only thing she says to me for the rest of my life.

Remember when you drove ten hours just to turn right back around with your tail between your legs?

What have I done?

"Wait. You're moving down here?" Josh finally says.

Is that excitement or horror in his voice? I really hope it's the first one, otherwise I completely misunderstood the "I wish you lived closer" comment from dinner the night before he left. "Yep. That's the plan."

"That's fantastic, babe."

The tension in my chest uncoils, and a shaky breath blows through my lips, knocking my gnat enemies off course. "You're not freaked out or anything?"

"Why would I freak out? We need to go out and celebrate. Let me know where you are and I'll come pick you up."

"I'm currently stranded at Waffle House."

"Shit. Are you okay?"

"Yeah, but my car isn't."

"Send me the address, and I'll be there as soon as I can."

———

A white Range Rover rolls up parallel to the curb, and the tinted window slides down, revealing a handsome face smiling from inside the cab. "Hey, girl. Need a lift?"

"Josh!" I scramble to my feet, knocking over my purse in the process, which of course means the clean underwear and toothbrush I threw in before the tow truck drove away with my car and my bags tumble out onto the sidewalk.

I'm not so worried about the underwear. All going well, Josh is going to see them at some point anyway. My toothbrush landing bristles down? That's a different story.

I scoop them up and throw them back into my purse, then scramble over to the driver's side to awkwardly hug his neck through the window.

He smells like expensive cologne and leather. Actually, the leather is probably coming from the car seats.

It's so crazy how a dire situation can turn around when the right person shows up to rescue you. "You don't know how happy I am to see you."

"Same here." His lips graze mine. "I've missed you every second since I left."

It's a relief to hear. I'd be mortified if this thing between us was only one-sided.

"Now get in and tell me everything."

He doesn't have to tell me twice. I trade the heat for the cool confines of his luxury SUV. I never understood why they called them that until the leather envelops me in its buttery embrace.

He shifts into drive and away we go, the Waffle House slowly vanishing in the rearview, my new life spreading before me like the open road. And would you look at that? His charger works on my phone.

Things are finally looking up.

"So you you're really moving here? What prompted this?"

"I wasn't happy back home." Existing isn't living. "I think it took meeting you to finally do something about it." I shudder to think how long I would've stayed stuck if we hadn't bumped into each other.

He reaches across the center console to give my fingers a squeeze. "Glad to be of service. What's your plan now?"

"Find a place to rent and a job. Any suggestions?"

His lips purse as he stares out at the road, weaving between cars as traffic starts to pick up. "I think all the apartments in my building are full, but I can always check around to see if there's a place close to downtown that would work for you. On the job front, I have a few buddies who might be looking for staff. What's your degree in again?"

"Marketing."

"That's right. It's too bad I didn't meet you a few months ago when our firm was looking for a secretary."

Oh, a secretary. I imagine that wouldn't be so different from what I was doing back home. The scheduling and organizing part, not the hearse driving.

Working with Josh would've been amazing.

Maybe the person they hired won't work out.

Wouldn't that be fate?

He flicks his blinker and zips around the car in front of us. Man, this car has some power. "You could always try headhunters."

Yeah, I don't know what that is.

"A recruiting agency," he clarifies. "A lot of companies use them to find their employees. That's where we got Naomi."

I've always liked the name Naomi. It's fun to say. Naomi. Nay-ohh-meee. "Naomi is...?"

"Sorry. Our new secretary."

Recruiting agency, huh? Sounds like a great idea. "I'll check them out. Thanks."

His smile lights up his whole face. "What would you like for dinner? Sushi or flatbread?"

Good question. Considering how hungry I am, both sound amazing. Literally, I would eat both. However, I did just sit on my ass all day, so bingeing probably isn't the best idea for my stomach. "I had a lot of beige carbs on the way here, so let's go with sushi."

"Perfect." He brings our clasped hands together, pressing a kiss to my knuckles and making me melt a little bit more. "Just like you."

Gah! Could he be any sweeter? "You're sure it's okay that I'm here? You're not secretly freaking out? Because it'd be totally understandable if you were." If our roles were reversed, I'd be jumping up and down with excitement, but that's me.

This is Josh. Fancy lawyer from a city who wears sexy three-piece suits. He probably has women fawning over him wherever he goes.

"Not freaking out. More like...taken aback? I can't believe you'd abandon your whole life just for me."

Honesty. This is good. Healthy. Just because his confession floods my stomach with dread doesn't mean this can't turn into a good conversation. I'd hate to start a relationship based on lies.

"It's not just for you." Mostly, but not completely. He's more like the catalyst. "I think I was searching for a reason to leave without even realizing it." Almost like I was looking for permission from the universe or some higher power that it was okay to go.

To take a chance on myself.

Or on someone who could end up being the love of my life.

"Oh, thank God." Huffing a laugh, he drags a hand

down his chiseled jaw. "I really like you, Loren, but the fact is, we barely know each other. I'm looking forward to learning more about you, growing closer, but..." He blows out a breath. "If you came here just for me. That's a lot of pressure. I think we should take things slow. See where we end up."

"I totally get it. This is a zero-pressure situation. Just two people who like each other, hanging out." Spending every waking moment together. Falling desperately in love. Getting married and having babies.

No, Loren! Don't think about how cute your babies would be.

That's not slow. That's fast.

Don't be a waterfall. Be a lazy river. Drift along, float where the water takes you.

"Two people who like each other a lot," Josh says.

Some of the tension in my body eases. "Exactly." We do like each other a lot. Someone who wasn't as chill as me might even say we could be soulmates.

Only time will tell.

For now, I'm just happy to be here.

CHAPTER 3
LOREN

ONE EXPENSIVE SUSHI dinner followed by a night in a cheap motel later, my life is looking a little bit brighter. Not only is my car fixed, but also after Josh left last night, I found a place to call home.

Turns out, I can't afford to live anywhere near Nashville. The closest I can get to the city is a suburb called Mt. Juliette. Sounds pretty, right? It is. There's a lake and a ton of craftsman-style homes lining every street.

Did I find one to rent?

Not even close.

What I did find was a studio apartment that may or may

not have been a closet at one point. If I spread my arms wide, I can almost touch the opposite walls at the same time.

But hey, at least there's a balcony and a random door that's locked and painted shut. Not creepy *at all*.

The real bonus is I don't have to worry about a burglar hiding in here—something my mom has warned me about multiple times since I left.

There's nowhere for him to hide.

My kitchen consists of three lower and three upper cabinets, a two-burner stove, and a mini fridge like you'd find in a motel.

Another upside? The place comes "fully furnished." Meaning there's a single bed complete with suspicious brown stains and a table with two mismatched chairs shoved into the corner. There's no couch, which works because there's no living room. However, there *is* a fat TV sitting on top of a chest of drawers that reminds me of the one at my grandma's house. Is this one black and white too?

The bathroom isn't much better. At first, I thought the grout between the puke-green subway tiles was black. Then I realized it was mold. There's more in the corners and around the exhaust fan that sounds like a revving chainsaw.

Other than that, the place is great. Nothing a little bleach can't fix.

Or a lot of bleach.

Add that to the list of things I need from the store.

The best part is, it's only four hundred a month, and I budgeted five hundred for living expenses. Unfortunately, I forgot to include the security deposit in there, so I'm down an additional four hundred, plus the two hundred from last night's hotel, a hundred and fifty for gas, and the thousand it took to fix my car.

But my car is back in action, utilities are included, and tomorrow, I'm going to find a job.

It's all a little bit backwards but everything is going to work out. If push comes to shove, I can always waitress to earn a bit of cash while waiting for something more permanent.

What matters is, I've done it. All. By. Myself.

Which is why I pick up my phone and dial my mom's number.

She answers on the second ring. "Tell me you've come to your senses and are on the way home."

And she wonders why I wanted to leave. Who answers the phone like that? "Even better. I found a place to rent!"

Silence.

"You still there, Mom?"

"Yes, but I'm trying to find someone to remove this knife you stabbed into my heart."

I never considered Susan Piper to be a dramatic woman; it would appear I was wrong. "Why can't you just be happy for me?" I don't add "for once" but I think it. Boy, do I think it.

"Would you prefer I lie to you?"

Kinda. Yeah.

Unfortunately, Mom prides herself on her honesty. Who doesn't want to hear that their prom gown makes them look like a twenty-dollar hooker? Or that the serving size for ice cream isn't four scoops?

Why did I call her again?

Oh, yeah. Because I was proud of myself, and I wanted her to be proud of me too.

Looks like that was too much to ask.

"Hey. I have to go. Love you. Tell Dad I say hi."

Aaaand *END*.

My phone immediately buzzes with a message, and I take great delight in tossing it onto the counter unread. I'm about to sink onto the edge of the bed when I spot that disgusting stain.

How much do mattresses cost?

There's only one way to find out.

I collect my phone and purse, then venture from the dim confines of my apartment into the bright day. Before I can lock my door, I'm nearly bowled over by a dark-haired man and a blonde woman, tangled in each other's arms. It's impossible to get a good look at their faces with the way they're fused together.

Probably not the best time to introduce myself as their new neighbor.

Once they move past, I jog down the five flights of stairs to my car.

The moment my butt meets leather, my phone rings. Josh's smile flashes on the screen and those tummy flutters start flapping around all over again. "Guess what? That place I found last night is perfect." If mint-green walls are your thing. "I can send you my location if you want."

"That's great, babe. I can't wait to see it. Listen, I hate to do this, but I'm still in the office, and it looks like I'm going to be here for quite a while. Can we go to the movies tomorrow instead?"

But...I was hoping to see him tonight.

Come on, Loren. The man has a life and a job. He can't throw everything aside because you decided to move on a whim.

"That's no problem." On the bright side, now I can unpack and get settled in.

"Great. Can't wait."

"Neither can I."

Happily-ever-after, here I come.

———

Mattresses come in boxes now. Who knew?

Not me.

Pretty convenient considering there wasn't enough room in my car for an unpacked mattress, and I would've had to wait two days for the delivery folks to drop it off.

Now all I need to do is haul this sucker up to my apartment along with the rest of my purchases and I will officially be moved in.

Just because the mattress-in-a-box is compact doesn't mean it's lighter than any other mattress. By the time I reach the top of the stairs, I'm a ball of sweat and my arms feel like they're about to fall off.

Which doesn't bode well for carrying the disgusting old mattress currently hanging out in the concrete stairwell back down to its new home in the dumpster across the parking lot.

Come on, Loren. You've got this.

If all else fails, I can always slide the thing.

The problem with that plan is that the floor isn't smooth but scratchy, like Velcro, and the mattress doesn't want to slide anywhere. The stubborn thing doesn't want to bend either, which is something I learn the hard way at the first ninety-degree turn.

Dammit. This was supposed to be the easy part. Gravity is on my side; however, the mattress is not.

It's just me and the sweat dribbling down my back versus the world's heaviest and grossest single mattress.

And I'm losing. Big time.

The damn thing has to fit; someone brought it up the stairs, after all.

Unless the architects designed the entire building around my bed, which, I'm starting to wonder...

"Hey."

I whip toward the sound, finding the guy from next door standing in his doorway, a white lollipop stick poking from between his smirking lips.

Now that his face isn't fused with someone else's, I can safely confirm that he's hot. Not that I'm interested since I'm dating the potential love of my life, but I can label him as objectively attractive.

First, we have the dark brown hair that looks freshly washed. The ends curl slightly, which isn't surprising considering the amount of humidity in the air right now.

Then we have the black T-shirt that fits way too well. The word "tailored" comes to mind.

I've always wanted a tailor, especially for pants. When you're as tall as I am, all the legs are a little too short. Going up the sizes increases the length, but then they don't fit in the hips/butt region.

I could go on but there's no point when there's a mattress to wrestle.

My neighbor glances from the mattress to me and says, "Nice shoes."

I don't even remember which shoes I'm wearing. Oh yeah, the black ones I bought during my emo phase. I shove my hair back from my sticky forehead.

Now isn't the ideal time to discuss footwear, but my mom taught me to be polite when receiving compliments. "Thanks." They're not the cutest pair I own, but they are the most comfortable.

"My grandma has the same ones."

Very funny. Lucky for him, I have a fantastic sense of humor. "Sounds like your grandmother has great taste."

The lollipop clicks against his teeth when he chuckles, which of course prompts me to say, "Nice lollipop."

"Thanks, I got it at the bank."

Yeah. Okay.

"What's that snort about?" he asks, tilting his head and making his hair fall across his forehead.

Is he saying they mistook him for a child? I'm not buying it. "And you got one how? Based on maturity?"

"Wow. You talk a lot of shit for a woman who looks like she needs help."

"You're the one who came out swinging and dissing my shoes."

Mr. Lollipop rests his shoulder against his door. "I'd hardly call 'nice shoes' a diss."

"And the grandma part?"

"The truth. Now, do you want help or not?"

I'd love to say no but we both know I'm not getting this mattress down these stairs on my own. Maybe I could launch it over the railing and let it fall. Except then it might bounce and hit one of those cars parked in front of the building. I don't have the spare money to handle being sued right now.

"That would be great. Thanks." Beats listening to him tell me his great aunt owns the same jean shorts or that his mother has the same ratty Southern High School T-shirt.

He closes his door and comes over to where I'm wrestling to free the far end of the mattress from where it's stuck to the corner of the railing. "I've heard a mix of hydrogen peroxide, baking soda, and dish soap is great at getting out piss stains."

Not sure why he felt the need to spout that random fact

at me. Wait! "Is that something you suffer from? That's why they gave you a child's lollipop, isn't it?"

He gestures toward the brownish-yellow splotches coating the entire back side of the mattress. "This is your bed, sweetheart. Not mine."

Okay, I'm an idiot. "I'll keep that in mind. Unfortunately, I've a policy against sleeping in someone else's urine." Not sure why I said "unfortunately" but there's no taking it back now.

He lifts the back side of the mattress, forcing me to catch the front or be shoved down the stairs. "But sleeping in your own is fair game?"

Walked straight into that one, didn't I? "Obviously."

Carefully, I descend the stairs. Walking backwards carrying a heavy mattress wouldn't be so bad if my fingers weren't starting to cramp. Why don't they put handles on the ends of mattresses?

My new neighbor doesn't seem to be the least bit winded by the time we reach the second floor. I, on the other hand, sound like I ran a marathon and look like I bathed in a puddle. "Can we stop for a minute?" Otherwise, I may end up passing out.

He eases the mattress against the railing once more while I stretch my back and try to quietly catch my breath.

"I hope you don't mind me asking, but what do you plan on doing with this thing when we get to the bottom?"

Sweat burns my eyes, forcing me to use the hem of my shirt as a towel. "Why? Do you want to keep it? You're more than welcome. No judgement here."

"Funny."

I thought so.

"You know you're not allowed to put it in the dumpster, right?"

Crap. I didn't know that. "Yeah, I know." I lift the mattress and wait for him to do the same with his end.

I'll just... Um... Tie it to the roof of my car? Wait. I can't do that because I don't have any rope. Haul it back to my apartment? Leave it on the balcony?

My neighbor sighs. "I have a truck. I can take it to the dump for you."

"Really? Thank you.

I help him load the mattress into the bed of his truck and it isn't until he drives away that I realize that I never asked for his name.

AUGUST

Should've told me you were going to
the dump

I have a couch to get rid of

A HOT GIRL moves in next door and what do I do?

Insult her shoes.

Did I introduce myself to make things less awkward?

Nope.

But I did tell her how to remove piss stains from a mattress.

CHAPTER 5
LOREN

MONEY ISN'T TIGHT.

It's non-existent.

All it took was a month to drain my poor account drier than the Sahara.

A few months ago I had money, but then I decided to be fiscally responsible and pay off my student loans.

Silly me.

My current woes began with the new mattress followed by the selfish desire for pots and pans with actual handles. I wasn't the biggest fan of the taste of rust either, so I bought disposable forks and spoons, but those kept breaking so I bit the bullet and got new silverware. No one tells you ahead of time how much freaking forks and spoons cost. Highway robbery, that's what it is. No wonder disgruntled servants in period novels stole the cutlery.

Don't even get me started on the ridiculous price of toilet paper. I've resorted to rationing single-ply. Sometimes I find myself sitting on the toilet, dreaming of the good old days when I didn't count unquilted squares.

Sadly, those days are no more.

My current situation is—I don't want to say *dire*, but that's the word that keeps popping into my mind. Every time I open my wallet, it's like one of those loud, creaking doors in a horror movie, only way more terrifying.

As I sit at the drive-thru counting the change in my car's cup holder so I can eat dinner tonight, I realize I might have to do the one thing I swore I wouldn't: Call Mom and ask for a loan.

This will lead to a lecture about responsibility and how I should come home and work for them again.

The one and only time I let my financial troubles slip, they promised me a raise if I came home.

The idea of having a bank account with actual money in it again and a free place to live that isn't infested with mold is almost too tempting to pass up.

My head falls forward against the steering wheel. I really don't want to give up and go back, but if life doesn't start going my way soon, I might not have a choice.

Something silver flashes between the seat and the center console.

No way.

My hope builds as I wedge my fingers into the tight gap, straining and wiggling until I manage to snag the stray coin.

Not just any coin. A whole freaking quarter!

I've never been so happy to see George Washington's powdered wig.

Now I have enough for nuggets *and* fries. The *Hallelujah Chorus* erupts like a symphony in my mind.

My luck is finally turning around.

The pickup in front of me pulls ahead, and I ease off the brake pedal. My car rolls forward to the backlit menu where an androgynous voice crackles through the tinny speaker, asking for my order. When I drive around to the first window and hand the sour-faced teen a ball of change, she looks like she wants to throw it right back.

Instead, she takes her sweet time counting every penny.

That's right. I'm desperate enough to use everyone's least favorite coin to pay for fast food.

As concerned as I am for my arteries, when you're literally pinching pennies, you can't be picky about what you put in your stomach. Meg, my only friend at work, brings healthy, elegant lunches like exotic salads and sushi while I mainline peanut butter and jelly.

The joys of being a temp.

None of the benefits of working at a multi-national advertising firm apply to me since I'm not technically their employee, but a lackey for the head-hunters who hired me. I'm lucky to have gotten my foot in the door considering my lack of "relevant" experience.

That's something I'll never understand about the world of employment. Everyone wants you to have experience, but how do you *get* experience if no one will hire you?

That will all change in six months, when my contract ends, and my boss gets to choose whether to bring me on board as a permanent employee or send me on my merry way to whatever the next opening might be.

That's why I've been busting my ass since I started three weeks ago. We're talking first to arrive and last to leave, proving myself as a valuable asset.

Hopefully, someone notices soon because I'd like to have a social life at some point.

By the time I pull into my apartment complex, my hunger is sufficiently sated. Nearly. I would've loved one of those hot apple pies, but penny-pinchers don't get pie.

I swing my legs out of the car and tug down my pencil skirt to keep from flashing my underwear at the guy leaning against a black BMW, puffing on a cigarette.

"Hey, Tony," I say with a wave.

He lifts his hand in response, dispersing the cloud of smoke floating around his head like that cartoon donkey's raincloud.

I grab my purse and click the button on my key to lock my car before heading into the main office where Tony's scarier brother Toby leans back in his black leather chair, his bushy black mustache hiding his entire upper lip.

I don't need to see his mouth to know he's frowning. Toby always frowns.

His thick fingers drum against a stack of papers riddled with coffee-mug stains as he scowls across the desk. "Ah, Ms. Piper, Apartment 5136. Your rent is late."

"Sorry. It totally slipped my mind to come by yesterday." Pretty sure he knows it's a lie, but it's not my fault the first of the month fell on a freaking Wednesday. Payday isn't till Friday, so if he tried to cash my check before that, it would've bounced like one of those rubber balls you get from grocery store vending machines.

Since the banks are now closed for the night, Toby won't be able to cash the check until tomorrow, when my account will be a little less depressing.

I withdraw my checkbook and fill out the missing information. Tearing along the perforated edge sounds a lot like my soul being ripped in two. With a few careful swipes of the pen, I'm four-hundred dollars poorer.

Toby grimaces at the check like its covered in the mold I've complained about for the last few weeks. I've tried bleach, vinegar and baking soda, and just about every bathroom cleaner I've come across, but nothing kills that stuff.

"You know, you can always do the direct debit," he says in a thick accent that's impossible to place.

Man, I'd love to pay by direct debit and avoid him altogether—except that would require actual funds. "Maybe next month."

I leave before he can say anything else, my feet aching in my heels as I dart down the sidewalk. If I don't get out of this skirt and button-down in the next five minutes, I might turn into an actual puddle.

We had two weeks of crisp autumn and then reverted to scorching summer. Even the locals say it's never this hot in December.

The air is so thick, my lungs can barely take it in. It's like soup.

Hot, wet, thick, soup.

Don't even get me started on the fact that there isn't so much as a breeze to flutter the hair plastered to my neck. By the time I make it up the stairs, there's an actual river running down my spine, and my quads are starting to wobble.

Then I catch sight of broad shoulders encased in a black T-shirt and a tapered waist disappearing into a pair of low-slung jeans and my legs just about give out.

My neighbor, mattress guy, also known as Elliott.

How do I know his name when he's never properly introduced himself?

Because I hear a different girl screaming it every other night.

Is he hotter than Hades? You bet. He also has a brunette pressed up against his door.

More often than not, this is how we meet. On the rare occasion when he doesn't have a woman with him, I try not to stare directly into his beautiful blue eyes for too long, lest I fall under his hypnotic spell.

He drags a key from his pocket, fumbling as he tries to fit it into the lock.

I really hope they make it inside before he sticks his "key" in her "lock," if you catch my drift.

He comes up for air long enough to glance down at the doorknob while she slurps at his neck so hard, he'll definitely end up with a hickey. When I see the mark, I will absolutely be making fun of him for it. It's the least I can do considering he never misses a chance to give me crap.

After the pissy-mattress incident was the mis-delivered menstrual cup. Most recently, we had the Thanksgiving debacle.

Don't ask. You don't want to know.

Those deep-sea eyes catch on me and the corner of his mouth hitches. "Loren."

I fold my arms over my chest, waiting for him to move out of the way so I can get past. "Elliot."

His last name is Grant—something I discovered via a phone bill delivered to my mailbox instead of his. If only it had been for something embarrassing like a subscription to "Grannies Quarterly" or a penis enlarger.

His keys land on the concrete floor.

Sighing, I bend down to pick them up and unlock the door for him.

He mutters his thanks, then he and his latest conquest

stumble into the dark apartment. His hand emerges to swipe the keys, and then the door slams shut.

Unfortunately, our shared wall is paper-thin, so I get a front-row seat to every loud moan and rhythmic slam of what I assume is a headboard until I find the perfect song on my phone and turn up the Bluetooth speaker in the kitchen as loud as it'll go.

CHAPTER 6
ELLIOTT

WHEN THE FIRST lines of Def Leopard's "Pour Some Sugar on Me" vibrate through my wall, I can't help my smile.

Joke's on Loren. I fucking love this song.

CHAPTER 7

LOREN

DAD

Please call your mom

5:04 PM

Is it about tornadoes?

I'd rather not say

AFTER A TERRIBLE THUNDERSTORM that kept me up half the night, there's finally a nip to the air as I make my way through my office's very full parking lot. Which begs the question: Why is it so full? I check my watch for the third time in as many minutes. It's not even eight o'clock yet. Most people rock up at nine or even nine-thirty.

The joys of working for a "progressive" company with flexible hours.

The instant coffee I made before leaving my place sloshes in my takeaway cup as I jog up the three stairs to the main entrance.

The glass door swings wide, and Meg is there, holding it open so I don't have to. "You're late."

I check the gigantic clock hanging over the desks at reception. Same as my watch. "No, I'm not."

"Gah! You didn't get the email, did you?"

Freaking IT. They promised my email was fixed. Guess I'll have to put in another ticket this morning. "No. What did it say?"

Meg loops her arm through mine, towing me into the industrial warehouse turned modern office, all exposed brick, black metal, and glass. She leans in close so no one in the graphic design department can hear her say, "Dick got fired."

His name isn't really Dick. We call him that because it describes his glowing personality better than "Reginald" ever could.

"No way. Why?"

"Don't know. No one tells me anything. What I do know is that they brought in someone from an outside firm to take his place until they can hire a new marketing supervisor."

Great. I spent the last three weeks buttering up our terrible boss only to have him get the sack.

That may sound selfish and borderline bitchy but allow me to explain.

I would be concerned for a man who is now without a job, except his wife is some higher-up in the banking world, so I figure they won't have any trouble putting food on their table tonight.

Me, on the other hand? If this new hire doesn't think the company should be shelling out for temp workers, then I'm in big trouble. Rent might be paid for this month, but it'll be due again in four weeks, and I have no husband or wife to fall back on.

Our heels meet the polished concrete stairs at the same time.

"Do we know anything about our new boss?" I ask.

Meg shakes her head, her sun-kissed blonde streaks rippling in perfect waves over her slim shoulders. Believe it or not, she wakes up like this. I've witnessed the phenomenon on more than one occasion after a few too many glasses of boxed wine.

I'd kill for her dewy complexion. Even the little freckle above her lip is sexy.

I, on the other hand, wasted an hour trying to straighten my wild curls only to step out into the damp morning air and have them defy gravity all over again.

Growing up, I used to get highlights to try and lift the drab brown color. The moment my mom decided I should be paying for my own hair treatments, those highlights stopped.

Meg's manicured nails bite into my arm when she gives me an excited squeeze. "All I know is that we're meeting in the conference room at eight to find out."

Well, that's great, isn't it? There isn't even time to throw my stuff in my cubicle. All these weeks of arriving early won't count for shit if I can't show up to meet the new manager on time.

"I hope he's hot," she whispers.

So do I.

Not that I'm interested.

Josh and I grow closer every time we're together. Still, it wouldn't be so bad to have a little eye-candy at work. No harm in looking.

Meg and I slip through another set of gleaming glass

doors and file in behind a couple of media buyers from her team.

The excited buzz dies the moment a perfectly polished Jessica Rabbit strolls into the conference room in a pinstripe pencil skirt that shows off curves that need no photoshopping.

Meg and I aren't the only ones gawking. Pretty sure that random thump was the IT guy's jaw hitting the floor.

"Good morning, everyone. My name is Rebecca James. As I'm sure you've all heard, LC Advertising has done some restructuring and brought me on board to streamline processes in the marketing department." Rebecca scans the faces surrounding the long table as she explains her new role.

I'm listening. Sort of. What she's saying doesn't really apply to a lowly traffic manager.

Don't know what a traffic manager does? Neither did I.

When I first found out an advertising company was hiring, I pictured Mad Men-style shenanigans and glamor. Instead, all I do is send commercial spots to stations and make sure they run them correctly.

It's even less exciting than it sounds.

Once we're dismissed, Meg and I head over to my cubicle so I can finally give my shoulder a break from my purse that weighs as much as a small elephant.

Meg leans over the adjoining wall to retrieve a brown paper bag from her desk and an overpriced coffee that makes the instant crap I have taste like tar in comparison. "Holy shit," she says, handing me the cup. "That woman is a freaking goddess."

Inhaling the vanilla-scented steam brings me life. "Tell me about it. I was thinking of asking about her workout routine." What sort of exercises give her such a teeny, tiny waist? I'd kill for a waist like that.

Snorting, Meg pulls a croissant from the bag. "Why? You can't afford a gym membership." She pulls the thing in half and offers the largest piece to me.

How would I survive without her? God love friends who live next to artisanal bakeries.

"Yeah, but Rebecca doesn't know that." Maybe I can recreate her workout with my five-pound weights and resistance bands.

If I get a minute, I'm going to ask her anyway. Could be a great way to connect with the new boss.

I really, really want to stay here at the end of my contract. Meg is here, there's free downtown parking, and once a quarter they have a book club where they pay you to read books. It's only a hundred bucks and the books are all non-fiction, but a year of books equals a month of rent, so I am here for it.

Did I mention beer Fridays? Who doesn't love free beer?

"Rebecca doesn't know what?" a honeyed voice asks from the other side of the cubicle wall.

Meg and I exchange grimaces before turning to find the woman in question standing right behind us. How she managed to sneak across this concrete floor while wearing those stilettos, I'll never know.

"That I'm poor and can't afford a gym membership," I blurt. Because that's what I do when I get stressed or nervous. Blurt, blurt, blurt away.

Rebecca's manicured eyebrows inch up her forehead as she taps her shiny red nails against her hip.

Great. Now she thinks I'm weird.

I mean, I *am* weird, but she doesn't need to know that.

I need to play it cool. Be calm and chill and composed like her. Explain the blurting. "I was going to ask about your workout routine."

Her lips purse as she considers me while I do my best not to shift beneath her prolonged stare. Are there crumbs on my face? I bet there are. That would be my freaking luck.

I swipe my mouth, just in case.

"I do a ton of squats and lunges." Her teeth flash in a blinding smile. "You don't need a gym for those."

No, you do not. I return her smile. Pretty sure I have a girl-crush on our new boss. "Thanks."

She looks between us, then down at the croissant being strangled in my fist. "What're your names?"

"Loren Piper," I say with a weird half-wave sort of gesture.

Meg lifts her own coffee in a toast. "Meg Benson."

"You're both in the marketing department?"

Our heads bob in unison.

"Good to know. I guess I'd better let you get back to work. It was nice to meet you both. Have a great day."

"You too," I say with another wave. At least this one is normal.

"I kinda love her," Meg whispers, watching Rebecca walk to the end of the hallway where Dick's former corner office overlooks downtown.

Actually, "walk" isn't a fair description. That woman saunters.

I want to saunter like Rebecca.

"Me too." I take a bite of squished croissant, hope building in my heart. "Do you think she'd want to hang out with us after work sometime?"

Moving to a new place has been tough. Not only is there financial strain, but also I had to make new friends. As an adult, that's crazy difficult. It's not like you can walk up to another girl on the playground, tell her you like her necklace, and then become besties. Women can be jealous, vicious creatures. You don't know which ones are fake until it's too late.

Case in point: my three-day stint at a call center.

I sat next to a nice woman, introduced myself, thought we were jiving. Next thing I know, she's talking shit about me in the bathroom to a bunch of other petty mean girls.

Thankfully, Meg is nothing like those witches.

We have bonded over a shared love of cheap wine and our mutual disdain for Dick.

Our former boss, I mean. Not actual dicks. We're both pretty into those.

Sighing, Meg sinks down on the corner of my desk. "God, I hope so. I bet she has a massive closet. Do our feet look like they're the same size?" She wiggles her foot encased in chunky black patent leather. "Those heels she had on would look great with my slinky black dress."

"I don't know." I stuff another bite of croissant into my mouth as I pretend to consider her feet. "You kinda have man feet."

"Excuse me, bitch." She throws what remains of her breakfast in my face, which I catch and plan to save for lunch. "I'll have you know, my feet are small for my height."

We both laugh until Carson, the man on the other side of the cubicle we have lovingly named "the librarian," hisses for us to be quiet.

"Sorry, Carson," we say in unison. With a roll of her eyes, Meg retreats to her own cubicle and I open a new helpdesk ticket so IT can get my email fixed for real this time.

CHAPTER 8
LOREN

THIS IS IT. Tonight is *the* night.

My first time having sex with Josh.

We've been dating for a little over month and haven't moved past third base. Or maybe it's second base.

Which one is under the clothes again?

Either way, he always puts a stop to things before they get too hot and heavy, saying he wants to take it slow.

Slow is good.

Slow lasts.

You know what else lasts? Being so horny you can't think straight.

Tonight is going to be different, though. I can feel it in my soul.

The scene has been set: We had a fabulous steak dinner, shared a bottle of expensive wine, and then he asked if he could come up to my apartment with a wicked gleam in his eye.

That flat stomach I'd glimpsed when he was carrying boxes from his great aunt's house are currently on full display. There's no "Let's take it slow" on either of our lips. From the way his tongue assaults mine, it's clear he wants this as much as I do.

I've only hooked up with two guys in my life. William Mattingly: high school flame and long-term boyfriend, and Sean Malloy.

Sex with him was about as exciting as his job.

But this, tonight, is going to be different. I can feel it in my bones and my very, very aroused lady parts.

"You know what we should do?" Josh murmurs between wild kisses, my chest firmly gripped in both his hands.

"What?" I pant against his mouth, so ready. More than ready.

Drawing back, Josh looks deep into my eyes before nudging my head down.

Looks like we're starting off with a good, old-fashioned blow job. I know a lot of girls don't like going down there, but I find it empowering. Anything I can do to make my man a weak pile of mush is a win in my book.

The key is enthusiasm.

I'm pretty sure most guys are into it, but if *you're* really into it, then it blows their minds.

And I am ready to blow Josh's mind.

"Oh, yeah," he groans, keeping hold of my ponytail, urging me to move faster. "You're so good at that, babe. Fuck. I knew you would be."

Fire blazes in his hooded brown eyes as he watches me. I keep going until he gives my hair a tug and tells me to stand up. Not wanting to look like a slobbering dog, I drag a hand over my swollen lips and do as he asks, standing in front of him in nothing but my matching bra and thong bought specifically for this glorious occasion.

Who needs gas money, right?

Meg and I can always carpool to work if necessary.

Josh scrambles for his wallet and pulls out a condom. Once he's all set, he drags my underwear down my thighs and settles me on top.

Not my favorite position, but we have time to figure out what feels best for us both.

We fit together well enough, although it's been quite a while for me so there's a bit of stinging. The pain should go away soon.

With his hands braced on my hips, he urges me to start moving. Groaning, his eyes roll back in his head as he settles deeper against the pillows. "That feels so good, baby."

Does it? Because to me it feels like I'm bouncing around on a pogo stick.

"Oh yeah. Right there. Just like that. Keep going."

I brace my hands on the headboard for purchase and keep going until my thighs start to burn. Wonder if this counts as squats? I'm using the same muscles, right?

Yeah, this totally counts as my workout for the day. I'm even starting to sweat.

Josh's hold on my waist tightens as he starts to thrust up into me, our bodies meeting with loud smacks. I try to tilt forward to get a bit more friction, but he keeps pushing me back because he "wants to see my tits bounce."

Not really the romantic, first-time vibe I was hoping for, but we can chat about it later.

His eyes squeeze shut. "I'm almost there."

What? No! He can't be there yet. I'm not even close.

I try to slow down, make it last, but he's having none of it.

Three more thrusts and I can feel him pulsing inside me.

I know I'm gaping down at him, but I honestly can't figure out what else to do when he nudges me off and rolls over onto his side to remove the condom, letting it drop to the floor.

First: Ew.

Second: Is he serious?

"That was so good," he mumbles, scratching his chest as his eyes fall closed.

For *him* maybe. I'm kneeling here feeling pretty freaking unsatisfied.

I could blame these unrealistic expectations on romance novels, but I know for a fact that sex should be more than this. Even Sean put in the effort.

It rarely worked, but at least he *tried*.

I poke Josh's shoulder. "I need to talk to you."

His response is a snore.

That's right. A freaking snore.

"Josh!" I whap his arm as hard as I can.

He shoots upright, his head whipping this way and that before his unfocused eyes land on me. "What is it? What's wrong? Sorry, babe. I must've fallen asleep."

No shit. They could hear him snoring in Texas.

He falls back down with a sigh. "I'm sorry. I'm just so tired. Work is killing me."

He's been putting in twelve-hour days getting ready for some big case. How can I expect a sex god when he can barely keep his eyes open?

That must be the problem. Next time will be better.

It certainly can't be worse.

I tell him its fine and climb off the bed to snag my robe from the hook, slipping the cool silk around my shoulders. Josh is already asleep again, so he doesn't see me grab my phone and escape onto my balcony to call Meg, who answers on the third ring because she was almost as excited about tonight as I was.

"Well? Did you do it? Tell me you did it."

I hold my phone away from my ear so her squealing doesn't rupture my eardrum. "We did."

"And? Was it everything you dreamed it would be? I need all the details."

I grimace at the stars. "He fell asleep right after."

"Ugh. I hate when that happens. Did he at least get you off?"

I wish. "He didn't even try."

Silence ensues.

If there's one thing I can't stand, it's silence. "But it's totally fine. He's just really tired from work."

"Okay, I don't know this guy and I understand you're head over heels or whatever, but I'm going to tell you here and now that if you decide to ever hook up with him again and the same thing happens, you've gotta cut and run, sister."

Is she right?

I mean, sex isn't the only indicator of a healthy relationship, but it's certainly a big part for me. I don't want to end up with someone who doesn't even *try*.

I glance back into my apartment, where Josh is panned out on my bed.

Have I been wrong about him all this time?

Soft chords of the Rolling Stones "I Can't Get No Satisfaction" lift behind me.

Slowly I turn, my stomach sinking when I see a

shadowy figure on the next balcony over. "Hey, Meg. I gotta go."

"See you tomorrow. Love you, girl."

"Love you too." I end the call and clench the phone in my fist. If I didn't need it, I'd throw the thing at my neighbor's smirking face. "You're such an asshole."

Elliott's deep chuckle washes over me, lifting the hair at the back of my neck. "Sounds like I'm not the only one."

I cinch the tie at my waist a little tighter. "You know, most people would be polite and not eavesdrop on someone else's private conversation." Or at least pretend they didn't hear. Honestly. Who raised this man?

"Most people would make sure they're alone before they *have* a private conversation. I was out here first."

He has me there—not that I'll ever admit it. "Don't you have anything better to do?"

He lifts what looks like a bottle of beer to his smirking lips. "Nope."

Of course he doesn't. Why would I be left in peace when I could be plagued by Elliott instead?

I glance back through my door to see if sleeping beauty woke up yet.

Looks like my boyfriend is out for the count.

As tired as I am, I really don't feel like going back in there and listening to him snore and there isn't room for us both on the single bed.

Narrowing my eyes, I watch Elliott take another sip. "Turn down that music." Wouldn't want Mick Jagger's singing to ruin Josh's nap.

Damn, that beer looks good. So good, in fact, that I'm willing to endure my neighbor's presence if it means I can drown myself in alcohol. "You have another one of those?"

"Nope. This is the last one."

Thanks for nothing, I guess.

Elliott turns down the volume on his phone, stands, and drifts over to his railing to hand me the bottle. "But from what I heard in there, you need it more than I do."

Normally, I wouldn't drink after someone else, but this guy is right. I need a drink.

The bottle is still cold when I wrap my fingers around the glass and take a deep swallow.

I really thought Josh was perfect. It's like he distracted me with his smile and his shoulders, and my brain malfunctioned—

From what I heard in there...

Elliott's comment strikes like lightning.

My hand tightens, squeezing the bottle almost hard enough to shatter the damn thing. "What do you mean, what you heard 'in there?'"

Elliott leans closer, resting his elbows on the railing between our units. "Let's just say that the next time you decide to have sex, you should probably close the window."

Looks like this night *can* get worse.

I drink until the final drop of beer splashes down my throat only to realize this isn't going to cut it. I need something stronger and then I need to pack up my things and move far, far away from this guy. "I can't believe you listened to me having sex." I thought him overhearing my conversation was embarrassing.

"Sorry. I didn't realize you were having sex too. All I could hear was your boyfriend moaning."

"You're a creep. You know that, right?"

With a chuckle, Elliot pushes off the railing and disappears inside his apartment. I wait for him to return, but he never does.

When I head back inside, Josh is still asleep in the

middle of the bed, so I end up curling up on the floor with a spare blanket. A couple minutes later, Radiohead's "Creep" seeps through the shared wall.

I really shouldn't smile, but my lips don't get the memo.

I guess I can't be too annoyed that Elliott overheard me. I mean, I've heard him and his plethora of women more times than I care to remember.

I only wish I'd been the one moaning instead of Josh.

CHAPTER 9
ELLIOTT

I STAND IN MY KITCHEN, coffee mug in-hand, literally banging my head against the wall as my mom's syrupy voice oozes through my phone's speaker where I've abandoned it on the counter. It was either that or squeeze the damn thing so hard the screen cracks.

"Your Dad's making himself sick over this. He could really use your help."

Thump. Thump. Thump. Hello, wall, so good to see you again. "I'm busy, Mom."

"With your *job?*"

She knows saying it like that makes me angry. That's why she does it.

I let my forehead fall, unable to hold myself up any longer. Even my bones are tired, which, according to my darling mother, is my own reckless fault for not sticking to finance.

I could be CFO by now—her words, not mine.

But no. I had to go and throw it all away on some fool-hearted venture. That her brother willingly invested in said venture should've been enough to prove I'm not a fool. Instead, it drove a wedge between them.

We both know what's coming next: The guilt trip.

You're our only child...

The one thing I ask you to do...

You will never understand the toll having children takes on a woman's body. You were ten pounds, Elliott. Ten. My vagina never recovered.

Yeah, my mom tells me about her vagina.

Since I want to avoid that conversation at all costs, I say, "What do you need?"

Turns out, Dad has been "making himself sick" over hanging a couple of massive paintings Mom bought online. According to her, my dad doesn't want to get it wrong.

More like he doesn't want to hear her complain about it every time they go into the living room until she decides to buy something else to put behind the couch.

I agree to swing by on my way home from the bar, and she takes away some of the sting by offering to make baked steak for dinner.

At one point in my life, I dreamed of moving far away, but as my mom reminds me on a weekly basis, I'm her one and only, most precious child. I can't tell you how many times I wished I had a brother or sister to take on some of their "love" and "attention."

———

The promise of food makes the twenty-minute drive to Mom and Dad's almost bearable. The houses gradually thin out, leaving room for sprawling yards and white picket fences.

That's the south for you. One minute you're in the suburbs, the next, you're neck-deep in tractors and cows.

Mom and dad bought their ridiculous brick rancher not because we needed the six bedrooms, but because it happened to be right next to her sister's house and it was twice as large.

I flick my blinker, but as I go to turn, my foot slams on the brake pedal instead. The car behind me swerves to avoid ramming my bumper, their horn blaring as they speed past. I can't even bring myself to wave in apology because right next to my mom's white SUV sits a cherry-red Volvo.

My throat is as tight as my fists on the steering wheel.

This isn't about hanging pictures and feeding her only son. This is a fucking ambush.

Mom can hang her own damn pictures.

Come to think of it, I wouldn't be surprised if the whole scenario was a big fat lie and there weren't any pictures at all.

I drive around the corner so they can't see me and pull into the Nelson's stone driveway. Dragging my phone from the center console, I type out a quick text.

6:13 PM

Work ran late.

I won't make it tonight. Sorry.

Since I'm not having my mom's cooking for dinner, I might as well swing by The Pearl for some seafood. Back to town I go, stopping at my favorite restaurant down the street from where I work. With the smell of fried food filling my car, I pull into my apartment complex full-on drooling.

My neighbor stepping out of her car right next to mine doesn't help, especially when her black skirt rides up her tan thighs. She gives it a swift tug back down, setting off at a clip toward the stairs.

Annoying Loren is one of my favorite things to do, so I get out, grab my Styrofoam container, and jog up behind her.

She glances over her shoulder and finds me smiling, then whips back around before I get a good look at her face.

She's always doing that. Turning away before I really see her.

With my long strides and her shorter ones, we reach the landing outside our apartment block at the same time.

Since she's stuffed her keys somewhere into that massive black bag looped over her shoulder, she's forced to pause and acknowledge me with a clipped, "Elliott."

I bob my head. "Loren." I haven't seen her in the week since I accidentally listened in on her conversation about the guy she's dating. I didn't hear everything, but I heard enough. I thought the guy was a dick the first time I saw him milling around the parking lot waiting for her instead of coming up to her door, and my opinion has only gone downhill since.

"What's in the box?" she asks, eyeing my dinner as she withdraws receipt after receipt, a tube of Chapstick—a pair of socks? She's like that Poppins lady with her bag. You never know what's going to emerge from the chaos.

The deeper she digs, the redder her cheeks turn.

I give the Styrofoam a shake. "Only the best crab cakes on the planet."

For some reason, that makes her snort.

I might not be a very good cook, but I take eating food very seriously. "You don't believe me?"

"I grew up thirty minutes from the beach," she says, finally extricating her keys with a victorious jingle. There are so many key chains dangling from the thing, it's a wonder she had trouble finding them in the first place. She jams the key in the lock, giving the knob a twist at the same time. "I don't see how anywhere in Nashville can have better crab cakes than I'm used to."

Didn't know she was a beach baby. Although, from the tan she's sporting, I could've guessed. "So you're a seafood snob."

"When it comes to eating seafood hundreds of miles from the sea, yeah. I guess I am."

I've heard this argument plenty of times. Then I bring folks over to The Pearl and they change their tune. The crab might not have come scuttling straight out of a crab pot, but it's still fucking delicious. "Since freezers aren't a thing."

"Tastes better fresh," she insists, about to step into her apartment.

Normally, I'm against sharing food, but the chance to prove her wrong is too good to pass up. I pop open the lid and hold it out to her. She frowns down at my dinner like it's poisoned.

"Go on. Try it. You know you want to."

"I bet that's your go-to pick-up line," she says with a sassy roll of those honey-gold eyes.

This girl always says the funniest things. You never know what's going to come out of her mouth.

Loren pinches a hunk of crab meat between her fingers and brings it to her lips to chew quietly. Then she has the audacity to scrunch her freckled nose and say, "It's fine."

"Fine?" Now she's definitely fucking with me. I may not be from the coast, but I know when food tastes phenomenal, and these crab cakes are mind-blowing.

"They're average at best. Too much filler. I have a recipe that puts those to shame." She swings the door open and tosses her bag inside with a loud *thump*.

What else does she have in there? The body belonging to those socks?

The way I see it, I can play this one of two ways.

I can either let her little comment slide or I can try to wrangle myself some free crab cakes.

Since crab cakes happen to be my favorite food of all time, I go with option two.

"Sure, you do," I say with a smirk.

She whips around, her dark brown curls catching on her pink lip gloss. "I do."

"Yeah, okay."

"I can prove it. I'll make crab cakes this weekend and bring you some."

Looks like Elliott is eating seafood twice this week. *Score.* "Looking forward to it."

———

It's been a fucking week. Between the late delivery at the bar Wednesday and pulling a double today, my body is this close to falling apart. I ease my head back against the plastic chair on my balcony, overlooking a bunch of evergreen trees doing a shitty job concealing the concrete mayhem of the highway.

My eyes fall closed as icy drops of condensation from the cold beer in my hand drip down my fingers. My arms are so sore from the gym yesterday, the thought of lifting my beer to my lips brings tears to my eyes.

Despite my exhaustion, when the door to my right creaks open, I have to bite my lip to keep from grinning.

Loren's voice comes out a little shriller than normal. "Here."

When I open my eyes, I find my neighbor standing on her balcony in a pair of paint-splattered black leggings and a white sweater, her hair piled on top of her head, making her look like a demented poodle. A very cute demented poodle holding a chipped white plate across the gap between our balconies.

Looks like she came through on her promise to cook and it couldn't have come at a better time. I'm starving.

I push upright and set my bottle on the small round table in exchange for the plate. The golden-brown delicacy on top smells delicious. Not that I tell her that as I cut into the crab cake with the fork provided and take a bite.

Holy shit.

She's right.

From the smug smile on her lips, she knows it.

Again, I'm faced with an important decision.

I'm not proud of what I'm about to do, but these crab cakes are giving me life, and one can never have too much life. I poke the patty with the fork and say, "You didn't make this."

Her shapely brows slam down over narrowed eyes. "Yes, I did."

I take another bite and nearly expire in my chair. I don't

know what spices she used in this thing, but they're divine. From what I can tell, there isn't any filler either. Straight crab and spices. *Get in my mouth.*

"No way. You bought it somewhere." I set the fork down long enough to take a swig of my beer. What a heavenly combination. Downright euphoric. "Tell the truth, Loren. Was it Waterfront? My cousin said they got a new cook."

She clutches her railing like it's taking everything within her to keep from leaping over the gap and stealing back the most amazing dinner I've ever had. "I made those in my own damn kitchen."

"Sure, you did."

"Fine. I'll tell you where to get the crab next weekend and I'll cook them right in front of you."

Hiding my smile behind another bite, I chuckle and say, "If you insist."

CHAPTER 10
LOREN

REBECCA SAUNTERS PAST MY CUBICLE, coffee mug in hand, rocking a black pantsuit that makes her look like a total girl boss. When I wave to her from my desk, she does a double-take before coming to a dead stop. "You're here early."

"I'm more efficient in the mornings." That and I fell asleep early, so I was awake before my alarm went off.

"Oh, my goodness, me too. By the time I leave, my brain is complete mush."

"Same here."

"Well, have a good one."

"You too."

That might be my first ever normal interaction with

Rebecca. I think I'm finally getting the hang of this social-izing thing.

I lift my arms over my head for a long, luxurious stretch. Okay. Time to get back to it. First up: email.

Looks like the company's quarterly book club meeting is scheduled for next week, which couldn't come at a better time. I could use an extra hundred bucks. But first, I have to force myself to read about outliers. Whatever that means. There are copies of the book down in the library.

That's right. This place has a library.

Oh, and the company Christmas party is in a few weeks. I still need to RSVP. I'll talk to Meg before I do though. Not sure I'll want to go if she doesn't. Unless Rebecca wants me to. Maybe I should ask. Wouldn't want to look like I'm not a team player or whatever. I *need* them to take me on as an employee after my contract ends.

Twenty minutes later, all the notifications are clear and I'm ready to send out some traffic.

There's an email with all the codes for each new commercial so that when I select the stations to send them to, I send the correct ones. There's also information about rotation and split and a bunch of other boring stuff that is thankfully straightforward enough.

By the time I'm ready for a break, it's ten thirty.

Man, I love traffic days. Makes the hours pass by so much faster.

When I stand to stretch my legs, I find Meg working away at her own desk, doing whatever media buyers do. Negotiating contracts with stations. Being rockstars. That sort of thing.

When she catches me peering over the low wall like a meerkat, she tosses her headphones aside. "Good morning, busy bee. I was going to say hi earlier, but you looked like you were in the zone."

"I really was." Most days are laid back but not traffic days. "I have a lot of spots to send and wanted to get an early start so the reps can get back to me before the end of the day." There's something so satisfying about crossing off all the confirmations, mostly because it means I don't have to worry about chasing them down tomorrow.

Her chair squeaks as she leans back, twisting from side to side. "Speaking of reps, do you think you could talk to Holly about the importance of confirmations? She doesn't seem to be grasping the concept, and I can't ask for any make goods if the stations never verified receiving traffic."

Make goods are kind of like reparations for when a station doesn't run the correct commercials. Basically, the client gets free exposure in exchange for the station's screw-ups. At least that's my newbie take on the whole process.

All I know for certain is that we're supposed to have written confirmation from all reps that the commercial spots were received and will be updated on the requested date.

That's Traffic 101.

"No problem." I need to stretch my legs anyway.

Meg thanks me and then throws her headphones back on. I grab my empty travel mug and fill it up in the break room before heading over to Jolly Holly's desk.

She's probably the nicest woman you'll ever meet, thus her nickname. Not that anyone else calls her that. It's a little trick I've come up with to help me learn names. Like Carson "the Librarian" Cooper or the IT guy, Marty "the Gray Ghost" or just "Ghost" Simpson.

That guy really loves the color gray. Meg and I have tried to determine whether or not his shirts were once white and just faded into gray, but the results from our observations are inconclusive.

Jolly Holly is at her desk, humming as she munches on one of those granola bars that are so dry, they turn to sand in your mouth. "Hey, Holly."

Her smile lights up her whole face. "Good morning, Loren. What brings you all the way over here on this lovely day?"

"All the way over" being four cubicles away and "lovely day" meaning wind and rain battering the windows. "I just wanted to check in. See how you're doing."

"Just peachy because it's traffic daaay!" She does this little shimmy and ends up spilling crumbs from what's left of her granola bar all over her khaki pants, which sends her into a fit of giggles as she shakes her head and swipes them onto the floor.

There are rumors that she drinks on the job, but I've never smelled alcohol on her, so I figure that's just folks trying to make sense of her general jolliness.

Holly hooks her fingers through her own mug and knocks it against mine for an enthusiastic toast. "How are *youuu* doing, Loren?"

It sucks being the one to pop her happy little bubble.

Maybe there's a way to broach this subject without making her feel bad. "I'd be better if these dang reps would get back to me. I've sent out almost all my spots this week and have only received confirmation from one station." It's only a little lie.

She takes a big gulp of her coffee before setting it back down next to the framed photo of her pug named Doug. "Oof. I hate it when that happens."

"Do you have any problem stations?"

"No, thank goodness. My reps are all incredibly sweet and confirm receipt the moment I call them."

Oh, Holly... No wonder Meg is frustrated. "You call your reps?"

"Of course. Don't you?"

"Only as a last resort when I can't get them to email me back." Like we were instructed during orientation. "I always make sure to get written confirmation to cover my own butt. I'd hate to get into trouble if the client doesn't receive the spots they've paid for."

For the first time since I met the woman, her smile falters. "Huh. I guess I should probably do that too."

Not probably. It's her freaking job. She should know this; she started the same week I did. Went through the same training.

She frowns down at her mouse. "But email feels so impersonal."

Now I understand.

This job can feel quite isolating. We don't film the commercials; we only send them out. We don't negotiate with reps; we only ask for a quick email confirming receipt. I don't mind, but for a social butterfly like Holly, it could be an issue.

But how do you make one of the most boring jobs in an advertising company a little less monotonous?

"What if you..." I scan her desk for inspiration. Oh! "What if you include little quotes after your signature line? Or jokes! Just something to jazz up your emails."

She takes another slurping drink from her mug. "That could be fun."

"Exactly. And as a bonus, you'd be doing your clients a huge favor when they get those free spots."

Her smile is restored once more. "Thanks, Loren."

I tap my mug against hers. "Anytime."

Hopefully, she takes my advice. I leave Holly's cubicle feeling a little jollier than before. I wave to Levi, the other traffic manager, on my way past his desk, then quietly slink by Carson so he doesn't grumble at me for my shoes being too loud.

Meg's head pops from behind the gray wall. "Did you do it?" she whispers.

I give her a thumbs up and she high fives me on my way past.

"You're amazing. Thank you."

"Shhh!" Carson hisses.

"You're welcome," I mouth.

Time to get back to work.

CHAPTER 11
LOREN

MEG BURSTS into the break room, her purple lunch box swinging from her arm as she hurries over to the table we've commandeered as our own between twelve thirty and one every single day. "You'll never guess what I found."

I slide my PB&J from the same plastic baggie I've been using for weeks. Don't worry. I wash it out every night. I'm not a monster. "An original Tiffany lamp at a thrift store."

Her nose wrinkles as she pops the lid off her salad full of colorful vegetables. "What? No."

Hmmm... "A priceless piece of jewelry that used to belong to the Astor family?"

"No, Loren. What is wrong with you?"

"I've been watching a lot of Antiques Roadshow, okay?" I can't afford any of the streaming services and the cost of cable is criminal, so I've been watching highlights on YouTube. I've learned a lot over the last few weeks. Mostly that I should be attending more yard sales in search of hidden treasures.

Too bad it's winter and there are no yard sales.

Thankfully, Nashville and the surrounding areas have plenty of second-hand stores. Not that my weekend visits have yielded anything fruitful. Yet.

"Never change, okay?" Shaking her head with a laugh, Meg stabs a piece of lettuce. "So last night I was bored and decided to go for a drive to look at the Christmas lights in our neighborhood."

"Awe. I used to do that with my mom and dad when I was little."

"Me too!"

We're basically the same person and I love that for us.

She shoves the lettuce into her mouth, too excited by whatever she's about to say to chew before speaking—which makes me love her even more. What are manners between friends?

"Anyway, while I was out, I discovered this place that serves one-dollar beers every Wednesday night."

"You're kidding!" Usually, our Wednesdays are reserved for boxed wine, but that stuff can leave you with the worst hangover. Not that I can see beer that only costs a dollar being any better in that regard, but I'm willing to give it a go.

"Nope! What do you say? Should I swing by your place tonight so we can check it out?"

I take a bite of my sandwich, but I was a bit heavy handed with the peanut butter and the damn thing sticks to the roof of my mouth. My tongue can't seem to dislodge it, so I have to use my finger. Gross. I really need to start packing something different.

"Is that even a question? Of course I want to go." It'll be nice to go somewhere besides one of our apartments so I can pretend to have a social life.

"Yay! I'm so excited!" Her face falls. "There is one tiny thing though..."

———

Turns out the "tiny thing" is that the place selling one-dollar beer is a bowling alley with faded white siding and a flashing neon sign of a ball and pins clinging for dear life to the grimy windows.

The trees surrounding the building lean over the tin roof like a silent threat. Definitely not somewhere you want to hunker down during a storm.

Thankfully, it's not storming tonight as Meg and I rock up in her car and park between two old trucks that are more rust than metal. The inside smells like nicotine and sweat, and the sounds of heavy balls slamming onto wooden floors and pins being knocked over fill the air.

Most of the patrons look like they've been here since the place was opened—which was sixty years ago in 2020 according to the faded banner hanging over the shoe rental counter.

A man with an unlit cigarette pinched between his lips

moseys over, a spray can in one hand and a rag in the other. According to the name tag pinned to his striped button-down, his name is Dave. "Evening, ladies. You here for a game?"

Meg's glossy blonde locks sway when she shakes her head. "Not tonight. We're actually here for the one-dollar beers."

Speaking of beers, where is the bar? There's a little hut over by the two empty pool tables that has a menu taped to the side but no bar stools or tables as far as I can tell.

The man sets the can on the counter, his cigarette wobbling as he speaks through the right side of his mouth. "I'm afraid the Wednesday special is only for bowlers."

Meg turns to me, a sparkle in her blue eyes and a smirk on her lips. "What do you say? Are we bowlers tonight?"

That depends on one very important factor. "How much is a game?"

Dave's cheeks hollow before he blows out a heavy breath. "Five dollars per game per lane."

Even if we stayed for a few hours that would still be cheaper than anywhere else we've ever gone drinking.

"Does that include shoes?" Meg asks with a bat of her thick lashes.

Dave smiles, revealing a whole mouthful of brown teeth. "It does tonight."

Looks like we're bowling.

We pay for our game and then take our hideous red and navy clown shoes over to lane ten and plop onto the hard plastic chairs bolted to the ground.

Meg unties her heeled booties while I toe off my sneakers. Good thing I wore matching socks. Not that Meg would judge me anyway.

"When was the last time you went bowling?" I wonder aloud.

"Never."

"You've *never* been bowling?" That can't be right.

"Why do you say it like I just admitted I've never driven a car?" The ends of the yellowed laces that I'm pretty sure are meant to be white *ping* off the edge of the chair as she loosens them and stuffs her foot into the shoe.

She has a point; that came out way more incredulous than it should've.

"I'm just shocked." To me it feels like going bowling is a right of passage. Surely someone in her life must've had a birthday party at the local bowling alley at some point.

"When was the last time *you* went bowling?" she shoots back.

That's a good question.

Not college—none of us had the money for extracurricular activities back then. In high school I was too busy falling in love with stupid boys, and in middle school I was too busy being edgy to partake in sports of any kind. "Probably elementary school."

Katie Sincell's fifth grade birthday party. Hawaiian themed with the leis and all. There was pizza, ice cream, and, of course, bowling.

Meg knocks her knee against mine. "And you're giving me shit."

"Who? Me? I wouldn't dare."

A woman in a faded denim shirt and jeans balancing two beer cans on a little black tray strolls over to where we're sitting. "Two beers for lane ten." She sets them on the table next to a computer screen that looks older than I am.

"We haven't ordered any drinks," Meg and I say in unison.

"These are from the gentlemen in eight."

A bunch of grandpas in matching turquoise bowling shirts wave from their lane. We snag the beers and raise them in a silent toast, which earns us a few gruff cackles.

The beer is...

Well, it's shit, but I've had worse.

At least it's cold.

Fueled by terrible beer, Meg stands and straightens her jeans. "What do we do first?"

Apparently, Katie's birthday party makes me the expert on the matter. "We need to find balls." There are plenty of them sitting in racks behind and in between the lanes.

Meg heads toward the one at the back, and I follow. "Oh! This one's pink. It even matches my nails."

"I don't know. That number stamped on the front means it's only six pounds."

"Is that good or bad?"

"I have no clue."

She picks it up as if testing the weight, then tries to hold it properly. "Yeah, it's not going to work. I can't even get my fingers into the holes."

"That's what he said."

She snorts. "This might be my new favorite night."

Mine too.

While I enjoy going to the odd bar, they all start to feel the same after a while. At least here, we have something to entertain us besides alcohol. Always a good thing.

Eventually, we find balls that work and then settle down to put our information in the ancient computer. Meg insists we're not supposed to use our real names, citing lane eight's listings as a reference. According to their screen, Big Billy is up next, followed by Thunderman.

Big Billy makes sense—the man has to be at least six foot five.

But how does one earn the name "Thunderman?" If I wasn't so anxious to get started, I'd stroll over there and ask myself.

"What's your nickname going to be?" Meg asks, her fingers skimming the keyboard.

"I'm not sure nicknames are the sort of thing you come up with yourself."

"Hmmm... you're probably right. How about you come up with mine and I'll come up with yours?"

"Sounds like a plan." Let's see... A nickname for Meg. Oh! I know. I nudge her out of the way and type her name for the night into the computer.

"Megalodon? Really?"

"What? It's fierce, includes your actual name, and you're a bit of a man eater." The perfect name, really.

"All true. Damn. Now I have to think of something just as epic for you." She taps her lips as she considers.

I end up bowling as "Great Pipes" because, my rendition of "Don't Stop Believing" on the drive over here gave her goosebumps and we should definitely do karaoke sometime.

Have I mentioned lately how much I love her?

Turns out we are awful, but I don't think we've ever laughed as much. At some point, the bumpers emerge from the gutters and we're marginally better. Then the woman who's been serving us all night brings a silver contraption for rolling the balls straight.

This helps Meg get her first and only spare.

I, on the other hand, knock down all ten pins. Not at once. Oh, no. It takes the entire ten frames for me to get that many.

The other players point at our scoreboard and shake their heads. Dave comes over to take a picture, saying he's never seen anyone so terrible at bowling.

We don't care though. It's the perfect escape from responsibilities and relationships and work. Not once did I think about how awful my one and only sleepover with Josh went.

Our laughter echoes through the space when we bowl our final frame and stumble over to return our shoes. Dave chuckles along with us, saying we should come back next week.

We leave with a decent buzz and a promise to return.

Outside in the crisp winter air, Meg frowns down at her fingers as we wait for our ride share. "My thumb is throbbing."

"I told you that you needed bigger holes."

Snorting, she huddles closer to me. "No one's ever complained about the size of my holes, thank you very much."

We both snigger.

Linking my arm through hers, I rest my head on her shoulder. "Tonight was so much fun." The most fun I've had since moving down here.

I try not to think too hard about the fact that it wasn't with Josh.

"Right? I was thrilled about finding such cheap drinks, but the bowling really stole the show."

I draw back, my breath a puff of white between us. "Are we bowlers now?"

"I think you have to knock down more than ten pins to call yourself that."

"Says old twenty-pins herself."

She bumps her hip against mine. "Hey! I'm proud of those twenty pins."

"Watch out. I'll be gunning for you next week, Megalodon."

"Bring it on, Great Pipes. Bring. It. On."

CHAPTER 12
LOREN

THANKS to the emergency root canal two days ago, my jaw feels like it's been punched. On top of that, the exorbitant cost means I don't have enough to pay rent at the start of January. Which means I shouldn't be out to eat right now, but since I'm with Josh, I'm taking full advantage of him picking up the check.

That's right. We're talking appetizers ordered under the guise of "sharing," a full dinner, *and* dessert. I'm not leaving this table without having to unbutton the top of my jeans.

The best part is, no one will even notice because my loose cream sweater hangs at mid-thigh.

It's the perfect ruse.

We talked about what happened two weeks ago and he seemed to understand where he went wrong. Unfortunately, we've both been so busy with work that we haven't had time for a do-over. It didn't help that he decided last minute to visit his parents for Christmas.

Was I bummed that he didn't invite me? Sure. But this is still the start of our relationship, so maybe it was for the best. At least that's what I told myself over my takeout turkey dinner.

Part of me missed going back to see my parents for the holidays. Mom suggested I use the Christmas money from my grandma for a flight back home, but I needed it for my tooth so...

Besides, I don't want to go back until I can prove I'm not a complete failure.

Soon.

The new year is going to be *my* year. The year of Loren Piper. I feel it in my bones.

Josh smiles at me from over his cobb salad but the look doesn't quite reach his eyes. He's been distant since he got back from Colorado, probably mentally preparing for his big work trip to California.

It sucks that he won't be around for New Year's either, but we can celebrate when he gets back.

I squish down the top of my burger bun so the mammoth monster will fit into my mouth without giving me lockjaw. "You all packed?"

His lips flatten as he spears a tomato. "Not really. I still have a few loads of laundry to wash."

At least he has a washer and dryer in his apartment. I have to use the community laundry room in our apartment complex. "Any fun plans for while you're away?"

His fork slips, landing on the edge of the salad plate with a *clang*. The tomato on the end pops off and rolls across the table, leaving a wobbly orange trail of French dressing in its wake. "For the last time, Loren, this is a *work* trip." He snatches back the tomato and drops it into the salad. "We'll be in meetings all day, probably have dinner with the higher-ups in the evenings, and then get ready to do it all over again the next day."

Geez. Someone's testy tonight.

I set down my burger to wipe my greasy hands on the cloth napkin stretched across my lap. "You don't have to snap at me. It was only a question."

A long breath passes between Josh's lips. After a beat, he offers an apologetic smile and reaches across the table to give my arm a tender squeeze. "I'm sorry. I'm used to people assuming all this traveling is fun. All I want to do is stay home."

I want him to stay home too. Work is important but it shouldn't be your life. "What would we do if you were here instead?"

The muscles in his square jaw flex as he chews slowly, considering. "We'd probably brave the crowds on Broadway, listen to the bands, have a few drinks while we wait for the fireworks, and then go back to my place."

That sounds like the perfect night. Especially the part where I get to sleep in a luxurious bed with Egyptian Cotton sheets and an apartment with a working HVAC system. Mine's been on the fritz since before Christmas.

"Maybe next weekend?" We could make some fireworks of our own.

Candlelight sparkles in his eyes when he grins. "It's a date."

The rest of dinner goes by without incident and by the time the check arrives, I'm reaching under my shirt to unfasten the top button on my jeans, giving my poor, swollen stomach a chance to expand the way she needs to.

As much as I don't want to say goodbye to Josh, I can't wait to take off this damn bra and slip into a pair of sweatpants.

Josh balls up his napkin and drops it onto the table next to what's left of his cheesecake.

Would it be weird if I asked the server to box it up so that I can have the rest at lunch tomorrow?

He flips open the black checkbook, drops in a few bills, and stands from his chair.

Guess that's a no on the doggie bags.

No worries. I fold up what's left of my apple pie inside my napkin and stuff it into my purse like my grandma used to do. I always thought it was strange and embarrassing, but she was on to something.

I sling my purse over my shoulder and as we make our way out of the restaurant, I check my email. There aren't any, but my reminder to pay rent this week flashes on the screen.

So much for enjoying the rest of the night.

Josh steps closer, his musky cologne drifting over me. "Everything okay?"

I stuff my phone back into my purse. Outta sight, outta mind and all that jazz. "Yeah. Sorry. I've just gotta pay rent before the weekend." We've received multiple letters saying payment must be received by the first.

The hostess holds open the door for us, and we step out into the chilly evening air. Josh hands the valet our ticket with a smile.

With my apartment's heating jacked, the thought of going back makes me want to scream. Even with the window open, it's going to be hot as hell. I've asked the twins five times to have someone come up and fix it, but like the mold problem, they haven't done a damn thing.

Josh lives right around the corner, at one of the high-rise

apartments on the city's west side. If I lived there, I could walk to work *and* swing by my favorite coffee shop on the way. Sharing rent would mean I might even have the extra cash to buy a muffin for Meg every now and then instead of relying on her generosity all the time.

"Maybe we should just move in together," I say, half-teasing, half-hopeful.

His shower has not one, but two shower heads and there isn't a speck of mold in sight.

The arm draped around me goes stiff. From the horror on his face, you'd swear I suggested we go out and slaughter a bunch of puppies. "It was a joke," I quickly add. "We've only known each other for a couple months." Wouldn't want to look like a crazy person. You know, the kind that hangs out with a guy for a few days and then moves hundreds of miles to be with him.

Josh's arm falls to his side, and he takes a step back. "You know I care about you, Loren, but I'm not ready for that level of commitment. We said no pressure, remember?"

"Yeah, no. I know. Neither am I. Like I said, it was a joke."

There's no humor in his answering laugh, which is just freaking great. I don't want him to leave tomorrow and have this conversation haunting us all weekend. We need damage control. Stat. "I'm really happy in my own place. Honestly. I've got great neighbors, and the commute isn't bad at all." Plus, I get to listen to audiobooks on my drive to and from work. What's not to love about that?

Josh's white Range Rover comes into view at the top of the hill, but he doesn't seem to notice. He's too busy frowning at me. "I thought you didn't really know your neighbors."

"Only in passing."

The tiny white lie feels slimy on my tongue. I don't *really* know Elliott, but I have shared a beer with him and made him crab cakes. Elliott and Josh don't know each other, so I can't imagine how Josh would learn the truth.

Still, I would hate for him to find out somehow and think I was hiding it from him on purpose. Because I'm not.

Yeah, Elliott is hot, but he's *not* my type. Plus, he hasn't hit on me once, so I'm pretty sure I'm not his type either.

Regardless, better to clear things up, just in case. "I mean, the guy next door and I have talked a bit. I gave him one of my crab cakes once and he gave me a beer."

I can't believe Elliott thinks I'm lying about cooking them. He's going to eat his hat when he realizes I am a master in the kitchen.

Josh's eyes darken. "When was this?"

"I don't know. Before Christmas."

The valet pulls the car up to the curb. The teen hops out, and Josh rips the keys from his hand, stalking around the front without giving the poor kid a tip.

My face burns as I scrounge around in my purse for something to give the guy, but unless he wants a sticky quarter, a used tube of Chapstick, or what remains of my pie, I've got nothing.

With my head bowed, I slink into the car.

Josh seethes from the driver's side where he strangles the steering wheel. Before I can fasten the belt across my lap, he whips onto the road.

The belt retracts to the sound of squealing tires, and I shoot him a glare. "What the heck is your problem?" Is he trying to decapitate me or what?

"*My* problem? You're the one going out to eat with other guys."

Did he not hear a word I said? "It wasn't like that. I

made crab cakes for dinner and gave Elliott one. He was sitting on his balcony and gave me a beer. Not a big deal."

"You don't even have enough money for an oil change, and yet you buy this guy dinner? I don't think you should even be talking to him. For all you know, he could be a serial killer."

"Nah. There'd be more screaming next door." There is screaming but I usually see the women leaving the next morning when I head out for work.

Josh's eyes narrow, and if he doesn't slow the heck down, he's going to ram into the truck in front of us.

"It was a joke, Josh. Lighten up."

He takes a deep breath, then sighs before leaning across the center console and reaching for my hand. "I'm sorry, Loren. I don't know why I'm acting like such a jealous asshole. I trust you, and it's not my place to tell you who you can and can't talk to."

"You're forgiven."

Even though our first fight is over, awkward silence fills the cab the entire drive back to my place. Josh lets go of my hand when he shifts into park next to my car. I remove my seatbelt, expecting him to do the same. When he doesn't, my heart stumbles.

We won't see each other for another week, and he doesn't even seem to care.

I open the door slowly. Waiting. Climb out even slower.

Isn't he going to kiss me goodnight?

"Hey Loren?" Josh calls before I close the door.

Hope swells in my chest as I turn back toward him, the light from the console like a golden halo around his head.

"Call me when I'm gone?" he asks with a soft smile.

"Every night."

His brow furrows and he glances away, scrubbing his hands down his dress slacks like he's nervous. "I..."

Oh god. This is it. He's going to say it. Those three words have been on the tip of my tongue since the night we said goodbye back on his great aunt's front porch and now I can finally set them free.

Josh's gaze locks with mine, emotion swimming in his eyes. "I like what we have and really don't want to lose it."

Hold on. Did he just say he *likes* what we have?

He *likes* it.

Like our relationship is French freaking dressing.

Maybe I'm jumping the gun a little expecting him to say he loves me after only a couple months, but the least he can do is say he *loves* what we have. He doesn't even do that.

He *likes* it.

"I don't want to lose it either," I say for lack of a more enthusiastic response.

When I close the door and walk toward the staircase, a lead weight settles in the pit of my stomach, and it refuses to go away.

CHAPTER 13
LOREN

FOLKS HEAD in and out of the diner down the road from my apartment while I sit in my car munching on the remains of my pie, watching the clock on my dashboard.

Don't worry. It wasn't in my purse all night. I put it in my fridge the moment I got home and then transferred it to a plastic tub to bring with me to work because I am a grown adult woman and not a heathen.

The fur around my coat's hood tickles my cheeks as I snuggle deeper into its downy warmth. I could turn on the ignition and jack the heat but that would require gas, and the tiny gas pump icon came on before I went to work this morning.

At this point, I'm running on fumes in every sense of the word.

At five minutes to five, I grab my phone and make the call.

"Talbott Property Management, this is Tony."

"Hey, Tony. It's Loren Piper from Apartment 5316. How much longer are you going to be in the office? I'm stuck in traffic on my way home from work and need to pay my rent."

His response sounds as flat as a pancake. "We will be gone at five."

"Oh, crap. Is it okay if I just drop it off tomorrow?"

"Tomorrow is a holiday. The office will be closed until Monday at nine."

Perfect. "Crap. You're right. I don't know where my head is. I'm so sorry. I should've left the check yesterday."

"We'll see you first thing Monday morning, Miss Piper."

"Yes, of course. First thing." First thing after I get home from work, that is. By then, it'll be too late to cash the check and if I drop it off in the office mailbox but forget to sign it, that might give me until Tuesday after work. They're only open until noon on Wednesdays, but since I'm working all day, I won't be able to sign the thing until Thursday, which means they'll deposit it on Friday, also known as payday.

I drive into the apartment complex with a smile on my face.

That is until I pull into my parking space and find Toby coming down the stairs of my building.

When he sees me, his eyes gleam like one of those cartoon villains, the ones who twiddle their fingers together while laughing maniacally.

Except he's not laughing.

He's coming over to the car and folding his arms over his chest.

So much for hiding in here until he's gone.

Cold air rushes into my vehicle when I roll down my window to offer him a wan smile.

"Just the woman I wanted to see," he says. "I'm not sure if you received the many notices we've slipped beneath your door, Miss Piper, but rent is due today."

"Yeah, I know. I called the office. Got stuck in traffic."

"It's a good thing I ran into you then."

Shit. "You want the check now?"

"That would be great."

"Sure. No problem. Just a sec." I rummage through the sticky napkins in my purse and shove aside random receipts. Would you look at that? Turns out I didn't leave one of my spoons at work, after all. "I'm sorry, but I don't have a pen on me. Can I drop it in later or...?"

Toby whips a shiny silver pen from his breast pocket.

How fortuitous.

With a wobbly smile, I take it from him and fill out the check, giving the man every last penny to my name.

He clicks the top before stuffing both the pen and my check into his pocket. "Happy New Year."

"Yeah, same to you." I watch him leave, that weight in my stomach growing so heavy I can barely drag myself over to the cube of tiny mailboxes outside our apartment block.

So much for letting loose this weekend.

Not that there's much I could have afforded to do anyway.

More good news waits inside in the form of a late notice for my credit card payment that I could've sworn I scheduled. *Dammit.* These interest rates are criminal. Whoever thought it'd be a good idea to let eighteen-year-old college freshmen sign up for credit cards should be thrown in jail.

I shuffle through the rest of my mail—mostly junk, thank goodness. All except for the final envelope from a bank I've never heard of. Probably because it's not my bank, but Elliott's.

I seriously hope he has more money in his account than I do.

I trudge up five flights of stairs, stopping by Elliott's apartment to slip the mis-delivered letter under his door. Right when I kneel down to dop it off, his red door suddenly swings wide open.

Elliott glances down at where I kneel, letter in hand, his eyes wide and a slow smile curving over his lips. "How did you know it was my birthday?"

Wait. Does he think I'm leaving him a birthday card? "What are you talking about?"

"You're on your knees at my door, Loren. I think you can see where I'm going with this." He waggles his brows, his grin growing.

What an idiot. How I'd love to offer a sarcastic remark in response to that, but I'm all out of money *and* humor. "Hilarious." I shoot to my feet and shove the letter at his chest.

He catches it, then my hand. That smarmy smile no longer anywhere to be seen. "Hey. You okay?"

No, I'm not.

"Sorry for the tasteless joke," he says. "It was inappropriate."

"You're the only tasteless joke I see."

His grin returns, and he drops my hand. "There she is. For a second I thought I offended you. We still on for this weekend? I've been looking forward to crab cakes all week."

Crap. I completely forgot that with all the holiday crazi-ness we had to postpone our dinner.

Josh may have apologized for playing the jealousy card, but my neighbor clearly bothers him. It feels dishonest to cook for Elliott the moment Josh heads out of town. "Actu-ally, I can't tonight. Something came up. Sorry."

"Sure, sure." He winks at me, which shouldn't make my stomach jump, but it leaps anyway. "Whatever you say. You let me know when you feel like 'cooking.'" His air quotes irritate me a hundred times more than his stupid joke.

Part of me wants him to press, to try and convince me. But he doesn't. He winks once more, turns on his heel, and heads back into his place.

I slip inside my stuffy apartment and throw open the windows before dropping onto my bed and praying for a breeze.

When Duran Duran's "Hungry Like the Wolf," drifts through the adjoining wall, I can't help but smile. That is until I realize that, in denying Elliott his crab cakes, I won't have anything to eat later either.

———

The knock at my door is as unexpected as the snow that's fallen outside on the balcony, dusting the concrete and the trees beyond in white fluff.

I pause the episode of *Antiques Roadshow* and mosey over to the door, completely stupefied when I whip the door aside to see Elliott down on one knee, a box in one hand and a sheepish smile on his face.

"Well, well, well." How the tables have turned. "You know, it's not my birthday but I do appreciate a man on his knees. Unfortunately for you, I have a boyfriend."

He pops back to his feet with a grin and a teasing, "Unfortunately for us both, you mean."

Okay, that was... well, it was the kind of banter I would normally die for. Single-Loren would clap back with something even more inappropriate; however, coupled-Loren thinks all these innuendos feel a little too close to flirting.

Instead of pointing out that he sounds awfully full of himself and having him say something ridiculously cringe like, "Would you like to be full of me?" I make the very mature choice to change the subject and save us both.

"What's in the box?" I ask, very non-flirtingly.

"Crabs."

"I don't want your crabs, Elliott Grant." That was the last one; I swear.

His chuckle is totally worth it. "I bought them for us the other day, so technically they're *our* crabs. They're going to go bad if someone doesn't eat them. Since I don't know how to cook, I figured someone might as well enjoy seafood this weekend."

As much as I'd love to have crab for dinner, this doesn't feel like a line I should be crossing, and taking this food from him without paying for it feels like theft.

What to do? What to do?

Suddenly his brow furrows, and he takes a step back. "Are you sick or something?"

"No. Why?" Do I look sick? I mean, I've lost most of my tan but didn't think I looked that bad tonight.

Elliott drags the sleeve of his blue henley across his forehead. "I can feel the heat pumping out of your apartment all the way out here. It must be like an oven in there."

That's an understatement. Before he knocked, I was this close to stripping completely. "My heating is broken, and the twins have an aversion to fixing it."

"Want me to take a look?"

"That depends? Do you fix HVACs for a living?"

"No, but the office where I work had a thermostat that was all out of whack, and I figured out how to fix that."

It would be nice to sleep without the window open, especially given the recent snowfall. There's no harm in letting him take a look, is there?

"Give me two minutes." I close the door in his face and proceed to sweep all the random clothes sprinkling my floor into the hamper. The good part about having an apartment the size of a matchbox car is that it's easy to clean—mold in the bathroom notwithstanding.

When I open the door once more, Elliott carries the box of crab into my apartment. He turns in a circle, his eyes wide and jaw hanging.

I wave him in with a formal bow. "Welcome to Chateau Piper."

"More like the Den of Chaos."

He's a den of freaking chaos. "I'd give you a tour but, as you can see, that's not necessary."

"You're not kidding. This place is like a fucking closet."

"Pretty sure it was. See that old door right there? I think it's meant to connect to your place, but it's been boarded up."

He sets the box onto the counter next to my empty fruit bowl. "Good thing, too. Wouldn't want you breaking in to stare at me while I sleep."

"Since that's something I do."

"You can never be too careful these days. Where's your thermostat?"

"Through that door, next to the toilet."

"Can you legally have a thermostat in a bathroom?"

"Why are you asking me?" I don't know anything about

thermostats or HVAC units besides the fact that you're supposed to be able to set the temperature and the air in your apartment is meant to then become that temperature.

With nothing better to do, I snag the box of crab and head into my meager kitchen-living-dining-bedroom. I still have all the ingredients from the last time I cooked crab cakes, along with my secret ingredient that isn't really a secret if you're from Maryland.

While Elliott fiddles with my thermostat, I take out my pan and start cooking. When he finally emerges some time later, I feel it: the sweetest breeze—and not from the open window.

"You fixed it?"

He shrugs. "I think so. You seemed to be having the same problem we did. Just needed a good clean." He drags a hand down the back of his neck. "Speaking of cleaning, you have a shitload of black mold in your bathroom."

"Which has been here since I moved in, so stop giving me that look."

"I'm not giving you a look."

He totally is, but there's no point arguing because he can't see his own face right now. "Jut like with fixing the thermostat, I've asked the twins to have it removed, and you can see how well that's been received."

Elliott glances over his shoulder toward the open bathroom door, his lips pressed flat.

He already helped me escape another night in the fiery pits of hell; the black mold is a problem for tomorrow.

"Thank you, Elliott." I'm so happy I could cry.

He leans his hip against the counter and nods down at the pan. "Give me two of those crab cakes and we're square."

That, I can do.

I rinse out one of my only reusable containers from my lunch, dry it, and then throw three crab cakes inside for good measure. I thank him again on the way out and then head back into my apartment to enjoy dinner beneath a working heater.

CHAPTER 14

ELLIOTT

THREE WEEKS AGO, our newest hire quit unexpectedly to go walkabout in Australia, which means August and I have been busting our asses to cover his shifts at work and hire folks to take his place. With today being a holiday, it's going to be insane in the bar, but our GM assured us she and the rest of the staff could handle things. I'm looking forward to getting way too drunk and blowing off some steam.

Usually, I'd be trudging up the stairs to my place but today, I'm running. The sooner I shower, the sooner I can head into town and start celebrating the new year.

Loren waves at me from where she digs through that purse of hers, a bottle of wine in a brown paper bag at her feet.

"Searching for buried treasure in there?"

"Ha-ha. I wish. I can never find my damn keys in this thing."

"Maybe you should clean it out."

Her eyes narrow as she shoves a chestnut curl from her forehead back into the chaos behind her ear. "Oh, really? You think so? How often do you clean your purse, Elliott?"

She has me there.

She lets out this little squeal of delight which I assume means she found them.

I drag my own keys from my pocket. "You have any big plans for tonight?"

"Josh is in California for work, so I'm staying in with this." She swipes the bottle from the ground and gives it a hearty shake.

Doesn't seem fair to me.

Then again, maybe she doesn't have many friends around town. The only person I've seen at her place is her dick of a boyfriend.

The thought of Loren being all alone on New Year's Eve makes me sad. It's tough trying to meet people when you're working all the time. "You could come into the city with us."

Her lips flatten as she twirls her keys around her finger, the plethora of keychains clanging against one another. "I distinctly remember hearing you say that you hate the city."

Did I say that? Probably.

I really do hate the city. More specifically: Broadway. Bars on both sides of the street blaring the same fucking songs by different bands dreaming of making it "big" some-day. Playing for tips and cheap beer. Tourists in cowboy boots and sequins.

Talk about hell.

It's worst in the summer. Not only is it busier, but it's

sweatier too. Because who doesn't want to smell redneck BO and spilled whiskey for hours on end?

But tonight is New Year's Eve and the fireworks in the city are fucking beautiful. Last New Year's, I stayed at the bar and got a little too drunk after we closed. Then my thumbs thought it'd be a great idea to send a text to my ex.

You can imagine how well that went down.

I shrug and say, "I make an exception for fireworks."

She shifts her weight from one heeled foot to the other, chewing on her lip. "Who else is going?"

"Just me and my cousin August. We're meeting a few women he knows." He called them a "good time."

For some reason, the idea of fucking some stranger tonight doesn't appeal to me.

"I don't know." She looks so conflicted, I can imagine her on an actual fence, swinging her long legs back and forth, glancing from one side to the other, unruly hair blowing in the breeze.

"Suit yourself." If a woman doesn't want to do something, I've learned not to pressure her because it almost always comes back to bite me in the ass.

The invitation has been extended. Short of throwing my neighbor over my shoulder and carrying her down to my truck, there's not much more I can do. "If you ever make up your mind and want join us, we're leaving at seven thirty."

———

My hair falls into my eyes as I let the shower beat me clean. There's no point rushing since August will be running late. He wouldn't be on time if he were made of clocks.

When I step out of my apartment at exactly seven

thirty, I consider knocking on Loren's door one last time to see if she's coming but ultimately decide against it.

If she wanted to tag along, she'd already be out here.

Something that feels a lot like disappointment fills my chest, but I shove that shit right down with every other unpleasant emotion and start for the stairs.

August waves up at me, looking ridiculous in a pink and black button down and a pair of black cowboy boots.

I love the guy, but his outfits are getting more absurd by the week. A couple days ago, he showed up to dinner in a pair of jean shorts and a tank top with one of those built-in bras.

Apparently, he lost some bet with his sister and now he has to wear whatever she picks out for him. Not sure how long that's going to last. Hopefully not long—for both our sakes.

I'm about to take the first step when my name echoes through the hollow stairwell. Loren stands outside her door, a shimmery black skirt skimming her thighs and an unsure smile on her lips.

"Got room for one more?"

Damn, those legs of hers look even longer than they normally do. It really is too bad that she has a boyfriend. "We do, but you might want to change into flats." As good as those heels look, I've been around enough women in my life to know what's bound to happen in about an hour. "I feel like your granny shoes would be more practical."

"Aren't you hilarious? Lucky for me, these heels are just as comfortable."

Women always say that, and yet ninety-nine percent of the time, I end up having to carry at least one of them on my back by the end of the night.

Still, it's not my job to convince her, so I shrug and say, "Suit yourself."

Surprisingly enough, she keeps pace with me on the way down the stairs.

The moment August sees Loren, his gaze drops straight to her legs encased in black hose with the thinnest black line running down the back.

He'll want to put a stop to that before we get to the city. I'm not dealing with his disappointment at the end of the night when she doesn't fall madly in love with him.

August has a very fragile ego.

"I need to grab something from my car really quick. I'll be back in a sec." Loren saunters off to collect heaven knows what. All I know is that she needs to bend over to get it. You can't see anything, but if you took a step to the right, then—

"Holy shit." A rush of breath whistles through August's teeth.

He knows I hate it when he does that, which is probably why he did it in the first place. I introduce my elbow to his stomach. "Not a chance, dipshit. She has a boyfriend."

"I can look, can't I?"

"At her face and that's all." Definitely not at her chest in that tight black sweater. That would be rude. *So rude.*

Loren's door snaps shut, and the lights flash when she locks it. She comes over with a smile on her face, seeming pretty damn happy about joining us.

I think I might be a little bit happy too.

I clap August on the back of the neck, giving him a little squeeze for good measure. "Loren, this asshole is my cousin, August. August, Loren Piper."

He must know what's good for him, because he sticks out his hand like this is some sort of business meeting. "Pleasure."

Her hand slips into his a little too quickly. "Nice to meet you, August. I really like your shirt."

"Why, thank you, Loren."

The compliment leaves him smiling way too widely. Guess he didn't recognize the sarcasm in her tone.

Before I get a chance, he opens the front passenger door for her.

I can feel my eyes narrow. "Behave," I mutter under my breath.

His answering smirk makes me wonder if this was a terrible idea. "Where's the fun in that?"

———

Loren crosses then uncrosses her legs like she can't seem to get comfortable in the front seat. Each time she does it, her skirt rides a little higher. Not that I'm looking. That would be incredibly dangerous considering I'm doing seventy miles an hour on the highway.

Closing the vent on her side, she settles back against the headrest before glancing at me, then at the irritating asshole breathing down my neck. "So, you two are cousins?"

August sticks his head farther between the two seats and pushes my arm away so he can rest his elbows on the center console. "Practically brothers. Born a month apart and grew up right next door to each other."

"Our Moms are sisters," I add, feeling a bit like the third wheel.

August squeezes his shoulders through the gap, his big head cutting off my line of sight entirely. "Speaking of sisters, do you have any, Loren?"

Loren's curls sway when she shakes her head. "Only child, I'm afraid."

Just like me.

Wonder if her parents drive her crazy too.

My mom has already called me five times today asking me to do this, that, and the other. The giant wooden Christmas tree my grandma painted needs brought in from the front yard and returned to the attic. She bought a new mirror that needs hung up in the "good" living room. She found a new podcast she thinks I'll like. She made home-made chili and froze two quarts along with a few cornbread muffins.

Granted, I didn't mind that last call quite as much.

"Cousins?" August tries again.

Since I can't see her face because of August's big, stupid head, I find myself watching the way Loren's black-tipped fingers toy with the gold zipper on her purse. "A few but they're like twenty years older than me."

August huffs a disappointed sigh. "That's too bad."

Enough is enough. "You know what'd be too bad? If I had to slam on the brakes and watch your head fly through the windshield. Sit your ass back and put on your damn seatbelt."

I'm not above pulling over and making him walk.

Although he grumbles, August does as I ask.

That's better.

At least now I can see our guest. She looks beautiful tonight—not that I'm going to say that out loud and make it awkward for the whole damn night.

There's no rule against thinking it, is there?

August's bony finger jabs into my shoulder. "It's going to be too busy downtown. Park on the East side. We can walk across the bridge."

"I know where to park."

"You think you know, but I can guarantee that you don't."

God, I hate him.

Loren unzips her purse, and it really shouldn't be sexy, but watching those fingers drag down that zipper makes me think of the zipper on my jeans that suddenly feel a lot tighter than they were a few seconds ago.

"I have my parking pass," she says, withdrawing a red hanging pass. "My office is near the Gulch. Does that help?"

I didn't realize she worked all the way in the city. That drive is a bitch with traffic. Back when I worked in finance, I used to make it every day.

One of the many things I don't miss from my stint in corporate America.

"That's great. Thanks." It'll be a bit of a walk downtown, but at least we don't have to park across the river.

Her arm brushes mine when she leans forward to slip the pass onto my dashboard.

It should be an innocuous touch but even a graze has me firing on all cylinders.

Time to distract myself before I start getting ideas that have no place in my head.

When I ask what she does, she says she's a temp at an advertising agency. I don't know many people working as temps who like their jobs, but from the genuine smile on her cotton-candy lips, she appears to be the exception.

I think I might even like her job too when I find out the parking lot is right at the top of the hill, behind the museum.

Loren's hips sway as she walks, those sequins catching the streetlights like a disco ball. I don't normally pay too much attention to what I throw on, but being next to her makes me feel underdressed. If I'd known beforehand that she was going to come, I would've worn a button down instead of my plain black henley. Not that you can see it under my jacket.

August knocks my hip with his, giving me a knowing glance.

Looks like I got caught doing the one thing I told him not to do. Not that I'll ever admit it. "What?"

"You know what," he mutters under his breath so Loren doesn't overhear.

"Mind your own damn business."

He grins. "But minding yours is so much more fun."

CHAPTER 15
ELLIOTT

10:23 PM

THE WHOLE BOTTOM half of Broadway has been blocked off by barricades—not that a car could get through the swarm of people spilling from the bars into the street even without them.

Some bro country band plays too loudly from the stage that has been set up down by the river. There are a shitload of cowboy boots, sequins, and stupid glasses made of glow sticks.

August comes back from buying the first round with a black and gold top hat perched on his head, looking like an idiot. Loren asks where he got it, and he whips out a pair of glasses with the year as the frame for her.

Loren thanks him for the beer and the glasses, which look damn good on her, I must admit.

"Fear not, Elliott. I didn't forget you." August takes off his hat, revealing a second underneath.

"Yeah, I'm not wearing that."

"It's New Year's Eve. Don't be such a Debbie Downer."

Loren's plastic glasses slip down her nose when she nods in agreement. "Yeah, Elliott. Don't be such a Debbie Downer."

I hate the hat almost as much as I hate August's smiling face. "Fine." I take the damn thing and shove it on my head. If I don't, he's liable to end up calling me Debbie for the foreseeable future.

One night at work he called me Freddie Frowner the entire shift.

Loren salutes me with her bottle, saying the hat doesn't look half bad. Not exactly a compliment, but the closest thing to it that this woman has ever given me.

Loren's glossed lips wrap around the top of the bottle, and her throat bobs when she swallows.

I'm not proud of where my mind goes next, but the gutter and I are well-acquainted when it comes to my neighbor. Started the first day I saw her outside her apartment wrestling that mattress and hasn't gotten better since.

The rest of the assholes around us nudge each other and stare blatantly at her. So sue me if I step a little closer to make it look like we're together. I'm only doing it for Loren.

Who wants to spend their night fending off unwanted advances?

It's too loud for a proper conversation, so we drink to the tune of whining steel guitars and pounding drums while August's thumbs fly across his phone's screen. I'm nearly finished with my beer when two petite women in matching pink sequined dresses and hot pink cowboy boots appear out of nowhere, throwing their arms around August's neck and kissing his cheeks. Their lipstick leaves smudges all over his face, but I decide not to tell him and snap a picture instead for future blackmail situations, should they arise.

As if they realize Loren and I are staring, the two women turn and offer matching smiles.

Twins.

Of course they are.

August introduces them as Tamela and Tamille, tapping his beer bottle against mine, his dark eyes filled with humor. Since it's my round, I offer to buy everyone another drink. When Loren doesn't immediately respond, I lean down close to her ear so she can hear me. "You want another one?"

A smile and a loud "What?" are all I get. Well, that and a waft of peaches.

Shampoo? Perfume? Unclear.

Either way, it's hazardous for my self-control.

My fingers strangle the empty bottle in my fist. "Do you want another beer?"

"Nah, I'm good," she shouts, giving me a thumbs up. "Don't really feel like drinking too much tonight. Just here for the fireworks. If you want to have a few more, I don't mind driving."

I don't like people driving my truck, but the longer I look at Loren, the drier my throat gets. I'm starting to worry that the only way I'm going to survive a night with this woman is through copious amounts of alcohol. Still, I feel guilty even thinking of having another drink when this is supposed to be her night out too. "I didn't invite you just so you could be the DD. We can grab a ride share later, and I'll get my truck tomorrow."

"I know you didn't. I'm the one offering. Besides, I'd say all the ride shares have probably been pre-booked, so we'll be waiting forever. Go." She shoves me toward one of the vendors selling beer from a cart.

The woman is stronger than she looks.

I fish my keys from my pocket and drop them into her palm. "They're my only set. Don't lose them in your ridiculous purse."

Although she makes a point to roll her eyes, she tucks them into her bag, and I wonder if she'll ever find them again.

———

LOREN

Freaking Josh.

That's all I can think as I check my phone for what feels like the hundredth time only to find no messages and no missed calls.

I haven't spoken to my boyfriend since he left for California. I guess it's my fault for assuming when he asked me to call him that he'd answer.

If Meg hadn't gone back to Ohio for the weekend, I'd be out with her, drowning my sorrows in cheap beers at a stale bowling alley.

Instead, I'm here with my neighbor and his cousin, who is currently making out with one of the hot twins.

This wasn't the plan.

Wine and leftover crab cakes had been in my future, but the thought of sitting around my apartment stewing for yet another night sounded like hell, so I made an executive decision.

It's not like there's anything going on between Elliott and me.

We're friends.

Sort of, anyway.

Josh will get over his jealousy.

Or he won't.

To be honest, I'm starting to not care either way.

What kind of boyfriend leaves without calling even once, just to say he made it safely to the hotel?

This coming year is supposed to be the year of Loren Piper but with the way this one's finishing up, I'm not so sure the next one is going to be any better.

The second twin rolls her hips to the beat of the music, both hands raised over her head.

How is she not freezing in that dress? She's not even wearing any hose.

Elliott returns with four plastic cups pinched in one hand and three in the other. When he hands me mine, I ask what it is.

"Diet Coke."

Huh. "How did you know I like Diet Coke?"

"There were at least five empty cans in your trash can."

Maybe I should be appalled that he noticed what was in my trash; instead, I'm reluctantly impressed. This is how low my standards have become. "Thanks."

"No problem." He mixes what I assume is a shot of liquor in with the sodas, handing them out to the others in our party. His twin doesn't stop moving even as she swipes the cup and drains the whole lot.

"Your date seems fun." I feel bad for shouting at him, but it's the only way to hold a conversation with all this ruckus.

His top hat tilts as he eases closer. "Yeah. She does."

"Don't you want to dance with her?"

"I'd rather jump off that bridge naked."

Not a dancer. Good to know. "That's one way to celebrate the new year."

He chuckles into his drink, sipping slowly.

If I had a few more, I'd be out there with her. Unfortunately, sober Loren has no rhythm.

I've been told drunk Loren doesn't either, but this has yet to be proven with hard evidence. Even if it were, drunk Loren wouldn't mind. She's impervious to judgment.

A breeze cuts through the crowd, finding its way straight through my sweater. I thought the chunky cable-knit would be warm enough but, like many things this week, I was wrong.

Should've worn a coat.

I glance up to find Elliott no longer staring at his gyrating date, but at me, his brow furrowed and a frown on his face. "Are you cold?"

"Nah. I'm good." Alcohol would warm me right up, but since I offered to drive, I shall die on this frozen hill.

"Don't be a hero, Loren. We still have two hours before the countdown."

"I'm honestly fine."

Rolling his eyes, he slips his arms from his coat, and I know what's going to happen next because I've seen my fair share of movies but when he drapes his coat over my shoulders, my immediate reaction is a high-pitched squeal.

That's right. I've gone full pig.

Elliott leaps back, spilling his drink all over his comfortable-looking boots.

I'd rather have those than his coat, to be honest. Not that I say as much.

I shall take my aching feet to my grave.

"What the hell was that? Are you part bird?"

"Shut up. You startled me." Turns out, a jumpy Loren is even weirder than a calm one. Who knew? "You don't have to give me your coat. You're only wearing a long-sleeved shirt," I say even as I hold my purse between my knees and slip my arms into the sleeves. The thing hangs off me, but it's warm and smells heavenly.

This coat might be mine now.

"I dressed appropriately and wore a thermal top under this."

"This is appropriate for the occasion." Everyone knows New Years calls for sparkles, and I didn't have a cute jacket to wear over this sweater. My warm, downy one would've looked ridiculous and covered my skirt.

I've heard "beauty is pain," but what no one tells you is that beauty can be a frigid bitch, too.

"Are your feet hurting yet?"

"No." This earns me a smirk, which I don't like one bit. "Why don't you go bother your date?" If she's anything like her sister, who is currently wrapped around August like a sparkly pink blanket, I bet Elliott's twin would be more than willing to keep him warm.

"Seems like she's having more fun without me."

She does seem to be having a lot of fun grinding between those two guys. Not sure why she's wasting her time with them though. They're not half as hot as Elliot. Objectively speaking, that is.

I bump my shoulder against his. "Jealous?"

"Of someone I just met dancing with other guys? Not in the least."

Considering what I know about Elliott Grant, he doesn't seem like the type to get too attached.

Unlike myself.

Maybe Elliott can give me some pointers on how to care less and avoid falling hopelessly for every handsome face that looks my way.

CHAPTER 16
ELLIOTT

MAYBE LOREN IS RIGHT. I probably should at least try to make small talk with my date after August went through all the trouble to set us up. Although, from the way he and Tamille are wrapped around each other, I'm not sure his motives were entirely selfless.

Either way, I don't want him to give me shit for not even trying, so I take a deep breath and push my way onto the pavement dance floor to sidle up next to my date.

"Hey."

A slow, coy smile teases Tamela's glossy lips as she peers up at me through lashes that are way too long and thick to be real. "Hey," she says back.

Now what?

Let's see...

"Having fun?"

"Oh, yeah."

Not really a lot to work with there. Time for a drink, I suppose.

And August wonders why I don't go out on "proper" dates. Isn't it painfully obvious? I don't know this woman, have no clue if we have anything in common at all, and I'm just supposed to learn everything there is to know about her in a couple of hours?

At least at the bar, there's not much small talk.

A woman flirts with you, you flirt back. At the end of the night, you ask her to your place, she says yes, and the deal is done.

We still have a couple of hours until the end of tonight, and I'm not exactly sure how to fill them when all Tamela seems to want to do is dance and I have zero rhythm.

Less than zero. We're talking negative rhythm here.

I squeeze my cup a little tighter. "So what do you do?"

Why did I ask that question? This isn't an interview. We're not swapping resumes. Also, I don't really care about her answer, so the question feels hollow.

Fuck. I hate small talk.

She pushes my shoulder, never losing the beat. "Right now, I'm dancing."

I can see that.

I am way too sober for this. "What about when you're not dancing?"

"Oh." A giggle. "I'm sort of on a journey of self-discovery at the moment." She twists her arms above her head while simultaneously rolling her hips, knocking them against mine. "Trying to find what brings me joy."

Unemployed then.

No judgment here. I did my fair share of "self-discovery" a few years back. It just looked a lot...darker.

Less dancing and more drinking.

Her hands flatten on my chest, then slide down my stomach before heading north again.

I'm all for casual touches, but the way she squeezes my pecs feels dangerously close to groping.

Yeah. I don't like it.

I step back so her hands fall away.

"You have a great body," she yells.

Heat climbs my neck, spreading all the way to my ears. "Thanks." The gym is the best place to blow off steam. With a mother like mine, there tends to be a lot of it.

Apparently, my running away wasn't hint enough because Tamela does this little side-shuffle to close the distance once more. Then she rakes her nails down my arms, and I use the term "nails" in the loosest sense of the word. They're more like long neon pink claws that sparkle like her dress.

"A *really* great body." Her teeth drag along her lower lip, which I figure is meant to be seductive or whatever, but feels too calculated.

Even when I do bring women back to my place, there's at least a little connection, superficially. Tamela is hot, but I'm as attracted to her as I am to August.

Strike one.

"Do you come downtown often?"

"Oh, all the time. I love Broadway."

Strike two.

I'd venture to say most folks who "love Broadway" aren't from Nashville—or Tennessee for that matter. That or they're desperately trying to break into the country music scene. Or both.

"Where are you from originally?"

"Oregon."

"What brought you to Nashville?"

"The music. What else is there?"

The restaurants, the history, the parks, the weather, the lakes, the rivers… I could go on, but there's no point.

"Can I tell you a secret?" She catches my collar and drags me down so she can shout in my ear. "I'm a singer."

Strike three.

Not for being a "secret" singer, but for the grabby hands. Normally, I can get on board with grabby, but there needs to be some sort of connection first.

Extricating myself from her hold once more, I force a smile. When my gaze finds Loren's, she gives me two thumbs up. I must admit, she makes those silly glasses look good.

Too good.

Her cup is empty. Does she need another drink?

She's not your date, dickhead.

She belongs to someone else.

Maybe so, but technically she's my guest tonight so the least I can do is ask if she wants another drink. Or food. There are a shitload of vendors.

Probably should ask my actual date first though. "Are you hungry?"

"No!"

Thank goodness. "I'll be back." Or not. Tamela doesn't seem to care as she bobs her head and goes back to dancing with someone else.

The tension in my chest eases a little more with each step I take away from her. Or maybe it's because of whom I'm walking toward.

Loren bobs her head to the music, her grin growing when she sees me coming.

Probably best not to overanalyze. "Hey."

She drags her glasses down her nose to waggle her brows over the plastic rims. "Sweet moves, Travolta."

"Very funny." I wasn't even dancing. More like... swaying awkwardly. "I was going to ask if you were hungry but if you're going to make fun of me—"

"Me? Make fun of you? Never. Also, I'm starving and the smell from that BBQ truck is making me swoon."

Me too. I'm going to demolish a pork BBQ sandwich. "Come on then. My treat."

Loren practically skips next to me, but then she stops. "Don't you want to ask your date?"

"She doesn't want anything."

"You sure about that? From the way she was grinding on you, it looked to me like she wanted an Elliott sandwich."

See? This is how you hold a conversation. Give and take. Ebb and flow. Maybe Loren could give Tamela lessons. Although I'm still not sure I'd want to get to know her that badly.

———

Everyone is counting down, shouting and laughing, but all I can do is stare at Loren in those glasses, my jacket hanging off her thin shoulders.

She has a boyfriend, dumbass. Stop gawking like you've never seen an attractive woman before. My gaze drops but only makes it as far as her lips. The gloss she applied a few hours ago is long gone. Those lips of hers are bare and smiling.

"Happy New Year!" erupts around us but all I can hear is my thundering heart. My feet think it's a good idea to bring me a step closer.

Abort. *Abort!*

I must be a fucking superhero because I manage to turn away, only to find Tamela blinking up at me with fireworks reflected in her pale blue eyes a split second before her hands fly to my cheeks and she smashes her mouth to mine.

The force knocks my hat clean off.

I'm so stunned, I don't even have time to close my eyes.

When my gaze meets Loren's, pink stains her cheeks. I know I probably shouldn't do it, but I hold her stare a beat too long before screwing my eyes closed and kissing Tamela while imagining my date tasting like peaches instead of stale beer and cigarettes.

Imagining the sequins beneath my hands are black instead of neon pink.

Fuck. Okay. Who knew all I needed to feel attracted to Tamela was to pretend she was someone else?

I should probably pull back before things get out of hand. Get my head on straight. Banish these thoughts back from whence they came.

Don't ask me how Tamela ended up with her legs around my hips, but as I ease her back to the ground, my gaze finds Loren's once more, like a ship lost along a dark shore, searching for the lighthouse to warn them of impending danger.

Loren's tongue sweeps across her own lips, and part of me wonders if she's imagining the same thing.

"You need a New Year's kiss!" Tamela shouts at Loren. My neighbor opens her mouth, presumably to protest, but Tamela takes that as an invitation to stamp her lips over Loren's.

And I thought her cheeks were pink before. This time, her blush goes all the way down her neck, disappearing under my jacket's collar.

Loren stumbles back, giving Tamela a jittery smile.

The moment Tamela turns toward her next victim, Loren swipes a hand across her mouth.

Drink.

That's what I need to wash away the disgusting taste clinging to my tongue. Our gazes catch, and I nod my chin toward Tamela spreading the love to another guy. "You know, if it doesn't work out with the boyfriend, maybe you can get her number."

Loren's throaty laugh wreaks havoc on my self-control. "I would, but I could never date a smoker."

Neither could I. Not seriously anyway. "Yeah. It's like making out with an ashtray."

Meanwhile, August has his tongue down her twin's throat, his ridiculous top hat sitting cockeyed on his head as they grope each other like no one's watching.

Get a fucking room.

I shift a little closer to Loren so I can speak to her without going hoarse. "Did you have a good night?"

She bobs her head. "It beats hanging out by myself in my apartment like I did for Christmas. Thanks again for inviting me."

Hold on. She spent Christmas all by herself? I thought she was going to spend the holiday with family or her boyfriend. Shit. Now I feel like a dick for not stopping by to wish her a Merry Christmas. Not that it was my job to do that.

I thought I hated her boyfriend before.

"Anytime." I mean that. She's easygoing, which is rare in my experience. Then again, it could be because she has a boyfriend and isn't trying to pressure me into something I'm not interested in.

A boyfriend who left her alone on Christmas *and* New

Year's. What a dickhead. "So, what's your boyfriend doing in California?"

She scoots her New Year's glasses onto her head, like one of those headband things, pushing back her curls. "He had to go for work."

"What does he do?"

"He's a lawyer."

Yeah...I'd bet every cent in my bank account that he's not really working right now.

I take a sip of warm bourbon and coke to keep myself from saying something I shouldn't. It's not like Loren asked for my opinion. If she wanted it, I'd be more than happy to share, but as it stands, my lips are zipped tight.

The sulphury smell of fireworks hangs in the air as the crowd starts to thin. When Tamela asks what my plans are after this, I may or may not lie and tell her that I need to get up early tomorrow as an excuse to go home alone.

August doesn't have the same reservations. He tells us goodnight and slings an arm around his twin, leaving me with a crowd of people, my neighbor, and thoughts that don't belong in my head.

CHAPTER 17
LOREN

4:58 PM

Hey! I hope you made it to the hotel safe
and sound.

9:56 PM

I miss you

Wish you were here

12:07 AM

Happy new year!

AUGUST DITCHED US.

Not that it should be a surprise since he and his date
barely came up for air all night. Still, I'm sorry he's not here
to ease this weird tension that seems to be crackling in the
air between Elliott and me. It's probably all in my head
because my neighbor doesn't seem the least bit affected as
he strolls up the hill, hands in his pockets and eyes straight
ahead.

Meanwhile, my head is spinning like the Scrambler at the county fair.

To make matters worse, my feet are killing me, and we still have a long way to go before we get to Elliot's truck.

Maybe if I focus on the pain, I can use it to distract myself from the lust overcoming my loins.

That's right: Loren Piper is hella-horny.

Are we still saying hella?

Either way, it's facts.

I may have a boyfriend, but right now, I can't even picture Josh's face.

All I can see is Elliot claiming that woman's mouth. The way his big hands slid around her waist. How his biceps flexed when he lifted her up so her legs could wrap around his slim hips.

Elliott Grant wins New Year's hands-down.

All I got were sloppy seconds.

Should I tell Josh I kissed someone to celebrate?

The thought makes me chuckle. Then again, he'd have to answer his phone for me to share the big news.

Elliott glances over at me, his brow furrowing. "What's so funny?"

"Just wondering if I should tell Josh that I kissed someone else tonight."

For some reason, the confession doesn't make him smile. He's looking at me, so he must've heard what I said, but he doesn't respond.

I guess that's the end of our conversation.

Oh, well.

With nothing better to do, I take out my phone to check for a message from Josh.

Nothing.

He could've at least responded to my last text considering he read it almost as soon as the thing went through.

Whoever invented read receipts must be some sort of masochist.

Pain. Focus on the foot pain to distract yourself from the ache in your chest.

We're not even to the top of the hill when the balls of my feet start to cramp, and I'm pretty sure my heels are more blister than skin at this stage. Elliott keeps walking, but I stop so I can covertly slip out of my shoes and let the cold pavement soothe my feet.

It's only meant to be a temporary fix, but after I see the blood gluing my hose to my poor heels, there is no way I'll be putting these devil shoes back on.

I turn around to find Elliott's hands planted on his hips and a scowl on his face.

"I fucking knew it."

"Knew what?" I swallow my grimace as I hobble forward, shoes hooked in one hand and my purse looped in the other.

"That those shoes were going to hurt your feet."

Surprise, surprise. Another man saying, "I told you so." Exactly what the world needs since we don't hear the phrase nearly enough. "I'm in pain. I need sympathy, not judgment."

Elliot drags a hand down the back of his neck and curses again before turning around and squatting down. "Come on."

I stare, not sure what he wants me to do. Am I supposed to squat too?

"Get on my back, Loren."

Uh, yeah. That is not happening. "I'm not getting on your back."

He rises and stalks toward me, his eyes narrowing with irritation. Not gonna lie, it's kinda hot if you're into the whole "dark-haired, broody guy" thing.

I wish I could say I'm not but I am. I totally am.

"You're going to step on a rusty nail and need a tetanus shot, and then I'll feel guilty," he grinds out.

So much for a knight in shining armor. He's more like a snarly dragon. Something I also happen to be into thanks to my latest Romantasy obsession. "I'm sorry, but I don't really feel like flashing all of Broadway with my underwear tonight."

The outfit might be cute, but the underwear beneath is *not*.

In my defense, life has been hella busy (I'm bringing it back, okay?), and I haven't done laundry in a while.

Just when I think he's going to drop it, Elliott picks me right off the sidewalk and throws me over his shoulder like a fireman.

Now, *that* is a sexy job. Firemanning.

Elliott could be a fireman. He certainly has the strong arms and the ass for it. Damn, he fills out those jeans.

Stop looking!

Horny Loren is the worst, especially when she notices the largeness of the warm, calloused hand now resting on the back of her thigh.

Logically, I know it's to keep my skirt from flipping up and giving the whole city a good gander at my underthings, but the orgasm-deprived part of me wonders what it'd feel like to have that hand slip under the material instead of holding it flat.

That, ladies and gentlemen, is the true reason I didn't drink tonight. Not to avoid a hangover, but because I could feel myself being pulled like a magnet to this man, and drunk Loren has been known to make poor decisions. Like the time I stripped bare and jumped into a frozen lake in the dead of winter.

I had to lock her down and remind that wild child that she is in a committed relationship and sexy neighbors who make out with other women right in front of her do not get to ride this merry-go-round, no matter how big his hands are.

My purse flops against the back of Elliott's thigh with each step he takes. Meanwhile, there's nothing for me to do but wait for him to get tired and put me back down.

Up, up, up the hill he goes, waiting at crosswalks, dodging rowdy crowds drunkenly making their way up and down Broadway.

He's had quite a few drinks. Shouldn't he be the one getting carried? Not that I'd have a hope of lifting him if he were to fall over.

"This is ridiculous," I grumble.

"No, those shoes you wore are ridiculous."

"*You're* ridiculous."

"Next time, you're not getting into my truck unless you have on proper footwear."

"I'll have you know that I've owned those shoes for years and never gotten one blister." It's true. Mostly. The first time you wear something doesn't count.

He snorts like he knows I'm a lying liar. We make it up the hill, and he still hasn't put me down. Which is pretty dang extraordinary considering I'm not a small woman.

If I were a tiny little teacup poodle like Smokey Pam (the name I've given Elliott's date), it'd be no big deal. But I'm more like a...a mastiff. Or a wolfhound. Yeah, a wolfhound. That's what I am. So while I am still very annoyed by the time we reach the truck, I am also quite impressed.

Elliott puts me down, not on the ground, but on the running board on the driver's side. I have to hold onto the roof rack to keep from slipping off.

"Aren't you going to thank me?" he says.

I blink down at him with an innocent smile. "For what?"

He rolls his eyes and folds his arms across his chest.

Is he seriously going to stand there and wait for me to thank him? "Thank you, Elliott."

Still, he doesn't move.

"What are you doing?"

"Waiting for you to find my keys."

Right. Since he gave me the keys.

Now, this should be a fairly simple task; however, I brought make-up in case I needed to reapply so there's a good bit more in my purse than there normally would be.

Like mascara. Lip gloss. A pack of tissues. Let's see...

"Tell me you didn't lose them in the black hole."

"Don't call my purse a black hole." Although that is an apt description. I'm sorry I didn't think of it. "Hold this." I hand him the makeup and continue rooting around. Oh god. I think I just touched something furry. Whew. Just my scrunchy. I toss that at Elliott as well. There are my keys, but where are his?

Crap.

"Loren?"

"They're in here. Just give me a sec. Do you have a flashlight?"

"Black holes eat light," he mutters, shifting my stuff into his other arm so he can retrieve his own phone from his pocket and flick on the flashlight.

Now that I can see, I manage to locate his keys under the reusable straw Meg gave me the other day. "Found them."

A grumbling Elliott drops my stuff back into my purse and then rounds the front of the vehicle to climb into the passenger seat. By the time I slip into the driver's side, he already has his seatbelt fastened.

Even as tall as I am, Elliott's seat takes forever to slide into place, and I can feel his eyes burning a hole into the side of my face.

"Why do you keep looking at me?" It's unnerving and I don't like it. Mostly.

"Just making sure you know what you're doing."

He can't be serious. "I know how to drive." Got my permit at fifteen-and-a-half and haven't had so much as a speeding ticket except that one time. In my defense, they dropped the limit in town without telling anyone.

He leans against the center console, draping those long fingers of his over the gearshift. "But do you know how to drive *well?*"

I give his knuckles a flick. "If you get your hand off of this, we'll find out."

While I have been driving for over ten years, I should probably mention that I haven't driven anything bigger than the hearse. This thing has a steering wheel and a gas pedal, so it can't be *that* different.

At least that's what I believe until I need to squeeze out of this teeny-tiny parking space.

The worst part is, Elliott thinks he's being helpful by telling me what to do. Like I don't see the neon green Jeep parked behind us.

Newsflash: I do.

With all his side-seat driving, I'm so flustered by the

time I pull out of the damn parking lot, that I nearly miss the turnoff for the highway.

"I'm surprised you didn't want to stay with Pamela." At least then I could've driven home in peace.

"Who?"

"Seriously, Elliott? Don't tell me you're one of *those* guys." I glance over to find him watching me with a blank expression. "You literally had your tongue down the woman's throat thirty minutes ago."

"Her name was Tamela."

I think I'd remember if the woman's name was Tamela. "No, it wasn't."

His lips twitch. "Yes, it was."

"You're wrong."

"Why don't I text August and find out?" He reaches into his pocket and withdraws his phone. The bright screen highlights the stubble on his chin and casts his eyes in shadow.

Eyes on the road, Loren.

"Go right ahead." Because I'm right...right? Of course, I am. "What do I get if I'm right?"

He drops his phone into the empty cupholder. "What do you want?"

Excellent question. Something good. Something embarrassing for him. Something like... "You have to feed me for a week. And you have to buy whatever food I say." Might as well get something useful from this bet.

"Done."

Okay, that was unexpected. Why did he agree so quickly? I could tell him I want filet mignon every day or lobster.

Mmm. Lobster.

"When I have proof that you're wrong, I want crab

cakes every day this week," he says, that cocky smile back in full force.

I can't afford that. Crab is expensive.

Not that it matters because her name wasn't Tamela.

"Fine."

Elliott taps the screen on the dash and turns on some music. We catch the tail end of Bon Jovi's "Living on a Prayer," then the beginning chords of Def Leopard's "Pour Some Sugar On Me" blare through the speakers, which of course makes me think of the time I blared the very same song so I wouldn't hear my neighbor banging his latest conquest.

Elliott huffs a laugh and cranks the volume, singing along remarkably in tune for a guy who's had so much to drink. It's Def Leopard, so of course I join in. I'm not a monster.

By the time we get to our apartment complex, we've made it through eight power ballads.

I park kinda far away, but it's the only space that looks big enough for this mammoth vehicle.

The moment I shift into park, his phone lights up with a message. I grab for the thing, but of course his big hand gets in the way, and he gets to it first.

Elliott's laugh booms through the cab, rattling my eardrums.

When he holds the phone across the center console, my stomach sinks.

AUGUST

Really, dude? Her name is Tamela

"I like to eat dinner at six," Elliott says, handing me my purse from where he threw it on the back seat.

I drop the keys into his palm with a glower. "Fine, but you buy the crab."

His laughter follows me all the way into my apartment.

As annoyed as I am, I find myself smiling as I throw the deadbolt.

But then I call Josh, and it goes straight to voicemail, and my smile disappears.

MEG

Meg: I'm drowning here.

Can't wait to see your face.

MUST. Have. Coffee.

Even after going to bed at three am on Saturday night, my body thought it'd be a great idea to wake up at seven on Sunday. After spending all day walking around like a zombie, could I sleep last night? Nope.

Now I feel like roadkill.

Thankfully, Meg met me the moment I stepped into the break room with a big, fat lemon poppyseed muffin. Rebecca swept in a moment later, looking like a total girl boss in a black pantsuit paired with one of those silky tops that ties in a bow at the neck.

I've always wanted one like that.

Someday.

"You look fabulous," I say around a bite of muffin, since I'm apparently a monster who never learned to swallow before starting a conversation.

Rebecca fluffs the end of the ribbon, her cherry-red lips lifted in a friendly smile. "Oh, thanks. I picked it up last week."

What must it be like to see something you like and just *buy* it?

I can hardly remember.

She leans a hip against the counter. "How was your New Year, ladies?"

Like the responsible adult I want to be, I swallow my bite before responding. "Great. I came into the city to see the fireworks with some friends." And I'm still paying the price. Late nights have become my enemy.

"Ugh. I should've just stayed here," Meg mutters, adding another creamer to her cup.

"Why?" Rebecca and I ask at the same time.

"Just some crap with my ex I'd rather not rehash."

Sounds like fodder for bowling on Wednesday night.

I blow on my coffee so that I don't burn my tongue. Again. "How about you, Rebecca?"

She pours herself a mug from the pot next to the microwave, her whole face lighting up. "So amazing. My boyfriend and I took a trip out to see my parents in Carlsbad, then we went to the ballet in LA. It was magical."

New Year's at the ballet doesn't sound very magical to me. But if that's her thing, good for her.

"Oh!" She smacks my arm with an excited squeal. "You'll never guess who we met at dinner! Branson Mills."

I have no idea who that is.

"No way!" Meg seems impressed, so now I feel really left out.

I'll have to Google the guy when I get back to my desk.

"Yes! Look." Rebecca hands me her phone and starts talking about how this Mills guy bought them a ridiculously expensive bottle of champagne and all these words keep coming out of her mouth, but I can't stop staring at this picture.

Not at Branson Mills—I've seen the guy on some TV show or whatever, but that's not what steals all my focus.

That goes to the guy with his arm around Rebecca.

Not only do I know his face. I also know he snores when he sleeps and hates when people eat in his car.

Her boyfriend is Josh. *My* Josh.

Maybe I'm wrong.

Maybe Josh is her brother? Cousin? Some other distant relative? Maybe they both happened to be in the same place at the same time and both wanted to get a picture with the Mills guy.

I tap the screen. "Who is this next to you?"

"That's my boyfriend, Hinds." She laughs and rolls her eyes. "I mean, Joshua Hinden," she says with her nose wrinkled. "Now that he's been named partner at his father's law firm he hates the nickname, but it's a hard habit to break when I've been calling him Hinds since we were at Vandy."

Different last name. Does that mean my Josh gave me a fake freaking last name?

Wait. If they were dating since Vandy, that means they've been together since college!

Oh no...

He isn't *my* Josh at all. He's *her* Josh.

Oh, shit.

That means *I'm* the other woman.

Rebecca squeezes my arm, her concerned expression only making me feel more guilty. "You okay, Loren?"

"Oh, yeah. Fantastic." Handing back her phone, I swipe my sweaty palms down my skirt. This is bad. This is so, so, *so* bad. Rebecca is literal perfection incarnate, and Josh is cheating on her *with me.*

Do I tell her?

How can I? This isn't exactly morning-coffee conversation. This is the sort of thing you say in a text after you've moved countries and changed your name.

I should really get a passport.

Not that I have the money for an international flight.

Unless I sign up for another credit card.

No, no. Credit cards are the devil, and my credit is already shot.

Keep it together, Loren. You'll figure this out.

Meg gives me a weird look, like it's obvious I'm totally not keeping it together at all. "Why are you smiling like a serial killer?" she asks with a chuckle, taking Rebecca's phone to have a look at the picture herself.

I'm not smiling like a serial killer.

Am I?

I catch a glimpse of my reflection in the microwave door. Balls. She's right.

Meg chokes on her sip of coffee and starts coughing and gasping. I take the mug from her so she doesn't spill it all over her tan dress slacks and pound on her back, silently pleading with her to get it together so we can figure out what to do.

Meanwhile, Rebecca runs over to the sink to fill a glass with water.

Why does she have to be so amazing?

Not that it would make sleeping with her boyfriend any less wrong if she were a raging bitch, but at least it would make sense why the hell Josh would waste even a second on me when he's dating someone like Rebecca.

"Are you okay?" Rebecca's brow furrows as she holds out the glass toward Meg.

"Yeah. Sorry. Sometimes I choke."

That's what she's going with? *Sometimes I choke?*

Looks like this is a wave we're riding together. "It's true," I say, nodding way too quickly, but I can't seem to stop myself. Once I get going, there's no end in sight. "She chokes all the time. One time we were having lunch, and she choked on soup."

"Yup. Me and soup do *not* jive."

This is going from bad to worse. Someone needs to save us from ourselves.

As if he heard my mental cry for help, a man with a silver handlebar mustache steps into the break room. "Ms. James? Can you come into my office, please?"

Saved by the boss's boss.

If he wasn't the CEO, I'd hug him.

"Here." Rebecca hands Meg the water, grabs her phone and coffee, and leaves us to our disaster.

When the coast is clear, I drag Meg by the arm into the bathroom.

"Oh my god! Her boyfriend is your boyfriend," Meg blurts the moment the door falls shut.

"I know." I think I'm going to puke.

How could Josh do this to me? To her? What kind of asshole cheats on Rebecca James? And to let me move all the way down here without coming clean? To let me stay without telling me the truth...

What a scumbag.

Meg presses her hands to her red cheeks, her eyes wild. "Her boyfriend is *your* boyfriend!"

"Please, stop saying that." The more I hear it, the worse it sounds.

"What're you going to do?"

That two-timing piece of shit doesn't deserve to get away with this heinous crime.

I drag my phone from my pocket, finding his name at the top of my favorites. *Not for long.* My stomach roils when I see the last message he sent, telling me he can't wait for dinner tomorrow night.

Lying piece of shit...

My hands shake as I type out a message. "What sounds better: Hey Ratbag or Dear Dickwad?"

"Ratbag. Definitely." Meg steps closer, looking over my shoulder. "What else are you saying?"

"I'm telling him that I know everything, and he has until Friday to come clean to Rebecca or I will."

"Oh, yeah, that's smart. Put it back on him."

Send.

The screen has barely gone dark before the phone goes berserk and Josh's lying, cheating face flashes like a warning sign. If I didn't need this phone, I'd flush it and him straight down the toilet.

This explains why Josh never called me after he got to the hotel like he said he would. Why he was MIA the entire weekend.

Because he was out with his *actual* girlfriend.

So much for eating bad sushi and going to bed early, which was his excuse when he texted this morning.

I take great satisfaction in pressing that red button.

A barrage of texts flood in all at once, growing more and more aggressive.

As if I'm going to respond to him telling me to "answer the fucking phone."

I press and hold the power button, and the screen goes black.

Good riddance, asshole.

CHAPTER 19

LOREN

RAT BAG

Call me now.

SOMEHOW, I managed to keep it together until the end of the day, but the moment I get back to my apartment, madness descends, and I spend the next hour deep diving into Rebecca's socials and kicking myself for not stalking her sooner. At least then I could've found out the news in private.

Okay. Time to regroup.

If I stay in this apartment, this disaster is going to consume me.

I need to get out of here.

I need Meg.

Thankfully, she answers on the first ring. "How are you?"

Terrible. Shitty. Angry. Sad. Spiraling. "I want to go out." Scratch that. "I *need* to go out."

"Tell me when and where, babe."

"Meet me here in an hour."

"See you in sixty."

We hang up, and I head into mold-central for a quick shower to wash the stress sweat from my skin. Then I change into a silky green dress that I was saving for a special occasion.

Being cheated on seems like as good a reason as any to wear the outfit. It's not as if I'll be celebrating anything worthwhile any time soon.

Hidden beneath is my favorite bra of all time. My secret weapon.

Meg arrives right as I'm putting the finishing touches on my mascara. "Damn, girl. Your boobs look fantastic."

"Thank you." I always feel like a superhero in this bra. It's like a hero cape for my boobs. "Meg, meet sex bra." My best-kept secret that has seen too little action of late.

"That thing is doing wonders for your rack. You are getting some tonight."

After what happened this morning, "getting some" is the last thing on my mind. "Oh, no. I want every single man who sees me in this to suffer in agony when they realize they'll never get a glimpse of what's under here." I don't care if Harry Styles himself waltzes into the bar. This girl is off-limits.

Agreeing that going back into the city sounds like a particular brand of torture neither of us want to endure, we decide to find a bar close by.

Meg offers to drive and then we'll catch a ride share home, which is smart because neither of us plan to be anywhere near sober enough to get behind the wheel.

The place where we end up doesn't look like much from the outside, with Christmas lights still dangling from the gutters and neon signs in all the windows, but the inside is packed. Unlike the bars and restaurants on Broadway, there isn't one pair of cowboy boots in sight.

As we make our way to the bar, the crowd seems to part like the Red Sea, and I discover a familiar face behind the taps.

"Holy shit." I grab Meg's arm, dragging her closer. "I know him."

Her head swings, and her lips kick up. "Which one?"

"The guy in the black shirt. That's my neighbor I was telling you about."

"Ohhh! Does this mean I finally get to meet Hot Elliott?"

I slap my palm across her lips. "*Quiet!*" Yeah, it's busy in here and there is almost a zero percent chance Elliott can hear her over the music and chatter, but it would be just my luck for him to find out that I have, in fact, referred to him as "Hot Elliott" on multiple occasions.

For that reason alone, I remain at the high-top table while Meg goes to order us drinks.

No men approach me while I wait, which is a relief.

I don't have it in me to play nice tonight.

Tonight is for drinking and drowning and bitching about the terrible monsters that are the opposite sex.

"Men are the worst," I moan into my glass of gin and tonic as the lime inside sways like a sad little boat all alone on the sea. That's me. I'm a sad boat. All alone. Drifting nowhere.

Meg rests her chin on her elbow with a heavy sigh. "Agreed."

"Why do we waste our time with them?"

"Don't know."

Neither do I. I tip my glass into my mouth and nearly drop the thing when the ice cubes avalanche into my face. "Do you know what else is the worst? Freaking ice."

"Awe, no. I love ice. I'd never drink water if it weren't for ice."

That's true. Maybe all ice isn't bad. Maybe it's just the ice in my glass.

A shadow passes over us and a man appears as if he heard us talking about how awful they all are and has made it his personal mission to prove us wrong. Unable to read the room, he props his elbow on the corner of our table. "Hey there."

Meg shoves her hand toward the intruder's smirking face. "No."

"What—?"

"I said no."

The man slinks off, but not before calling us bitches.

"Do you ever wish you could bite people?" Meg muses, spinning the ice cubes around her glass with the straw.

"Just ratbag." I catch a glimpse of Elliott smiling across the bar at a woman with purple hair as he makes her a drink. "And maybe Hot Elliott." For two totally different reasons.

Meg snorts.

"Not in a mean way," I add for clarification. "More like a your-biceps-look-edible-let-me-nibble-on-them sort of way."

"He does have edible biceps."

"He does." Should I tell him that? If someone thought my biceps were edible, I'd want to know. Might help my self-esteem. Not that Elliott seems to have any issues with his self-esteem. Look at all those women drooling over him.

Still, sometimes our outsides don't match our insides and we're more self-conscious than people think.

I slide off my stool and saunter across the sticky floor to the shiny bar, nudging my way between two women in super cute dresses. Meg clambers behind me, squeezing herself into the gap as well so we're both squished together.

Elliott is too busy pouring a bunch of shots from one of those silver shaker things to notice us. I should get his attention. Say something suave and cool that'll be the perfect segue into a conversation about his edible arm muscles.

"I know you!"

Totally freaking nailed it.

Elliott's hypnotic blue eyes widen, and so does that lethal smile.

For the first time since we met, there's no guilt curling in my stomach over smiling back.

"I might have to sleep over at your place this weekend," Meg murmurs under her breath.

For some reason, thinking of her being one of Elliott's many conquests makes my stomach churn. Or that could be the gin swimming around in there. I really should've eaten more for dinner than that handful of stale corn chips.

Elliott runs the card for the man who bought the shots, then comes over to where we're waiting and braces his hands on the edge of the bar. His very large hands that were on the back of my thigh only a couple days ago.

Was he always this tall or has he had a growth spurt?

Remember this weekend when he carried me up that hill? Good times.

The memory makes me smile. Chivalry isn't completely dead. "You're a bartender."

"What gave you that impression?" he drawls, snagging a

towel from behind the bar and swiping it along the wood before throwing it over his shoulder like they do on TV.

Elliott could be on TV. He has the face for it.

And the ass.

"Funny." Hot guys shouldn't be funny. They don't need another weapon in their very full arsenal.

Meg extends her hand over the bar. "Hi. I'm Meg. Loren's very single best friend."

His hand dwarfs Meg's when he takes it. "Elliott."

Is he lingering?

He's totally lingering.

That's not fair. I want to shake his hand so he can linger.

"What can I get you two?" he asks, finally letting go.

I squint up at the shelves of bottles. *Soooo* many bottles. "Drinks."

"More specific?"

"*All* the drinks."

Meg holds up two fingers. Or are there four? "Two gin and tonics, please."

"Take a seat, and I'll drop them down to you."

Sounds like a plan to me. I slap my credit card onto the bar and say a little prayer that the payment I made yesterday cleared some necessary funds.

Meg snaps the card right back up and stuffs it into my purse. "As if I'd let you pay after what just happened to you."

Elliott's brows rise toward the bits of dark hair that have fallen over his forehead. My fingers itch to push them out of his eyes but then I remember the threat of hypnosis and figure it's better if they're covered.

Makes the hypnosis less effective.

Everyone knows that.

He's clearly curious about Meg's comment but there is no way I'm telling him my woeful dating story. Except his stunning eyes are locked on me and I have to say something to break this tension coiling in my chest so— "You need a haircut."

I am on a freaking roll here.

His full mouth breaks into another mesmerizing smile as he sweeps aside the strands with a careless hand. "Yeah, I know. It's pretty bad."

"It's not bad. It just gets in your eyes, and you have pretty eyes."

He leans an elbow on the bar, putting us way too close. Almost nose-to-nose.

Elliott has a nice nose. Straight and a little bit freckled. Never noticed that before.

The freckles. Not his nose. Clearly, I've noticed his nose. It's in the middle of his beautiful face.

"Oh, yeah? Anything else you want to compliment about me?"

Okay, flirty bartender. You're not going to hypnotize me. "You wish."

Mic. Drop.

His deep laugh booms over the thumping base as I turn and saunter back to our table in the corner.

Let the fun begin.

CHAPTER 20
ELLIOTT

IT'S ALMOST CLOSING time and Loren and her friend are still here. Normally, I'd be laying down the law and kicking them out so we can get home. But she's entertaining as hell when she's drunk.

Why is she so drunk though? From the dribs and drabs I've overheard from her conversations with her friend, it seems as though all is not well in paradise. How'd I come to that conclusion? Let's just say they've dropped the term "douche canoe" an insane number of times in conjunction with her boyfriend's name.

Called it the first time I saw the guy.

Loren's friend slips off her stool. They were at the far table for a couple rounds, then made their way to the open seats at the bar. "Time to go, doll face," she shouts. "We've got work in a few hours."

From Loren's pout, you'd swear her friend told her that someone ran over her cat. "It can't be time for bed already. I haven't even danced yet."

Loren has been on that dance floor tonight more than anyone else in this bar.

Not that there's any point in saying so. She seems determined when she heads to the center of the empty floor.

She looks shit hot in that green dress. If she were single and if she wasn't my neighbor and drunk as a skunk, I would absolutely shoot my shot.

Meg groans, dropping her face into her hands. "I'm never getting home."

"I can take her back if you want." The offer is out before I have a chance to stop it.

Meg narrows her eyes at me. "Why should I trust you?"

August chooses this moment to step out of the office. Should've known he'd be listening from back there. He's the nosiest Nellie there ever was. "Because he's basically Clark fucking Kent without the glasses. Unbutton your shirt, Elliott; show her the red and blue spandex suit you wear under those shitty T-shirts."

I'd take my "shitty T-shirts" any day over the Hawaiian button-up his sister made him wear for tonight's shift. "Nobody asked you."

August shrugs and heads over to the dishwasher to start unloading and drying glasses.

Loren's friend still doesn't look convinced. "You swear you won't touch her?"

I hold up three fingers. At least I think it's supposed to be three. "Scout's honor."

"Let me see your license."

I take out my wallet, and the woman snaps a photo of my ID. Knowing she's looking after Loren like this makes me feel a little better. There are a lot of shitheads out there. I'm glad they're being careful.

As I tuck my license back into my pocket, I ask if she needs a lift home as well.

"No, I'm good. I called a ride share. Is my car okay here tonight?"

"There are cameras on the lot, so it should be fine."

With that, she gives Loren a smack on the ass before disappearing into the frigid night.

I hang the cloths and towels on the edge of the sink, then shoot my cousin a glance. "You good to lock up?"

"Yeah, man. Get that girl home."

Loren is in her own little world, not even realizing there's no longer any music playing. The curls at her temples drip with sweat, and she's pulled the rest of her hair onto the top of her head. She looks like mayhem wrapped in one very sexy green package. "Come on, Chaos. Time to go."

Loren blinks at me, the hands that were twisting and flailing above her head slowly falling as she glances around the empty bar. "Where's Meg?"

"Went home to bed, I imagine."

"She left me here with you?"

"Why do you make it sound like it's the worst fate in the world?"

"Because it is."

Here I am, trying to be nice, and this is the thanks I get? Next time, remind me not to bother.

I hunch down so she can drape her arm across my shoulders, and together we walk to where I parked around the back of the bar.

At least I walk. Loren stumbles like a newborn foal.

Or a baby giraffe.

Yeah, that's what she is. A baby giraffe. What are baby giraffes called?

Leaning her against the side of the vehicle, I fish out my keys. "Don't puke in my truck, okay?" That shit is impossible to get out of the carpet. Don't ask me how I know.

Let's just say it involves August and tequila.

"Please. I'm not going to puke."

That remains to be seen. If I drank what she did tonight, I'd absolutely be introducing the contents of my stomach to the toilet when I got home. Work is going to suck for her *if* she makes it. Right now, it's not looking very promising.

She catches the handle and yanks before I've had a chance to unlock the damn door.

I press the button on my keys and hear the mechanism click, but Loren yanks at the same time and won't stop. "Hands off."

She throws her hands up in the air like I'm about to frisk her, and fuck, if that doesn't put some dirty thoughts in my mind. Like how good it'd feel to press those black-tipped fingers to the window, and kick her heels wider so I could slide my hands from her dainty ankles, over the swell of her calf and knee, up her inner thigh to—

Nope. Nope. Nope.

Eyes on the skies, Elliott. You are not touching this woman.

With her hands still over her head, it gives me the chance to open the door so she can climb in, which is easier said than done because her shoes keep slipping off the running board.

"Do you need help?"

"No. I've got it."

Doesn't look like it. "Just let me—"

"I said I've got it! I don't need a man's help. I am a perfectly capable, independent woman."

All right...

By the time I'm settled in the driver's seat, she's finally in. The engine roars to life, and I throw the thing into reverse, backing out of the lot.

Being cooped up in here with her peaches 'n cream scent slowly assaulting my senses is a torture I hadn't expected to endure tonight.

Time to turn on the radio and distract myself from the way her chest rises and falls with each breath.

Staring out the side window, she shoves her chaotic hair back from her face. "Why do men suck?"

"It's one of life's great mysteries." From the corner of my eye, I catch Loren frowning up at the moon. "Boyfriend trouble?" I assume, even though it's really none of my business.

"Yeah." She tugs one shoe off, then the other, and tosses them on the floor with a huff. "The *trouble* is he's not *my* boyfriend. He's someone else's."

No wonder she's been drowning herself in alcohol.

I never understood cheating. If you don't like someone enough to stay faithful, don't call them your girlfriend. Say you want to keep it casual or don't feel like being tied down.

It's common fucking sense.

It sucks for Loren that her boyfriend was a cheating asshole, but it sounds like she's better off—not that saying so aloud will help the situation. She needs to sit in the suck for a while before she sees it that way.

I tap my thumbs against the steering wheel, matching the beat of the Fleetwood Mac classic buzzing quietly from the radio. "How'd you find out?"

"I saw him plastered all over my boss's Instagram. They've been dating for years. *Years.* I can't believe I moved to Tennessee for the guy."

What a slimy fucker. "Does he know that you know?"

"I texted him as soon as I found out. He tried to call me a bunch, but I turned off my phone."

Half of me is worried he'll be there when I pull into our parking lot. The other half is sorry that he isn't because I want to call him a shithead to his face.

"I gave him till Friday to tell his girlfriend the truth," Loren goes on, collecting her shoes and purse.

"He's not going to tell her." No way is a guy like that going to admit he did something wrong.

"He might."

I may not know this dickwad from Adam, but I know men, and ninety-nine percent of them don't come clean when they're caught. They burrow deeper, like ticks. "The guy cheated on her. The last thing he's going to do is admit it. He'll wait until you do and then make it seem like you're the psycho."

Loren turns to me, her eyes wide as the full moon at her back. "What am I supposed to do? He shouldn't be allowed to get away with treating her like that, but I don't want her to hate me either."

The thing about a shit situation is that there's rarely a way around it without getting your shoes dirty.

Although she's right. That asshole shouldn't get away with it.

All she needs is someone to tell this woman the truth about her boyfriend. Her boss doesn't necessarily need specifics. "I could always message your boss."

The tiniest wrinkle appears between her shapely brows. "Out of the blue? Won't that be weird?"

I lift a shoulder. "Maybe, but I don't have anything to lose."

"Isn't there some sort of bro-code that forbids you from ratting out another guy?"

Fuck that. "People who cheat are the scum of the earth. Your boss deserves to know the truth, but you don't deserve the shit you'll get if she finds out you're the one he cheated with. You didn't know any better and ended things the moment you found out, right?"

"I ran into the bathroom and texted that ratbag straight away."

Ratbag. I like it. Suits him. "Exactly." I pull out my phone. "What's her handle?"

"Rebecca James. There's an underscore in the middle."

I tap on the Instagram icon and wait for the app to load. As soon as it does, I type in the woman's name. "Damn." She's a stunner. Does she look as good without all the makeup?

Every other photo is a picture of some exotic dish or another. Personally, I've never understood the trend. Food is for eating, not for posting.

Loren's head falls back against the seat. "I know, right? What kind of dipshit would cheat on someone like her?"

Someone like Rebecca, not someone like Loren. The casual distinction pisses me off. "He cheated on both of you." Rebecca isn't the only victim here.

Loren blows a raspberry through her lips. "I guess."

Seriously?

Sure, this Rebecca looks like a Victoria's Secret model, but Loren is pretty too. And she looks just as good with a fresh face.

Not that I tell her any of that because now is not the time to hit on my neighbor.

Even knowing the DM will go straight to Rebecca's "Requests" folder, I type out a quick message and hit send.

"I don't know, Elliott. Maybe we should wait and see if he tells her."

"Too late. It's already done."

"*What?*" Loren jerks out of her seat, leaning over the center console to grab my phone. "You sent it already? What did you say?" Her thumb swipes across the screen over and over again, as if there's more to see than a couple of lines.

"I said I saw him making out with another girl and thought she'd want to know." Which isn't a lie at all because I had seen dipshit and Loren making out in the parking lot one night.

She pushes the phone at me and falls back into her seat, pressing her palm to her forehead. "It's fine. It's *fine*. No one will know it was me."

"Exactly. Come on. Let's get you inside."

I jump out of the car and run around to the passenger side before she opens the door. It's a good thing, too, because she must not remember how high up she is and misses the running board completely, falling straight into me. I have to catch her to keep her from face-planting on asphalt.

Why did she put her heels back on?

I take her hand and help her climb. We reach the second floor before she tugs free of my hold and plops down on the concrete. "My legs are tired."

"Come on. Three more floors and you're home."

"I can't do it. You go ahead."

"I'm not leaving you behind."

"I'll be fine." She eases back on her elbows.

"Don't you dare lie down. Loren, get up. Loren? There's gum right beside your head."

She launches upright and glowers down at the hunk of pink next to where she was about to pass out.

"Up you come." I stretch a hand toward her, wiggling my fingers. "You can do it. I know you can."

Her hand locks onto mine, and I yank her back to her feet. She wobbles a bit and with each step she takes, she makes a keening sound like a dying hyena, but eventually we make it to her door where she roots around in her purse, muttering to herself.

I offer to look for her keys, but apparently, I've "done enough" and "should have let her sleep on the stairs."

Cursing, she squats down and dumps the contents of her purse onto the stoop. A wallet, tampons, chewing gum, two tubes of Chapstick, at least six hair ties, a napkin with— are those *chicken tenders?*—a ball of change, and a condom spill onto the concrete.

That thing really is like a black hole.

One more shake, and the keys magically appear.

Loren holds them up with a victorious smirk and proceeds to sweep the random assortment back into her purse, forgetting one thing.

Heat climbs my throat when I bend down to pick up the condom. "I believe this is yours."

"You keep it," she says, turning the key in the lock. "It's not like I'll be having sex anytime soon." Her maniacal laugh curls around my ears. "Besides, who needs men when you have vibrators?"

She leaves me standing alone in the hallway holding a fucking condom, wondering what other sex toys she might own.

CHAPTER 21
LOREN

SWEAT LEAKS from my palms as I walk into the office Wednesday morning. Meg and I both succumbed to the vat of alcohol we poisoned ourselves with Monday night and called in sick yesterday. She sent me a text this morning to say she still hasn't recovered, which means I must walk in alone. To make matters worse, my milk was expired so I had to choke down fistfuls of dry cereal between sobs and there's no scrumptious artisanal croissant or fancy coffee to make it all better.

Yesterday, I woke up with a hangover the size of Texas—and I use the term "woke up" in the loosest sense of the word because I didn't get out of bed the entire day.

That's right. I lay in my tiny bed in my crappy apartment and watched clips of horror movies—which I *hate*—on my phone all because every other video suggested was from freaking romcoms.

Whoever writes those things is a damn liar.

There is no broken hero with a traumatic past willing to change and do anything for the woman he loves. There are only assholes named Josh who lie and cheat and break hearts.

Now it's time to face the music, and I'm sick to my stomach with worry.

That Rebecca didn't get the message.

That she did and is devastated.

That Josh made me look like a psycho trying to steal her man.

That I'm going to get to my desk and find out I've been fired for sleeping with my boss's boyfriend, which means I won't have money to pay rent in February, and I'll get kicked out of my apartment and end up living under the bridge with all those mangey dogs.

What if they turn on me and make me their next meal? They have hunger written all over their scarred faces.

I could always go home. But to be honest, I think I'd rather brave the rabid wolf pack.

My hands keep wanting to ball into fists, but I force them to relax.

It'll be fine.

It'll all be fine.

I take the stairs nice and easy, focusing on breathing and putting one foot in front of the other. Past accounting. Past the design team. Up another set of stairs to the marketing department. All I have to do is make it to my cubicle. That's it. Wednesday's workload usually isn't too bad, so if I get to my desk, I'll be able to get through today.

"Loren?"

Slowly I turn, my heart jackhammering when I find Rebecca standing in her office's doorway. She doesn't look feral, but her boyfriend didn't look like a sleazy ratbag, so I don't trust my own judgement right now.

I start to wave but my hand refuses to cooperate and I end up doing this floppy-fingered sort of thing. And my smile? It's as stiff as a freaking brick. "Hey, Rebecca."

"I'd like to see you in my office if you have a minute."

Rabid dog meat, here I come. "Sure."

I try to saunter nonchalantly into her bright, airy office with a wall of windows overlooking the city, but my shoes feel like they're made of concrete blocks, and I end up trudging.

This is it. The beginning of the end.

The overwhelming floral scent from the mammoth bouquet on the corner of Rebecca's desk reminds me a bit of my family's funeral home. A bad omen, no doubt.

Rebecca settles onto her chair and folds her hands atop her desk. "Close the door and have a seat."

If I close the door, then no one will know I'm in here and they won't be able to hear me scream if she decides to shiv me.

Not that Rebecca seems the type to hide a shiv under that pristine black pencil skirt and classy white blouse, but I'm spiraling, so that's where I go.

The only reason I comply is because there's nowhere to stash a body. Unless the windows open.

Please, tell me the windows don't open.

With my heart in my throat, I ease the door closed. The latch lets out a shrill *click*. When I turn back around, she's still smiling. My wobbly knees knock together as I cross to the stiff office chair across from her.

Rebecca taps her blood-red nails against the corner of her keyboard. A ticking bomb. A death knell. "Are you feeling better after your day off?"

Oh no. She knows I was too hungover to move yesterday. That I got obliterated on a Monday night and called off work because of it.

"Yeah. A little. I stayed in bed all day watching slasher flicks." TMI, Loren. Dial it back or she's going to see right through you.

Her perfect brows arch toward her perfect hairline. "You like horror movies?"

Nope. Not at all. "Oh, yeah. The more gore the better. What about you?"

"I'm afraid horror isn't really my thing. I have a weak stomach." She reaches down beside her desk and heaves a black leather briefcase up and onto the top. Who carries a briefcase? Is she mafia? Is there a mafia in Nashville?

What's inside? My muscles tense as she flips open the top. A shiv? From this angle, it looks like a bunch of papers, but there could be some sort of weapon hidden underneath.

"Ah. Here it is." Rebecca returns the briefcase to the floor, leaving her clutching a stack of pages held together by a hot pink paperclip. "Sorry. I'm a bit turned around this morning." She blows out a breath, ruffling the perfect ginger waves draped over her shoulder. "We're looking for someone to oversee the traffic managers and I think you'd be a great fit."

Hold on...this is a *good* meeting? How is that possible? "I haven't been here very long."

"And yet in the time you've worked here, you've never been late on a deadline, your communication record with reps is brilliant, and everyone on the team seems to like you.

That's not necessarily a requirement, but it certainly makes the job easier."

To say I'm shocked is an understatement. "My contract isn't up for another four months."

"That's what I wanted to speak to you about. We've been in touch with the recruiting agency, and they said we can buy out your contract if we want."

My palms are so clammy, they're leaving a damp smudge on my dress slacks. Good thing they're black.

"You'd still be responsible for your daily duties," Rebecca goes on, flipping through the pages, "but you'd be asked to take the others under your wing and help them hit their goals like you do: Consistently. You would be fairly compensated, of course."

Compensated might be my new favorite word.

How do I ask about the pay without seeming like a rabid raccoon salivating over a juicy bag of restaurant garbage? "What's the salary?" It's gotta be a lot higher since I'll be doing my job *and* another one, right?

She skips to the pages at the back and frowns. "You're only on fifteen an hour?"

"I didn't have the relevant experience, so they started me at the lower rate." At least it wasn't eleven an hour like I was making at the call center.

The pages fall back into place and she steeples her fingers in front of her as she watches me through wide eyes. "Sorry. I didn't mean to sound like a bitch. I'm just surprised. You had a job before this, right?"

The call center probably doesn't count since it was for less than a week. "I waitressed in college and then worked for my family's business."

"That sounds like experience to me. I'd take a thousand waitresses over a bunch of pencil-pushers who haven't had to deal with the public." Her nail goes back to tap, tap, tapping on that keyboard, only this time, the noise doesn't set me on edge. "I think we can make this work for you. Most managers start off significantly higher, but I have a feeling they're going to balk if we shoot straight to that sort of rate. Would you be happy with forty-three?"

That seems a little low considering I'd be in charge of three other people *and* still have to maintain my own duties. But beggars can't be choosers. Either way, it's a ten-thousand dollar raise and that's nothing to sniff at. "That would be fine."

She props her elbows on the table and shakes her head. "Are you *sure*?"

My head starts shaking as well. "No?"

Her face lights up with a smile. "I can go to fifty."

Holy crap. Fifty-*thousand* dollars? That's almost what my mom makes, and she's been working for decades. "That sounds—"

Rebecca shakes her head again.

My knees bump the desk when I scoot forward in my chair. "A little low, actually?"

Her smile widens. "Fifty-five. But that's my final offer."

Holy shit. "That...um...that should be sufficient."

Rebecca holds a hand across the desk and gives mine a shake. "You drive a hard bargain, Loren Piper. It'll take a few weeks to get the contract sorted and your pay adjusted to the new rate. In the meantime, head down to HR and they'll go over the specifics of the job."

How can Josh cheat on this amazing, beautiful woman? "Thank you so much, Rebecca."

"It's my pleasure."

Her cellphone abandoned on the desk lets out a shrill

ring. Josh's face appears on the screen, and my stomach twists with guilt.

Rebecca's expression darkens when she picks up the handset. "I need to take this call. Can you close the door on your way out?"

I lurch to my feet. "Yeah. Sure. Of course."

Before the door closes, Rebecca answers in a clipped tone. "What the hell do you want?"

CHAPTER 22

LOREN

I BOUGHT MYSELF A STEAK.

I shouldn't have splurged on so much meat, but I did. The wine probably wasn't the best idea either considering the Tuesday I put down, but today calls for a celebration and since Meg and I aren't bowling, this was the next best thing.

The only problem is, I have no steak sauce. The steak gods are probably cringing over the fact that I use steak sauce, but they can enjoy their sauceless steaks in peace and leave me to mine.

The grocery store is ten minutes away, and by the time I go back there, buy steak sauce, and then get home, this glorious hunk of meat sizzling in the pan will no longer be at the perfect temperature, and I'm pretty sure microwaving a steak will anger the steak gods way more than a bit of sauce.

So I set down my dinner and head over to Elliott's.

He answers on the third knock, his dark hair damp and sticking to his forehead.

Did I mention he's shirtless?

Because he is very, *very* shirtless.

I knew he was fit, but this is...this is something else.

Not only that, but there is a towel wrapped around his waist. A very trim, very cut waist with those V's in his hips that you only see on TV.

He clears his throat, dragging my gaze up to his smirking face. "Did you knock just to stare at me or...?"

Of course, he had to open his mouth and ruin everything. I did come over here for some reason, but at the moment, all I can think about is licking the drops of water falling down the ripples of his very defined abs.

Let me see.

Promotion. Celebration. Dinner. *Steak.* That's the one. "I need steak sauce."

His dark brows jump beneath his fallen hair. "For what?"

"Tuna fish. What do you think? A steak, obviously."

"What kind of steak?"

"A ten-ounce filet." Not that it's any of his business.

At that, his eyes brighten. "What are we celebrating?"

"*I* am celebrating a promotion. Do you have any or not?"

He disappears into his apartment and returns with a bottle of steak sauce in hand. When I go to grab it, he holds the thing up over his head, just out of reach. "What do I get if I give you the sauce?"

"Why can't you ever just do anything out of the goodness of your heart?" He already won a week's worth of crab cakes that I'll have to make good on at some point.

"It's not my fault you mentioned steak at dinnertime." He pats his stomach, bringing my gaze right back to his bellybutton and the thin trail of dark hair that disappears beneath that towel.

Focus, Loren. He has sauce, you need it for your steak; you really don't have much of a choice. "You can have two bites."

"Half a steak sounds good to me."

"I said two bites. One. Two." I hold up my fingers so we're clear.

"No deal. I guess I'll see you later..." The knowing grin on his too-full lips expands as he eases the door closed nice and slow.

Here's the thing: my love of steak is only surpassed by my love of the sauce you smother it in. Sauce that is slowly disappearing through the shrinking gap in Elliott's closing doorway.

If I don't have sauce, then what's the point?

"Fine. You can have half my damn steak. But you have to put on pants."

He swings the door wide once more. "*Just* pants?"

"Clothes, Elliott. Put on all the clothes." Can't have the man sauntering over half dressed, distracting me from my party.

I snag the sauce and head back to my place to cut the steak in "half," leaving myself the bigger piece. This is my celebration steak, after all.

My neighbor doesn't arrive empty-handed. He brings over two Tupperware containers, one with spinach salad and one with leftover scalloped potatoes.

Maybe having him over isn't such a bad thing after all.

"Did you make these?" I pop the lid on the potatoes before throwing them into the microwave. Au gratin. My favorite.

"My mom did." When he douses his steak in sauce, I like him even more. Josh always had a smart comment to add when he took me out for steak and I asked the server for sauce.

I dump a little more over my own steak to spite him.

Ratbag.

"Does she live around here?" I assume, since this salad seems fresh.

"Yeah. About twenty minutes away."

I don't miss my parents as much as I thought I would. Sure, it would be nice if they were closer, but having them as close as Elliott's parents would give me a crutch, and I am determined to make life work without their help.

Thanks to this promotion, that might actually happen.

"Any word from your boss on the whole ex-fiasco?" Elliott asks, dragging a few spinach leaves onto his plate with his fork.

I shake my head and shove the bite I took to the side of my mouth so I can speak. Not the best manners, but this is my home and I'm hungry. If he wants to chat, he's getting heathen Loren.

I explain what happened in the office earlier today, the way she answered ratbag's call. The fact that I didn't see her again for another hour, and when she did emerge, the skin beneath her eyes was puffy and red.

"I hope Rebecca ditched him." I also kinda hope she lights him on fire, but that would land her in jail, and I like her too much to see her incarcerated. Maybe fate will light him on fire for us. Or strike him with lightning.

Yeah. That's what we need.

A lightning strike.

"So do I."

Of course he does. Why are men so freaking predictable? "What are you going to do next? Ask me to bring her by the bar?"

He reaches over to the counter to snag a paper towel from the roll, then dabs at his lips. "I'm not interested in your boss."

Yeah, okay. Do I look like I was born yesterday? I stab my steak, pretending it's his eye. "Why are men such liars?" Does it have to do with their DNA? At some point during evolution, were they all tainted by rats?

"It's not a lie. She's hot, but she's not my type."

"Rebecca is everyone's type. Hell, she might even be *my* type."

"Really? Tell me more."

"Shut up. Just admit that you'd date her, and we can move on."

Shaking his head, he tilts the wine bottle into my glass before filling his own. "Except I wouldn't date her."

"Right. Sorry. I forgot you have an aversion to commitment."

He sets the bottle back down.

I'd say his wide eyes look innocent if I didn't know better. There's nothing innocent about Elliott Grant.

"What makes you say that?"

"Did you forget we share a wall?" A very thin wall. "Guys like you don't settle down. You're always searching for your next conquest, thinking the grass is greener in someone else's pants."

The corners of his lips slant up. "If grass is growing in your pants, you should probably seek medical advice."

"Stop that. You know what I mean." He'll still be hot

and single well into his forties, maybe even his fifties, sleeping with women half his age.

Meanwhile, I'll be getting older and wrinklier but not wiser because my curse is to fall for guys who disappoint me. Sad, but true.

Elliott finishes his steak while I take my sweet time with mine, both of us falling into companionable silence that I feel no need to fill. For some reason, the blurting isn't quite as bad with Elliott. Maybe because we're not romantically involved and there's no pressure to go down that path.

Thank goodness for that.

He'd break my heart the moment I offered it to him.

Elliott sits back, resting one hand on his stomach as he sips his wine, watching me finish my last few bites. "So are you going to move back home since it didn't work out with shitbag?"

Talk about bringing down the mood. "Not if I can help it. I love my parents and all but their opinions on what I should be doing with my life do not line up with mine."

"How so?"

I set my fork and knife aside in favor of my drink, leaning back in my chair as well. Where do I even begin? "They think I should take over the family business."

"Which is?"

"A funeral home."

He blinks at me. "You're joking."

"Afraid not."

"I can't imagine you working in a funeral home. You're too full of life. You're like bubbles."

"Bubbles?" That's a new one.

"Yeah. Always rising up, effervescent, giddy. Shiny. Iridescent." A wince. "Sorry. That's weird, isn't it?"

"You're fine. I've decided to take it as a compliment."

"Good. Because I meant it as one." He glances down at his empty plate, his smile faltering. "I know what it's like to not live up to your parents' expectations. My mom always wanted me to be CFO of a Fortune 500 company. She was so disappointed when I quit to work at the bar with August."

Are we the same person?

Who knew I'd have so much in common with this guy? Does this officially make us friends? Heaven knows I could use another friend in this place, especially after losing the reason I moved here.

I could be friends with Hot Elliott as long as I don't let myself get hypnotized by his blue, blue eyes. "Elliott Grant, CFO. I can see it."

His nose wrinkles. "Really?"

"Yeah. I can." He'd look so hot in a three-piece suit. He'd look hot without one too. Moving on... "Did your mom threaten to disown you too?"

"Every single day since."

I hate that for him. For both of us. "Well, I'm proud of you, Elliott." His eyes widen. "I am. It's important to do what makes you happy, even if the people you love think you're wrong."

He holds up his glass of wine. "To being wrong."

Sounds like the perfect toast for tonight.

Smiling, I clink my glass against his. "To being wrong."

CHAPTER 23
ELLIOTT

MOM

Call your grandma and wish her a happy
birthday.

MY MOTHER IS WAITING on the front porch, a glass of
sweet tea in her hand and an apron over her dark skirt. She
looks like she walked straight out of a magazine from the
1950's. Not a blonde hair out of place, her makeup subtle
but fresh, nails painted a classy nude, and a demure smile
on her lips.

If August's family didn't live right next door, I
wouldn't have realized how messy life was allowed to be.
That your bed didn't need to be made every morning.
That some days it's okay to wake up and spend all day in
your pajamas. That sometimes cereal is the perfect
dinner.

That parents don't always know best.

I cut the engine and step out into the driveway, still

looking as freshly paved as the day last summer the crew came to tar it. "Hey, Ma."

"Elliott. So good of you to finally call."

What does she mean "finally?" I was here four days ago.

She holds out the glass, her smile as tight as the bun in her hair. "Would you like a drink?"

"Sure. Thanks. You know you don't have to wait outside for me, right?"

"Watching you pull into the driveway is one of my favorite sights. If only it happened more often."

Man, she's laying it on thick today. Should be a fun visit.

"Come on inside so you don't catch a cold."

Says the woman standing on the porch without a coat in the middle of January.

The house is as warm and cozy as a Thomas Kinkade painting—my mother's favorite artist as evidenced by the sheer number of his prints she has hanging around the place.

The foyer hasn't changed in all the years we've lived here. Still the same maroon walls that feel as if they're closing in on you. The same welcome mat where everyone is expected to leave their shoes the moment they arrive. Same silver hooks for our coats. The round mirror she inherited from my great-grandmother when she passed.

My mother waits with her arms folded until my shoes are next to Dad's boots. As if I would forget the rules. "How's life at the bar?"

There's always a tiny sneer curling her lips when she mentions my job. A hint of disdain. I bet she tells her friends this is a phase or that I'm taking some time off before heading back to Spencer Jones Investments.

"Work is great." January hasn't been very busy overall

but giving her anything less than glowing news only invites more problems.

Ammunition for her guilt gun.

"Where's Dad?"

"Out with Gerry's husband."

Gerry being August's mother. Aunt Gerry is three years younger than my mom, but I swear they were raised in two different families. Where my mom keeps the house tidy, Aunt Gerry thinks life is too short for cleaning. August's house always looked like a pack of wild apes lived there.

Having grown up with just my parents in the house, I found it difficult to adjust to all the noise.

Now, I'd rather go there for dinner than here.

If Dad is with my uncle, that can only mean one thing. "Is the feud finally over?"

The feud being my father losing his mind when August's dad had the audacity to hang a Kentucky Wildcats flag on his front porch. Never mind the fact that August's youngest sister just got into school there. That was obviously completely irrelevant.

Dad insisted Uncle Chip only did it to piss him off. My mother didn't help the situation, saying she wouldn't be surprised if one of my cousins stole our Tennessee pennant that's been hanging from the back deck since I got my acceptance letter, which of course led to Dad buying the biggest, most obnoxious Vols banner, which is currently stretched across our front lawn.

It's ridiculous, but I know better than to add my two cents to family matters.

Mother turns and starts down the hall, past just about every photo of me growing up tacked to the wall in matching oak frames.

August calls this "Elliott Alley."

I get that my parents are proud of me and I appreciate their support, but does everyone who visits really need to see a picture of me in the bathtub? It's like my mother has never heard of photo albums.

"They agreed to a tentative truce," she says. "At least until playoffs."

I make a mental note to avoid this place in March.

"So how's life outside the bar? Are you seeing anyone?"

Ohhhh no. I'm not making this mistake again. "Did you need me to get something from the attic or...?"

She whips around, her narrowed eyes freezing me in place. "What is it with your aversion to small talk? This is why you're single."

She knows exactly why I'm single, which is part of the problem. If anyone is ever wondering whether they should discuss their love life with their mother, allow me to advise against it.

Knowing she was once privy to such private information only makes that particular door even harder to close.

Why are you shutting me out?

I only want what's best for you.

You used to talk to me about everything.

That last one was because I didn't have any brothers or sisters to lean on instead. At least now I have August—not that I tell him shit. But I could. And I definitely would talk to him over my mother.

"The attic?"

She spins on her heel, huffing and puffing like the big bad wolf all the way to the living room. "The Christmas tree and those boxes over there need to go up in the attic. While you're up there, I hope you find some manners."

I doubt she has manners in one of her many plastic tubs,

but if she did, it wouldn't be hard to find because it'd be perfectly labeled.

The tree's prickly branches scrape my arms as I drag the largest piece into the hallway.

My mother stomps in behind me, lugging a box almost as large as she is.

Has she lost her damn mind? "Put that down or you're going to throw out your back."

"I know how anxious you are to get out of here and wanted to expedite the process for you."

I am anxious, but if she hurts her back again, that won't happen.

"Put the box down. Please?"

She sets it down and stalks back down the hallway, toward the kitchen.

I reach up and tug the string dangling from the ceiling. The spring on the stairs groans as I open the hatch and unfold them.

Fifteen minutes later, I have everything tucked away until next November, and the furniture that had been relocated to make room for my mother's twelve-foot, pre-lit spruce is all back where it belongs.

When I head into the kitchen to make sure there isn't anything else on her to-do list, I find her furiously scooping mashed potatoes into a Tupperware container.

She means well, I remind myself. The problem is that, for eighteen years, I was her job.

Now she doesn't know what to do with herself.

Dad has a few years before he retires from the bank, so he's gone Monday through Friday from eight until six.

She runs a craft group at church and volunteers for just about every fundraiser in town, but that's not enough to keep her occupied.

I do feel bad for her, but I have my own life to figure out.

I refuse to be another one of her projects.

"That's all done."

She snaps on the lid with quick, efficient movements. "Thank you, Elliott. I appreciate you coming all this way to help us."

"It was no problem." Maybe if I hadn't disappointed her by shirking corporate life, things would be different. But after everything that happened, I needed a change. Something completely different and out of my comfort zone that required all my focus and attention. Something that didn't come easily, so my mind couldn't wander.

Thanks to August, I found that.

I'm proud of what we've built together.

If only she could be proud of me too.

"I'm proud of you, Elliott."

Loren's words from last night come soaring back.

"It's important to do what makes you happy, even if the people you love think you're wrong."

She's right. It's so incredibly important, because at the end of the day, you're the one who has to live with yourself.

5:26 PM

GUESS WHAT I FOUND?

MEG

WHAT?

YOU'LL SEE!

THE MOST AMAZING, wonderful thing just happened.

It's like fate has decided to offer a reward for all my recent hardships. A reward sitting in the backseat of my car as I drive over to The Alley to meet Meg.

The moment I pull in next to her, the door of her car swings open and out she comes, her furrowed brow disappearing beneath her wooly red hat.

I throw open my door in time to hear her say, "You know I hate it when you leave me hanging."

"I know." That's why it's so fun to do it.

Her laughter puffs like white smoke in the frigid

January air. "Well, don't leave me hanging *now*. Tell me what you found."

I unzip my coat and throw open the lapels with a flourish, revealing the most glorious surprise beneath.

Meg bounces on her toes, her golden hair swishing as she screeches with excitement. "No way! Bowling shirts?"

"That's right." Every few weeks I swing by the thrift store to search for hidden treasures (thanks, *Antiques Roadshow*). Today's foraging session has borne more fruit than I could have ever imagined. "There were four in total, so I splurged." Another treat to celebrate the promotion. The whole set cost twenty bucks, probably because the thrift store didn't think anyone would wear mismatched shirts embroidered with the names Harry, Erwin, Glenn, and Ash over the breast pocket.

Joke's on them.

I've already claimed Harry as my own.

"Who do you feel like being tonight? Erwin, Glenn, or Ash?"

"Erwin, obviously." She swipes the hanger out of my hand and sheds her coat, leaving it in the back of my car and swapping her navy sweater for the red-and-blue striped button-up. "These are fantastic. Dave is going to love them."

My thoughts exactly. We might not look like a team, but at least we look like bowlers. "Shall we take these for a test drive?"

"I thought you'd never ask."

———

Meg stacks her feet onto the chair next to her, a plate of nachos balanced on her chest. "Hold up. Ratbag is still texting you?"

We have one more frame to bowl before Josh and all other negative subjects are no longer allowed. It's something we used to do during our wine nights and the best way to end the evening on a high instead of going home more depressed than we arrived. Back then, we used to count glasses. Now we count frames.

We've already talked about Meg's jerk of an ex, whose favorite pastime is gaslighting, *and* her parents' desire for her to marry and produce babies with just about anyone they can find. Her mother fixed her up on four dates while she was back home, which is impressive considering she was only there for five days in total.

"Yup." For some reason, Josh keeps texting and calling every other day. To be honest, I'm shocked he hasn't driven out to where I live. Or maybe he has, and I just haven't been home.

The new job has kept me pretty busy.

The chip crunches between her teeth, spilling crumbs back into the plastic container, thus the reason she puts it there. "What does he want?"

"To talk."

"About what?"

"Hell if I know." And I've no desire to find out. I grab the plain black bowling ball I've claimed as my own and make my way to the start of the lane. We're only four frames in and already I've knocked down more pins than the entirety of our last game.

We haven't even used the bumpers, either.

When we arrived, we found Dave behind the counter, having swapped his cigarette for a chewed-up blue ink pen. Our lane was free, and Sally dropped down two beers before we had even changed shoes.

I pull back and slide the ball down the center of the tiny arrows printed on the boards.

Come on.

Come onnn…

For some reason, my body leans to the right like the ball and I are connected and it's going to listen to me instead of veering left and—

Gutter ball.

Meg snorts when I head back, and I knock her feet to the ground so I can plop down next to her and steal a nacho.

She hands me the whole plate, swipes her hands down her jeans, and pushes to her feet with a groan. "Maybe they should call us the Unlucky Strikes." She tugs her collar, referring to the *Lucky Strikes* decal emblazoned on the back of her shirt.

Mine only has a couple of bowling pins. I'm a little jealous, but the name tag is what won me over in the first place.

"Enough about my lack of skills and my problems. What're you going to do about your ex?" An ex whose name I still don't know. She's referred to him as everything from the "devil himself" to "turd burger" but has yet to reveal any identifying detail beyond his many faults.

Meg snags her ball from the return like it's on fire. "Oh! Would you look at that? The fifth frame. No more depressing talk."

"You sneaky little…" She kept me talking this whole time about my own issues. "I'm onto you now. I'm coming for you next week, Meg Benson."

She holds up her free hand as she backs toward the lane. "Promises, promises."

Meg knocks down three pins, and my luck finally changes with a spare.

She taps her can against mine. "So, Head of Traffic Managers, huh? That's exciting."

"I still can't believe it. Feels like I haven't been there long enough to deserve a promotion."

"Whatever. You're amazing and they noticed. You deserve it."

Rebecca is the one who noticed. And how did I thank her? By ruining her relationship.

Since we've finished our bitching for the night, that little guilt trip will have to wait until next Wednesday.

"Honestly, the best part will be the job security." Being a temp sucks. Not that you can't get fired from any job, but being contracted puts your neck on the chopping block first.

"Not the paycheck?"

"That too." Thanks to my raise, I can pay for this whole night and *still* have money for a nice lunch tomorrow.

Is this how normal people feel? The ones who didn't spend their entire life savings paying off debt and then relocate on a whim?

It's nice. Freeing.

I take my turn, knocking down four pins. We're a long way off the other bowlers here, but at least we've reached double digits.

When I make it back to our table, Meg has traded the nachos for her beer. "So how's the house hunting going?" Ever since she made Media Buyer six months ago, she's been on the hunt for a place of her own.

"Not bad. I still haven't found anything I love that's within my price range, but it's fun to look. You won't believe how many people around here still have those lacy valances printed with roses."

"I forgot about those. My mom was obsessed with them when I was in elementary school." That and wallpaper. I've heard wallpaper is making a comeback, but I doubt it's the kind with little apples or roosters printed on it.

"Mine too. They're awful."

They are awful. It's a wonder my apartment doesn't have them.

Meg heads over to our lane, ball in hand.

Maybe someday I'll have enough money to buy a house. My mom would lose her mind. When I told her about the promotion, she advised me not to take it. Like turning down an extra twenty thousand dollars a year was even an option. My dad, on the other hand, congratulated me.

I'm learning to be content with a fifty-percent approval rating.

"You're up, Great Pipes."

I push to my feet, grab my ball, and bowl a freaking strike.

With my hands in the air, I whirl to see Meg standing on her chair shouting while Sally and Dave whoop from where they were flirting in front of the snack stand.

The other bowlers hoot and holler, one of them whistling so loudly the sound pierces my eardrum.

Now that the mess with my ex is behind me, maybe this really will be my year.

I SKIP up the stairs to my place, feeling rejuvenated and alive and, yes, a little buzzed, but mostly I feel as if anything is possible. Which is why, when I meet my neighbor on the landing, I smile and wave and seriously consider giving him a hug, because, why not? The world could use more hugs.

I don't though, because Elliott is staring at my bowling shirt, his brow furrowed and a question in his eyes.

My new favorite shirt might be lucky. Unfortunately, I can't be like those superstitious athletes and never wash it to keep the luck from rubbing off because the slice of pepperoni pizza I had at The Alley did me dirty.

He unlocks his door and tosses the bag he was carrying inside. "Hey there, Harry."

I reach into my purse, prepared to begin the long,

arduous search for my keys only to find them right at the top. Your girl's luck really is changing. "Hello, Elliott."

"You look awfully happy."

"I think I might be." What's more, I don't want this night to end. That's what happens when you're having fun, isn't it? You get worried tomorrow won't live up to today and all you want is to make the goodness last. I unlock my door and drop my keys back into my purse. "Would you like to come in?"

He glances around like he's searching for anyone else in the concrete hallway. After confirming we are indeed alone, he presses a hand to his chest. "I'm sorry. Are you talking to me?"

"Yeah. I have beer." And drinking alone is sad.

Drinking with friends is sociable, everyone knows that.

"In that case..." He follows me into my apartment, but instead of immediately taking a seat at the tiny table, he stands in the middle of the room with his hands tucked into his pockets.

I give him a beer and then grab one for myself. Can't have them taking up precious real estate in my mini fridge for too long. "You coming home from work?"

"From my mom's, actually."

Oh, fun. "That explains why you don't have a companion with you." Normally he's latched onto a woman like a leech. Or she's latched onto him. It's difficult to tell who initiated the latching.

His brow furrows beneath his unruly hair. "What does that mean?"

"Seriously? You get more action than Mark Wahlberg."

"That is oddly specific."

"No, it's not. He's been in a lot of action movies lately." Like the one where he's the hot ex-spy dad.

"It's cute that you've been keeping tabs on me."

Believe me, there's nothing cute about it. "Hard not to when the walls are so thin."

Although he chuckles, I'd swear the man's cheeks are turning red. It's probably the alcohol I've consumed messing with my perception.

Not nearly as much as last week, thank goodness, but enough to make me giddy.

Elliott wraps his lips around the top of the beer bottle and takes a deep drink.

How do guys like him make such a simple action look so scandalous?

Don't even get me started on the way his throat bobs.

His beautiful blue eyes get lost beneath his mop of hair when he glances up at me. "How's the promotion?"

"Amazing."

"And all the shit with your boss and your ex?"

"Behind me." The year of Loren has officially begun.

"That's good." He tips his bottle back and drinks. And drinks. And drinks.

When he stops, the bottle is empty.

I might not know Elliott very well, but every time I've seen him drink, he's nursing the thing. Something feels off. "You okay?"

He drags the back of his hand over his mouth, the stubble on his chin rasping against his palm. "Just feeling the weight of my mother's disappointment tonight."

"I see. And how have you disappointed her now?"

"It doesn't matter."

From the way he frowns, it would appear my dear neighbor is lying. Being well-versed in parental disappointment, I feel it's my job to help him gain a little perspective on the matter. "Did you murder anyone?"

His lips twitch. "I only commit heinous crimes on weekends."

"Did you kick any puppies?"

His mouth pops open in horror. "I'm not a monster."

"Exactly. You're handsome, successful, not living in your parents' basement—"

"Much to my mother's chagrin," he mutters.

Same, man. My mom would kill to have me stuck in her basement until the day I die.

But this conversation isn't about me. Elliott helped when I needed him most, and now I get to return the favor. "Even so, you're doing amazing. If she can't see that, it's on her."

"Easy for you to say. Your parents don't live in the same state."

It's easy for me to say because I finally had the guts to leave. Do you know what happened? The world didn't end. It went on.

Mom and Dad just hired someone new at the funeral home, and I'm living my best life in Mount Juliette. Yeah, I might not be living in the lap of luxury and things might not have worked out with ratbag, but things are looking up.

None of that would've happened if I'd been less of a "disappointment."

"Do you know what my mom said when I told her I got a promotion?"

He shakes his head.

"She told me I shouldn't take it. That I should come back home where I belong."

"Fuck that."

"Exactly. Now take that attitude and apply it to your own issues."

Chuckling, he tosses his bottle into the recycling bin.

"Yeah. I'll try. So *Harry*, are you going to tell me what's up with the shirt?"

Oh, yeah. The shirt that started this whole conversation. I tug on the hem, sincerely hoping the greasy sauce stain comes out. "I bought this gem at the thrift shop."

He bobs his head. "Interesting. Are they doing casual Wednesdays at work or...?"

"No, no. Nothing like that. Meg and I bowl every Wednesday." Which is quickly becoming my favorite day of the week.

"You're kidding. Where?"

"This little place on Woodbridge Road."

"The Alley? I heard a rumor they turned that into a laundromat."

"Nope. Sixty years and still going strong." On Wednesdays, anyway. I have no idea what the place looks like any other day of the week. Maybe Meg and I should swing by this weekend and find out. We do have two more shirts that need broken in.

"I never pegged you for a bowler."

"I'm not. But the beer is cheap, and no one tries to hit on us. It's quickly becoming our favorite bar."

He rubs his chest like I just shot him in the heart. "Ouch. That hurts."

"Sorry! I didn't mean it like that. We just love it there."

"I'm glad to hear it." He turns and starts for the door.

I am irrationally sad over the thought of him leaving. Stupid beer. "You don't have to go yet."

His eyes find mine, holding for a beat too long. Heat spills through my stomach, spreading. "I should get to bed."

I have a bed.

Okay. Can we just take a moment to appreciate the fact

that those words didn't accidentally slip out? "Yeah. Of course."

"Thanks for the beer and the pep talk."

"Thank you for keeping me company." He's fun to hang out with. Probably too fun, all things considered.

"Are you kidding? This is the first time you've invited me since you moved in. I wasn't going to say no."

"That's not true. You were here for steak the other day."

"Because I weaseled my way into eating half your dinner."

Good point. "What about when you fixed my thermostat?"

"You mean when I convinced you to make me crab cakes?"

"That's right! What is it with you and food?"

"I'm a southern boy whose heart is right here." He pats his stomach. His very flat stomach.

Moving on...

Elliott catches the door. "See ya, Harry."

"Goodnight, Elliott.

MEG

When you get here, just know I didn't have
a choice

"WHO'S READY TO—" I was about to say bowl, but the woman standing next to Meg at the rental counter stole the words right out of my mouth.

What the heck is Rebecca doing here? Not that I'm not happy to see her, but I also need her to like me, and I tend to overshare when drinking.

Not the best idea when you've been accidentally sleeping with your boss's boyfriend.

I could just not drink but to be honest, the whole reason I'm here is for the one-dollar beers and chats.

"Hey, Loren." Meg sweeps past Rebecca, clutching her rental shoes under her arm. As if she can hear me silently freaking out, she quickly adds, "Rebecca and I ran into each other after work and started talking, then our Wednesday-night ritual came up and I asked if she'd like to join us for bowling."

Something in her tone tells me there's more, but I'll have to wait to hear it because Rebecca is coming up to us with a pair of shoes dangling from her hands "Hey, Loren. I hope you don't mind me crashing your party."

"Not at all." Looks like Harry Great Pipes is going dry this evening. Probably for the best, considering the last few weeks I've put down. "Did Meg explain the rules?"

"The rules for bowling?"

"No. For girl's night. First four frames are for bitching. After that, we're only allowed to be positive so we end the night on a high."

Rebecca nods. "I think I can handle that. Any other rules?"

"Nope."

Rebecca tugs the hem of Meg's shirt, where its half tucked into her skirt. "These are so cute."

"I bet Loren still has them in her car if you want one."

I do have them in my car, but that's not the point. This is our night to bitch and moan and if our boss is here, we can't do that. It's fine that Rebecca showed up tonight, but if she has a shirt, she's liable to take that as an invitation to come every Wednesday.

I like Rebecca so much, but I'm not sure how I'm supposed to be her friend with everything that's happened.

"Really? I would love one. Thank you."

Looks like what I want doesn't matter in this situation. Maybe we can bowl on Wednesdays as like, a team-building exercise and get drunk in secret on Thursdays instead? "Glenn or Ash? Those are the names we have left."

"Let's go with Glenn."

"Perfect. I'll be right back." I run out to my car, take a

moment to mentally shout at the heavens for cursing me, and then retrieve Glenn from beneath the mountain of takeout containers in my backseat.

Back inside, Rebecca looks so overjoyed when I hand her the old bowling shirt that I feel guilty all over again.

"This is so great." She glances around the alley. "The bathroom is...?"

"On the other side of the snack bar," Meg says with a tilt of her head.

We both wear matching smiles as our boss heads that way.

Meg falls down on the chair behind the screen with a groan. "I think I tweaked my hamstring at the gym."

Rebecca vanishes into the bathroom.

"Are you insane?" I hiss.

"I'm sorry!" She throws up her hands, her shoes tumbling to the floor. "I didn't know what else to do. She was crying, Loren. Crying!"

"Really? Why?"

"I'll give you one guess."

"Ratbag."

"Exactly. Look, I know it's super weird, but I feel like she could use a friend, and I didn't want to leave either of you hanging. This is what bowling at The Alley is all about."

She's right. If I just keep my cool there won't be an issue. Everything will be fine.

"Three of you tonight, ladies?" Sally asks, three cans on her tray.

Afraid so. "We brought a friend."

"Happy to hear it." Sally leaves us to mosey over to the rental counter so she can flirt with Dave.

With her shoes on, Meg takes over computer duties. "We need a nickname for Rebecca."

Yeah, we wouldn't want to make her feel left out, especially if she's already down in the dumps. Let's see.... "I have the perfect one."

———

Rebecca James has done the impossible: made an old man's bowling shirt look like it belongs on a runway. The way she tied the front so that the hem hits at the smallest part of her waist is the work of a fashion genius.

"I hate and love her so much." Mostly, I want to be her.

Minus the jerky boyfriend, that is. Or ex-boyfriend hopefully.

"Same, girl. Same."

Rebecca places her shirt and purse down on the chair at the end where I dumped my own things. Her perfect white teeth flash when she grins up at the screen. "Let me guess. Meglodon?" She nudges Meg's shoulder, then turns to me. "And you must be Great Pipes."

"That's me."

"I guess that makes me Jessica Rabbit?" She laughs. "I'm flattered."

Meg kicks her heels onto the corner of the computer table. "Let's see what you've got, Rabbit."

Rebecca rubs her hands together, selects a ball, and says, "Here goes nothing."

———

Turns out, Rebecca James is good at everything, bowling included.

What is it like to be God's favorite?

If only I knew.

I'm bowling better than I ever have but it still doesn't compare to my boss, who is on her way to triple digits.

She returns from her latest frame wearing the biggest smile. She always seems pleasant at work but never so exuberant.

If only I felt the same.

Meg disappeared on us about five minutes ago, chatting to the old timers in lane eight, so it's only me, this too-hard plastic chair, the low hum of an old Willie Nelson song crackling through tinny speakers, and beautiful, perfect Rebecca.

I need a buffer so I don't accidentally blurt out the truth that's swirling through my mind.

But Meg doesn't look like she's coming back any time soon, so it's just me and Rebecca, and now she's smiling at me and asking if everything's okay, and I need to respond but make sure I direct the conversation away from dating or boyfriends...

You can do this. Be calm and cool. Breathe.

Give the woman a compliment.

"You have the most amazing shoes."

Rebecca huffs a startled laugh, pushing back the strawberry strands that fall across her perfectly contoured cheekbones. I bet she's like Meg and wakes up perfect. "Thanks. Shoes are my obsession."

"Mine too!" Okay, I did not mean to shout.

Turns out Rebecca and I have a lot more in common than I thought.

Yeah, like men.

Damn brain. Why can't you switch off for one freaking minute?"

"Really?" she says.

Well, they would be my obsession if I could afford them. I have a whole Pinterest board of pairs I'd love to buy. Once my finances are secure, I'm going to make that dream a reality. "Oh, yeah. Someday, I want an entire room just for my shoes."

She drops onto the chair across from me, her nails trilling against the can clutched between her hands. "I have one of those!"

"Shut up. No way."

"Well, it's technically the guest bedroom, but no one ever comes over, so my shoes moved in."

Too bad I couldn't move in. I bet her heating works all the time and there isn't mold in her bathroom. Imagine how awkward it would be when Josh came over. *Ratbag.*

Meg finally returns to rescue me, thank goodness. "Sorry. Mo was so excited when he heard I was looking for a house. Says he knows just the place that would be perfect for me, but it's not on the market yet."

"That sounds like the start of a horror movie." I would know. After that night of forcing myself to watch clips, all my ads since are for slasher flicks.

Rebecca shoves her hair back from her face, no longer smiling. "I'll give you a horror movie. One day you're happy, the next, the guy you've been dating since college cheats on you."

Oh no. Oh god. Why can't we be on the fifth frame so all the negativity can go away?

Meg, bless her heart, intervenes so I don't have to. "I'm so sorry to hear that." She presses a hand to Rebecca's shoulder.

"Not as sorry as me. This isn't the first time, either. Back in college he slept with one of my sorority sisters. I feel like such an idiot for forgiving him."

"You're not an idiot. He is." That, I can say with absolute certainty. Joshua lying-cheating-ratbag is the biggest idiot/jerk/asshole I've ever had the displeasure of knowing.

"I don't know how he does it. Every time I think we're done, he finds some way to wheedle back into my life. Not this time, though. This time, he's dead to me."

I raise my previously untouched beer into the air for a much-needed toast. "Glenn doesn't need a man."

Rebecca chuckles, tapping her aluminum can against mine. "Hell no, she doesn't."

Meg adds her can as well. "To Erwin, Glenn, and Harry. Three strong, independent women."

Meg was right. Rebecca did need this.

And maybe I did too.

CHAPTER 27
LOREN

MEG

Mayday! Mayday!

Get here ASAP

THANKFULLY, when that message came through, I was already pulling into the office parking lot.

My purse slams into my side as I jog toward the main doors

What could possibly be wrong?

The text sounded dire, but Meg has been known for crying "mayday" when the coffee shop she visits religiously has run out of her favorite vanilla creamer.

As I ascend the stairs to our department's floor, I don't know what I'm walking into.

It isn't until I round the wall of cubicles to see Levi and Holly standing by the whiteboard, staring blankly at the wall, that I realize Meg meant mayday-mayday.

I've never seen my department look so devastated. Even Holly is as white as the foam cup in her hand.

"What happened? Did someone die?" Freddie down in accounts, the oldest person in this company, celebrated his sixty-fifth birthday last week. Did something happen to poor Freddie?

"I wish," Holly whispers.

Well, that's dark, especially for the happiest woman I know.

The Librarian pops his head up from his cubicle. "Holly sent the wrong spots." It's the first time I've ever heard Carson speak at full volume.

Tears flood Holly's eyes as she confirms the accusation with a nod.

I don't believe it.

"You mean they ran them wrong?" Stations get mixed up all the time.

"No, he means I accidentally sent them the wrong commercials *and* the wrong spot codes. The station ran the wrong commercials for the wrong products at the wrong times. The client agreed to pay a premium for these spots on those particular days and now it's all..." Holly throws a hand in the air.

Empty. It's all empty because the client didn't get their spots, and it's not the station's fault.

It's our fault.

I need to speak to Meg, but she's not at her desk.

Dammit. Where the hell is Meg?

Rebecca appears at the end of the hallway, her smile from last Wednesday nonexistent. "Loren? Can I speak with you in the conference room, please?"

I find my best friend sitting at the conference room

table, a coffee cup clasped between her hands. When she sees me, she offers a wan smile.

Rebecca drops onto the chair next to her.

The only other free chair happens to be right next to the freaking CEO of the whole company, old handlebar himself.

Not even a full month in and the year of Loren has officially come to an end.

"You heard about the spots?" Rebecca asks as I sink into the leather chair.

"The team just told me."

"What I don't understand is how something like this could happen," the CEO mutters. His name is Fergal and he insists we call him that if we ever interact with him, which, thankfully, doesn't happen often because he's intimidating as hell.

He tries to pretend he's one of us, dressing in trendy jeans and acting like a "hi, how are ya" boss, but at the end of the day, he's still a CEO who drives a ridiculous sports car that costs more than I'll ever make.

Rebecca sits up straighter.

Meg grimaces.

And the CEO is staring at me as if he wants me to answer, but I was hoping the question was rhetorical.

How could something like this happen?

"Human error?" That makes the most sense.

Fergal's mustache twitches. "Is that a question?"

"No. No, it's not." Articulate your thoughts, Loren. You *deserved* this promotion. Earned a seat at this table.

Except I didn't.

I'm a fraud.

I've only been here a few months and whatever Rebecca

saw in me, she was clearly mistaken. I don't even know what the hell is going on.

GET IT TOGETHER!

Panicking isn't going to save you.

"Which spots were they?"

Meg slides a stack of papers to me from across the table. "Newman Systems. They make—"

"Medical devices. I know." What I don't understand is why in the world Holly was sending Newman spots when Levi is in charge of their account.

"When were the spots put into rotation?"

"They were sent out last Thursday to run at peak Saturday and Sunday."

Hold on. If they were sent out last week, then I know exactly what happened. "The Traffic Manager who sent out the spots was covering for a colleague on vacation." Levi needed to take a long weekend to drive his sister back to college.

It really was human error after all.

"You're the lead traffic manager. Why didn't you take the extra clients?"

Because I'm not a freaking robot. I may be the leader, but that doesn't mean I'm supposed to do *all* the work. I have a team for a reason. "It was a heavy traffic week. I took on over half of Levi's clients as well as my own." Not to mention that I stayed until after six to make sure all stations confirmed. "I gave the other remaining managers two extra clients each." The error could've happened to any one of us.

Rebecca winks at me from across the table, her lips lifting into an almost -mile.

The CEO blows out a breath before turning toward Meg. "You're the buyer on the account, Benson. What can we do to appease the client?"

Meg's shoulders droop. "Nothing. They're livid and want to close their account."

"*Dammit.*"

Newman Systems was one of Meg's biggest clients.

Why didn't I take their account myself?

Fergal rakes a hand down his face and then pushes back from the table. "We needed more oversight in your department, Piper. That's why Rebecca suggested you. Get your house in order or you won't have a roof over your head."

I realize he meant that as a euphemism, but he doesn't realize how right he is.

———

A heavy knock rouses me from a dreamless sleep. I peer up at my darkened ceiling, the low hum of the heat breezing through the vent.

Bam. Bam. Bam.

It's three o'clock in the freaking morning. Who the heck is pounding on my door?

There it is again.

Oh god. What if it's Josh? I am not answering. No way. He and I are done. I'm not jeopardizing everything to speak to that snake.

Bambambambambambam.

Would it really be my ex? He's given up trying to text me and barely bothered driving out here when we were dating, so why would he put in the effort now?

Maybe it's Elliott.

What if something is wrong? Like... Like a fire!

I roll out of bed, and sprint over to the door to peer through the peephole. My stomach bottoms out when I find a police officer on the other side.

Not a fire. Something worse.

Like a murder.

Stupid freaking horror movies hijacking my brain.

My hands shake as I slide the chain open and twist the knob. What if something bad happened to my parents?

Wait. That doesn't make any sense. How would they know my parents?

Maybe they have the wrong apartment.

Elliott's parents!

The woman frowns at me, then down at the notepad in her hand. "Loren Piper?"

Shit. They have the right apartment. "That's me."

She flips over the page. "Are you the owner of a silver Honda Civic, Maryland plates?" She rattles off a series of numbers and letters, and while I don't know my license plate number by heart, how many other silver Civics have Maryland plates down here? "Yes?"

"I'm afraid there's been an accident."

How is that possible? My car is in the parking lot, and I have the only set of keys. Maybe someone hotwired it. Is that a real thing or just something they do in movies?

"You need to come with me," she says.

I stuff my feet into my slippers and grab my keys, trailing her into the chilly night. Moths and bugs swarm the yellowed lights attached to the walls along the staircase. Blue and red lights flash in the parking lot, bouncing off the concrete walls.

The officer slips her notepad back into her breast pocket, leaving her hands free to hold the railing. "We have a suspect in custody, but your car's in pretty bad shape. You'll need to have it towed to a shop."

Tow trucks are freaking expensive, and I won't have my next paycheck till Friday.

Muddy skid marks streak across the grass, leading straight to my poor car.

The back bumper is completely torn off and the side looks like it's been stomped by elephants. Whoever did this must've been traveling at crazy speeds to inflict that kind of damage to a parked vehicle.

Another officer snaps photographs of a black Toyota I've never seen before, turned on its side next to a tree. Thank goodness no one was walking around at this hour.

Even though I'm pissed at the driver of the other vehicle, I hope whoever it was is okay.

The longer I stare at the bits of my car still laying in the grass, the more dread fills my stomach. "I can't afford to fix this." And I can't afford a new car right now.

The officer's lips press flat, her dark eyes swimming with sympathy. "You'll be able to claim the towing, damage, and rental car on the other man's insurance."

That's something at least.

It takes the officers another thirty minutes to wrap things up and tell me that I can head back inside. My alarm will be going off in an hour, but there's no hope of me getting any more sleep before work.

The closest rental car place isn't open until nine, but I need to be in the office by eight thirty.

I could call in and explain what happened, but how would that look after yesterday's disaster?

No. I have to go in.

I text Meg to see if she's awake yet, but even after I've showered, she still hasn't responded.

If I wait around and she doesn't get back to me in time, I'll be late.

I should just call a ride share, but...

Maybe this is a sign, the universe telling me to give up,

pack up my stuff, and head home. That I was never meant to be here in the first place.

Normally, I pride myself on my positivity, but after what happened at work yesterday, it's getting harder and harder to smile.

If I go back now and budget carefully, in a few years, I might have enough saved for a down payment on my own place. Yeah, I'll have to live with Mom and Dad until then, but there are worse fates than that.

Like...

Huh.

Actually, I can't think of anything worse besides maybe having to date Josh again.

These past few months haven't been easy, but I've loved (almost) every second of my time in Tennessee. I don't want to leave Meg behind, and maybe it's crazy, but I don't want to leave Elliot either.

Elliot.

That's it! I bet if I promised him food, he'd be willing to help me out.

CHAPTER 28
ELLIOTT

SOMEONE IS POUNDING on my door.

At least I think it's my door. It could be my neighbor's.

Whoever it is pounds a little harder.

Okay, that's too loud. It's definitely coming from outside my apartment.

I throw my covers aside and leap out of bed. Or at least that was my plan. But my left leg has other ideas and decides to give out. I try to catch myself on the mattress but miss completely and bruise my ass on the floor.

By the time I get to the front door, I'm this close to losing my fucking mind. When I find Loren waiting on the other side with tears in her eyes, my rage evaporates.

"I'm so sorry for waking you this early, but I need help and don't have anyone else to ask." She dabs at her eyes with the tissue strangled in her fist.

Her words take way too long to sink in, but when they do, my heart rate skyrockets. "What do you need?" Does this have something to do with her ex? A protective feeling surges in my chest as I glance past her, into the empty hallway bathed in an orange glow.

"Someone hit my car last night, and I don't have time to pick up my rental before work. But that also means I don't have a ride to the office. Is there any way you could put on a shirt and bring me downtown?" She clutches her purse to her chest like it's the only thing keeping her together.

Holy shit. "Are you okay?"

"What?"

"You said someone hit you."

"Not me. My car. While it was parked."

That's something at least. She's not hurt. She just needs a ride into the city. I glance over my shoulder at the clock on the microwave. At this hour, traffic will be a bitch. Even so, I can't stand to see those damn tears in her eyes.

Put on a shirt...

"You want me to drive you to work in my T-shirt and underwear?"

Her gaze drops, and her cheeks go all splotchy, like she didn't realize until right now that I'm standing here in a pair of black boxer briefs.

Loren clears her throat, but her voice still comes out squeaky. "You really need to start putting on clothes before you answer the door."

She's right, but from the crazed way she was pounding, I thought the place was on fire. "What can I say? I like watching you drool."

"I'm not drooling."

"Then what do you call this?" When I go to swipe my thumb over the corner of her mouth, she smacks my hand away. "You're awfully violent for someone who needs my help."

"I really don't have time for your teasing this morning. If you can't help me, I'll need to call a ride share."

I have a better solution. "Tell you what." I reach over to the counter and grab my keys from the bowl where I keep them. "Why don't you just drive yourself?"

Her wide eyes fly to mine, and she clutches her purse even tighter. "You want me to drive your truck alone?"

Why not? She's already proven that she can handle the thing. I lift a shoulder. "Sounds better than having to put on clothes."

Her quiet chuckle hits me right in the heart. Every time I've seen my neighbor, she's had so much fight. Even when all that shit happened with her ex a few weeks back, she still had a bit of life in her.

This morning, she looks defeated, like a deflated balloon in a puddle with a footprint on top.

Her fingers brush mine when she takes the keys and stuffs them into her too-large purse. "I'll drive really carefully and fill up your tank."

"Don't worry about it." The tank on the thing is huge, so a trip to the city and back will hardly make a dent.

Her eyes glisten, and she starts to blink rapidly. I assume she's going to leave, but instead she throws her arms around me for a hug, and my dick gets the wrong idea, swelling enthusiastically against the soft cotton.

"Thank you, Elliot. Thank you so much."

I draw my hips back so she doesn't accidentally bump

into my very noticeable erection. *Next time, put on pants before you answer the door, you idiot.*

I retreat into my dark apartment before she can see what's going on downstairs and shout, "Drive safe." The closing door cuts off her response.

Adjusting myself, I glare at my tented boxers. "Don't even think about it. We don't piss where we eat." Yeah, she's cute and the few times we've hung out together have been fun, but that is where this thing ends. We can be friends who borrow vehicles and occasionally have dinner. Nothing more needs to come of it. Besides, she is clearly the relationship type, and as much as I hated her calling me a commitment-phobe, she's not wrong.

I did the whole relationship thing and look how that turned out.

My gaze catches on the spare bedroom's closed door, and my chest tightens.

I like my very single life. I like bringing women home for a night and then sending them on their merry way after we're both sated.

Loren moved to a brand-new city for a guy she only knew for a fucking week.

She's a romantic at heart, looking for love.

I've found love and all it did was let me down.

I head back to my bedroom and flop onto my bed. After ten minutes of lying here staring at the ceiling, it's clear that I'm not going to get back to sleep even though I didn't get to bed until two this morning.

I reach over to my nightstand and unplug my phone from the charger.

There are a few messages from Mom asking if I want to come over for dinner. I blow her off and say I'm working.

There's another message from an unknown number that

I stupidly click open because I can't handle seeing those little red notifications anywhere on my screen.

UNKNOWN

We need to talk.

I don't need to have the number stored in my contacts to know who the cryptic message is from. She has some nerve texting me today of all days. There's just enough intrigue to keep me dangling on a fucking hook like some pathetic worm.

Deleting a message has never felt so good.

Why is it that every time I start to feel a semblance of peace, the past comes back to haunt me?

The longer I lie in this bed, the more I think about those four words.

Four fucking words that have the potential to ruin a perfectly good day. No way am I going to let that happen.

I find August in my recently called list and click his name. He answers on the second ring as chipper as a fucking daisy. Fucking morning person.

"Good morning, sunshine. To what do I owe the pleasure of this call?"

"Can't sleep. Need an extra set of hands today?" He's a firm believer in the old adage: Idle hands are the devil's playthings. That guy works more jobs than I can keep track of. Not only does he bartend with me, but also he pretends to be a landscaper in the spring and a barista at a coffee shop down by the lake in the colder months.

In the summer, it's the bike shop or the bait and tackle. Sometimes he even picks up shifts at the ice cream parlor.

I'd commend him on his hard work if I didn't know the real reason he keeps so busy is to avoid being alone with himself.

"Seriously? I can always use an extra set of hands. Especially ones as big and strong as yours."

I hate him so fucking much. "Swing by my place on the way. I'm riding with you."

———

The moment I climb into his Jeep, August tips his baseball hat like an idiot. Seriously. Who does that? August, that's who. Even from behind his sunglasses, I can tell he's scanning the parking lot. "Where's your truck?"

"Doesn't matter. Nice shirt, by the way."

I wouldn't be caught dead in a lime green V-neck sweater. Looks like his sister is still picking out his wardrobe.

He takes his hand off the gear shift and leans back against his door as he slides his sunglasses up to his forehead. "Where is your truck, Elliott James Grant?"

So much for distracting him. "Loren borrowed it, all right?" I do my best not to look at him, but then I do, and it annoys the shit out of me. "Don't give me that look."

"What look?"

He knows damn well what look. That wide-eyed, raised brow, smirky-mouthed look.

Now that smirk is growing into a full-blown grin. "I find it very interesting that you don't even let me drive your truck and we're related by blood. But you let this chick drive it, what, twice now?"

"She needed a ride to the city, and I didn't want to deal with the traffic."

"Mmmhmmm..."

"Whatever you're thinking, get it out of your head."

He shifts to reverse and backs out of the parking space,

a smirk still on his face. "You say that like it's easy to control my beautiful mind."

————

There's something about smelling like sweat and fresh air that makes you feel like you've done a hard day's work. My mom would be appalled if she saw the sweat gluing my shirt to my skin.

August's legs swing as he sits on the tailgate. Four hours of hard labor and our grandmother's garage is completely devoid of junk.

I don't understand how that woman gave birth to my mother.

Maybe she was adopted.

I take a bite of the chicken salad sandwich my grandma gave me, then glance over at August. That would explain so much.

As if he can feel me looking at him, August kicks my boot. "Mom won't shut up about the reunion this year. Think you'll go?"

As a kid, I used to look forward to those things every year. Everyone brings different covered dishes, and they have every single pie imaginable. There are puppet shows for the kids, skits for the adults, and a singsong at the end of the night around a mammoth bonfire.

Now that I'm older, I see them for what they really are: A chance to pry into everyone's private lives.

Southern families love some good, old-fashioned gossip and heaven knows I've provided them with enough to last a lifetime.

Which is why I say, "No fucking way."

August drops his head with a groan. Some of the filling

from his own sandwich slips from between the slices of homemade bread and *plops* onto the driveway. "Come on, man. Don't make me be the only single one there again."

Our family marries young and stays together, making August and me the black sheep of the Nolan clan for two very different reasons.

Our cousin Molly married her husband right out of high school. Most of the others were more sensible, waiting until after college. There are kids everywhere. It's impossible to keep up when all of them seem to have at least four. We multiply like rabbits.

I kick him back. "You still have a few months. Surely you can get a girlfriend by then."

The bread of his sandwich flops over when he shoves it toward me like that's going to help him make his point. "I could get ten girlfriends. But I'm not like you. I enjoy the single life too much to give it up."

"So do I."

"*Mmmhmmm.*"

I tear off a piece of crust and toss it at his infuriating head. "Don't do that shit."

He doesn't even bother dodging it, just lets the chunk land on the shoulder of his ugly sweater "What shit?"

"Act like you know something when there's nothing to know." He always does this to me.

"Says the guy without a truck."

CHAPTER 29
LOREN

MY STOMACH IS GROWLING like a hungry lion but there's no way I'm going to step out of line for my rental car to grab a burrito from the food truck outside. Whoever chose this lot to park that thing in is either a genius or a super villain.

After I dropped off Elliott's truck, Meg ferried me to the rental car place. Turns out everyone and their freaking mother is trying to snag a car for the weekend.

If I don't eat something soon, I might die.

The moment I get home, I'm going to throw on my comfiest sweats and order Chinese takeout from the good place, not the dirt cheap one like I usually do. But before all that, I need to swing by the grocery store and buy myself a whole dang cake.

Might even splurge on the cookies 'n cream kind instead of boring old vanilla.

What reason do I, a car-less Loren Piper, have to be celebrating?

Fergal spoke to Newman Systems and, after a great deal of sweet-talking, they agreed not to cancel their contract.

Fate must've taken pity on me for the whole car incident.

Either way, today is infinitely better than the last few days combined.

With this job and the subsequent pay raise, my time in Nashville is about to get a whole lot more bougie. Even the fact that I've spent the last hour standing in line waiting to get the car the guy's insurance company is giving me can't get me down.

When the elderly couple dragging suitcases finally get their keys, it's my turn.

This must be the guy's first day. It takes him forever to key in my responses and photocopy my ID, which baffles me because I already filled out all my details online.

We're talking DMV slow, folks. Then the tablet I'm supposed to sign goes dead and they have to go old school and print out the rental agreement. But of course, no one can find the paper and when they *do* find it in some back-office cupboard, the printer gets jammed. By the time they sort it out, I'm ready to chow down on the contract he clips to the board and hands across the counter.

"Sign here, here, and here. And initial here." He indicates each spot with the tip of a pen.

I pray the sound of ink meeting paper masks my howling stomach.

Maybe I'll forego the cake and head straight for takeout.

I'm about to hand back the clipboard when I notice one teeny-tiny detail that has completely slipped my mind.

Today is the first of February and—holy shit.

I check my watch.

No. No. *No.* It's almost seven o'clock, which means the office at the apartment will be closed and my rent check will be late.

Again.

I've been meaning to go direct debit but between the trouble at work and the whole car fiasco, that plan went right out the window.

Tightness grips my chest, and I have to smile through blinding panic as the guy leads me around a cute little sedan so I can check for dents and scratches. A couple more signatures and the keys are in my hand. I jump inside and sweat immediately collects on my forehead.

With the press of a button, the car rumbles to life. Hot air blasts my face as I fiddle with the dials to make it cold. Only then do I grab my phone to call my landlords, praying something kept them in the office past closing even as the call rings out.

The worst part is, for the first time since I moved in, I have more than enough money to cover rent.

If I leave a check in the mailbox, it's technically still paid on the first, right?

My head feels like it's being pounded by a gavel. It'll be fine.

It'll be *fine.*

The lies we tell ourselves.

After the week I've had, I know it won't be.

My worst fears are confirmed when I trudge up the stairs to my apartment and find a pink eviction notice taped to my door.

CHAPTER 30
ELLIOTT

IMAGINE my surprise when I stumble upon my neighbor sitting in the middle of the concrete with her head in her hands. This is just like the night I brought her home from the bar and she wanted to give up and sleep outside. Except it's a little early to be drunk. I'm about to ask what's the matter when I see the paper clinging to her apartment door.

Evicted? For what? Sure, she plays loud music at inappropriate times, but I've never complained to the jackasses who own the building.

Winter sunlight hits her cheeks, making her tears glisten like the ice clinging to the tree branches.

"Hey. You okay?"

She glances up at me through red-rimmed eyes. "What do you think?"

Yeah. It was a stupid question. "What happened?"

"I forgot to pay rent."

They kicked her out for that? Seems a bit harsh if you ask me. "Maybe you can talk to the twins."

Curls slap her cheek when she shakes her head. "They won't listen. I've never paid my rent on time. I thought... gosh, it's so stupid." She laughs to herself. "I thought my luck was changing. Should've known better."

She does seem to have had a shitty run of luck lately. That doesn't mean things can't change. "Can you stay with your friend for a while?" Maybe sharing rent with someone would help get her back on her feet.

"Meg's renting a room over someone's garage while she looks for a house."

Yeah, that probably won't work. "Do you have any other friends?"

"Yes. I have so many friends lining up to help me out. See. Look at all of them." She gestures toward the empty stairwell.

"There's no need for the snark. I'm only trying to help."

"I know. I'm sorry. I didn't mean to be a bitch."

"It's okay." That notice flutters in the breeze.

She must hear it as well, because she turns, glancing over her shoulder at the ominous pink paper. "I guess this is it. It's time to go home."

Wait. *Home?* "Back to Maryland?"

"Yeah. At least my parents will be thrilled."

Parents who didn't want her to move in the first place.

She catches her wild hair, pulling it back from her face and twisting it into that crazy poodle on the top of her head. "All I wanted was to make it on my own."

I understand exactly what she's talking about. My

parents would happily foot my bills for the rest of my life *if* I did everything according to their rules.

No, thank you.

Her head falls to her arms folded over her knees.

She looks so defeated. It's not fair that her asshole ex cheated on her. It's not fair that some drunk dickhead totaled her car.

It's not fucking fair.

Loren may be mayhem wrapped in a pretty package, but she's also sweet and funny and helped me when I was feeling down and... *Shit.*

I can't believe I'm about to say this. "You could always move in with me."

"Ha!"

Well, at least I made her laugh.

I throw myself down next to her, mirroring her position. "I'm serious."

Her eyes narrow as she watches me, the tiny wrinkle between her dark eyebrows gradually deepening. "I can't move in with you, Elliott."

"Why not? It makes perfect sense. You already know who I am."

Her nose wrinkles when she squints up at me. "Do I, though?"

She might not realize it, but she knows me better than most—which isn't saying a lot, to be fair, but it is saying something. "I let you drive my truck; we're practically best friends."

"I appreciate the offer. Really, I do. But it won't work. Maybe I'll find someone willing to rent me a cheap room."

Let me get this straight. "You'd rather live with a stranger than move in with me?"

"*You're* a stranger."

"You've cooked me dinner..."

Her hands fall to her sides, and she sits up a little straighter, some of that fight finding its way back into her spine. "You conned me into making you crab cakes and giving you half my steak."

Exactly. Dinner. "You've visited me at work."

A heavy sigh pushes through her lips as she throws her eyes toward the gray sky overhead. "I stumbled into a bar where you happened to be bartending."

"I let you drive my truck." So what if I listed that one twice? It's that big of a deal to me.

Her mouth opens but no protest emerges.

While she's silent, I keep going. "I never let *anyone* drive my truck, Loren. Oh! And you know my family."

"I met your cousin twice."

"Like I said, you know my family."

"Wow." Her eyes narrow. "You're really laying it on thick. Makes me wonder what you're getting out of the deal."

She's right. Why am I so adamant about this?

It's hard to explain, but something about Loren leaving doesn't sit right in my gut. If there's one thing I've learned in my thirty-two years on this earth it's this: When your gut speaks, you listen. Otherwise, you'll find yourself sitting in a courtroom across from the woman you love, arguing over who gets to keep the damn dog.

Loren's hand falls to my knee, bringing me back to the present. "Look, I can't put you out like that. You've already done more than enough for me. I appreciate the offer, but it's a no." She glances past me to my door across the concrete hallway. "Where would I even sleep?"

"In the spare bedroom."

"Your apartment isn't a studio?"

I shake my head. "The corner apartments are all two-bedrooms."

"Why do you need two bedrooms?"

To answer that would be opening a whole can of worms, and having both of us depressed at the same time isn't going to help the situation. So I keep it light and neutral. "I like my space."

Her head tilts, that poodle flopping to the side. "Yet you're willing to give up that space for me."

"Maybe I just want someone to pay half the rent."

She finally removes her hand, letting it fall to the concrete between us. "How much is half the rent?"

"Two-fifty."

"A month?"

"I've been here for a while."

"How long's a while?"

"Twelve years."

"And they haven't upped the rent?"

"They can't. My rate's locked in." That's why I haven't moved. One of the reasons anyway. The other one isn't relevant to this conversation.

"You're a saint for offering, but I won't do that to you. I'm sure someone online has a spare room. Maybe a bit closer to the city so the drive to work won't be such a slog."

I guess that's that.

Now I'm going to have to get to know a new neighbor and hope they can cook as well as Loren. Otherwise, I'll have to go back to going home for proper meals and listening to my mom harp on and on about my life choices in person instead of via text.

But the last thing I want to do is push her. Seems like a woman's mind is usually already made up before you even realize there's a problem.

If Loren does change her mind, she can let me know. Otherwise, it's time to let her go.

———

Loren smiles up at me from my doorway, a plate covered in aluminum foil in her hands. "So I was wondering if you could do me a teeny, tiny favor."

From the number of boxes stacked behind her, I have a pretty good idea why she's knocking.

Would you look at that? She brought what look like homemade chocolate chip cookies. "Let me guess. You want me to help move your stuff."

The plate presses against my chest, and she bats her long eyelashes. "Pretty please? The trunk on my rental is shockingly small. This would really help me out."

Damn, she works fast. It's only been a couple of hours since I left her in the stairwell. "Where are you going?" I fish out a cookie and take a warm, gooey bite.

"I found a place on Roomer near the airport."

Not the best part of town, but maybe this will be the exception. I stuff the rest of the cookie in my mouth, grab my keys, and help her lug box after box down the stairs. At least now I can skip the gym and not feel guilty for eating a few more cookies.

The house she found is a twenty-minute drive toward the city—which bodes well for her daily commute. But when we pull up outside the drab white craftsman, my optimism dies.

Loren parks behind me and slowly climbs out of the car. When she pushes her sunglasses onto her forehead, there's horror in her eyes.

I jump out of my truck before she can even set foot on the cracked sidewalk. "This place is a shit hole."

Her gaze flicks over to me before landing back on the tiny house with a sagging front porch and BEWARE OF DOG signs plastered all over the clapboard fence. "Maybe it's better inside?"

Yeah, I can't see that being the case. But she insists, so I take the box from her hands and follow her up the half-sunken walkway to a screen door that's hanging off the hinges. The skunky smell of weed wafts from beneath the faded green door. Before Loren can knock—or run away—a guy with muscles rippling from beneath a ribbed white tank top answers.

Loren offers him a sweet smile. "Hi. I'm not sure if I have the right place, but I was talking to someone named Mika on Roomer and she said there's a room for rent?"

He gives her a wolfish smile. "You have the right place, sweetheart." Over his shoulder, he shouts, "Yo, Mike! The new roommate is here!"

Somewhere inside, a dog starts going berserk.

Another guy, even taller than the first, steps into view, jacked as shit. What hope would Loren have if either of them turn out to be complete assholes?

"Hey, girl. Come on in. Room's down the hall." Mike/Mika nods to the right.

Yeah, this isn't happening. I get that Loren doesn't want to put me out and appreciate the sentiment, but what kind of man would I be if I let her stay here?

I adjust my grip on the box, freeing my hand to take Loren's. "If you'll excuse us for a second." I drag my neighbor back down the driveway until we're out of earshot. "You're not staying there."

"Elliott..."

"No way in hell. I know that's overbearing or whatever, but if you go in there, there's a good chance you'll never come out."

"It wasn't that—"

"I swear, if you say bad, I'm going to drop this box, throw you over my shoulder, and lock you in my car."

Tears fill her eyes. "It's bad."

"So bad."

"Are you *positive* you don't mind?"

I'm starting to mind less and less. "I'm not in the habit of saying things I don't mean. If you want it, the room is—"

She throws her arms around my neck, her soft chest pressing tightly to mine. "Thank you so much. This place is scary. I'd rather go back to Maryland than stay here."

Fuck. She smells good enough to eat, which doesn't bode well for my sanity. Thankfully, I'm a grown man perfectly capable of resisting temptation. "Well, now you don't have to do either."

Sniffling, she nods, running her fingers beneath her eyes, leaving black smudges of mascara. "I'll accept your offer on one condition: If at any point I get on your nerves or you want to reclaim your space, you must promise to tell me. I'll move out right away."

I press my hand to my heart. "I promise. Come on." I throw the box in the bed of my truck with the others. "Let's get you home."

Loren offers to pick up pizza on the way back, and I let her. Not that I plan on mooching off her for all my meals, but this gives me the chance to do something I've been putting off for way too long.

———

When I step inside my dark apartment, an unsteady breath escapes. My heart jackhammers as I cross to the spare room and twist the knob with a trembling hand. A wave of floral perfume wafts over me, making my head spin.

The boxes that have been sitting beside the bed for the last four years stare back.

I throw open the curtains and unlatch the window, letting the fresh air sweep inside, wishing it would take away the memories too.

Twenty minutes later, everything in the room has been reduced to three trash bags and four large cardboard boxes, and the place smells like lemon-scented cleaner and bleach.

Funny how something you've put off for so long builds and builds in your mind until it feels insurmountable. And in only twenty minutes it can be gone.

When I finish clearing out the room, I leave the door wide open, my heart feeling lighter than it has in a long time.

CHAPTER 31

LOREN

I RUN into Elliott in the hallway, a trash bag in either hand that are both heavy enough to make the muscles in his biceps bulge. Not that I'm looking.

Okay, maybe I am looking, but I'm not going to do anything about it. A week ago, maybe. But now that he's saving my ass from living under the bypass, that line will not be crossed. Not that he's given any indication that he'd be interested in stepping over said line anyway.

Focus, Loren.

"Getting rid of the bodies, I see."

Chuckling, he mutters, "Something like that." He nods

his chin toward his apartment. "The door is open and there's an extra key on the counter. Make yourself at home."

I've been in plenty of frat houses back in my day, so I have a loose idea of what to expect from Elliott's apartment. That is until I step into an immaculate sanctuary. Holy cow, this apartment is nice—so much nicer than mine. Yeah, the beige paint is dated, but other than that, the place looks brand new.

"You've been here for twelve years?" How is that possible? Even the fridge is spotless if you look past the stack of takeout containers and door full of different sauces. The oven? Not a smudge or greasy stain in sight. "You don't do much cooking, do you?"

"Not anymore."

I don't ask why and he doesn't elaborate and—*holy shit.* He has a washer and dryer up here, too? No more communal laundry for this girl. I'll be living in the lap of luxury.

The spare bedroom is small, but compared to where I was living, this place is a freaking palace. And there aren't any stains on the pristine mattress, like it's never been slept on. When I flop on top, there isn't one squeak or groan.

Not from the bed, anyway.

This mattress must be made of angel wings.

Elliott watches me from the doorway, his eyes shuttered as he leans a shoulder against the doorframe.

"This might be the most comfortable bed I've ever felt. Is it a queen?"

"Yeah."

I'll have to buy some new sheets, but it doesn't even matter because I'm in heaven. The cream headboard with matching nightstands and mirrored closet look like something straight off Pinterest. Who knew this guy had such good taste?

"We'll be sharing a bathroom. Hope that's okay."

Right. Totally forgot to ask about the whole bathroom situation. If it's as clean as the rest of this place, that shouldn't be a problem. "It's fine with me if it's fine with you."

"Wouldn't have suggested you move in if it wasn't. You need help with your stuff?"

Reluctantly, I push myself off the luxurious mattress. "I'll get it. You've done enough."

If he sees the state of my car, he'll absolutely change his mind about giving me the spare room.

It's not that I'm a messy person. I've just been busy lately and—

Oh, who am I kidding? I'm a slob.

That ends now. I'm not going to do anything to screw this up.

———

I take the steps two at a time, breathing heavily by the time I get to my car. Before I grab the next box, I collect all the takeout containers and receipts and the random assortment of other crap that I've collected and haul it all into the dumpster.

Then I grab the pizza inside so Elliott can enjoy a slice while I move in.

My suitcase bumps along behind me. Did I mention it only has three wheels? Don't know when that happened.

Elliott meets me at the bottom of the stairs, picks the thing right up, and carries it to my room.

I'm an idiot for not taking him up on his offer to stay

in the first place. It would've been a lot easier to move all my worldly possessions right down the hall—something Elliott reminds me of every time we pass each other in the stairwell. But I felt so guilty and helpless and upset, and he seemed to like his own space, so I didn't want to impose.

Thank goodness he's letting me impose. Otherwise, I would've left that weird house and driven straight to Maryland. I wouldn't have even worried about the boxes left in his truck.

When I return with the last armload of stuff, Elliott is on his phone. He looks up from the screen, then stuffs the handset into his pocket to relieve me of the box. "I'm gonna grab a drink with August."

A pang of disappointment spreads through my core. "You don't want any pizza?" I bought a large so we could share.

"Just put what you don't eat in the fridge, and I'll have some when I get back. You want me to pick anything up for you while I'm out?"

It's silly to feel disappointed that he's not going to be here this evening. What did I expect? That he'd help me unpack and we could Netflix and chill on the leather couch? Get it together, Loren. "No, thanks. I'm good."

I venture into the bathroom that smells like him. There aren't any toothpaste stains in the sink or spit marks on the mirror. The shower is mold-free, but there's no shower curtain, only a clear plastic liner. That won't work at all. What if I accidentally walk in while he's showering? Not that I don't know how to knock.

Still, better safe than sorry.

I grab my shower curtain from the suitcase. If Elliott hates it, I'll buy a new one. He doesn't have any throw pillows either. Not to worry. I can pick up a few from the store when I head out to buy sheets.

After I finish getting everything set up, I eat four pieces of pizza, not because it's good, but because I'm drowning my sorrows in cheese and pepperoni. Doesn't really help. You know what does? The bottle of wine I wash it down with when I get back from Target.

———

Do you ever have those days where everything feels like a slog?

Today was one of those.

Even checking my email felt like a monumental task. I'd blame it on stress and lack of sleep, but I slept like the dead last night.

Maybe I'm about to start my period. It's all doom and gloom when that happens.

When I finally get back to Elliott's, all I want is to curl up and die, but I'm also starving, so dinner first and then death.

I step into the apartment and find Elliott in the kitchen holding a takeout container overflowing with fried chicken, mashed potatoes, and collard greens. "That looks delicious." It's depressing to see him eating like a king when I only have a TV dinner in the freezer.

Tomorrow, I'm going grocery shopping. I don't care how tired I am.

"I'm glad you think so because there's one for you on the counter."

"You bought me dinner?" I think I might cry.

He shrugs. "It's the least I could do for the woman who redecorated the entire apartment."

Oh, right. The decorations.

By the time Elliott got home last night, the wine had done the trick, and I was happily snoring away in my bed of clouds, forgetting all about the beautifying spree I may have gone on.

The thing is, nothing matched my old apartment's sickly green paint so I never bothered buying decor.

Well, that and I never had any money.

Elliott's apartment, however, is beige and brown and is it my fault that I found the perfect forest green throw for his couch? I couldn't let the throw be the only spot of color, so I grabbed a couple of pillows to compliment.

Then this framed picture caught my eye, and I couldn't leave it behind either.

"Sorry. I went overboard, didn't I?" I always do that. Jump right in with two feet. Move in with your hot neighbor? Why don't you redecorate his entire house while you're at it? A manly man like him will love ruffles and floral patterns.

"Not at all."

"I'm sorry."

"Loren, it's fine. I'm only giving you shit. I told you to make the place your own, and you did." He kicks his feet onto the corner of the coffee table, right next to the scented candle I bought along with the two others in the bathroom and my bedroom.

They were buy two, get one free.

Everyone knows that's a deal you don't pass up.

Tears prickle the backs of my eyes when I flip open the lid on my own takeout container, feeling like the luckiest woman in the world.

CHAPTER 32

ELLIOTT

ALL I WANTED when I got home from work was a beer and an hour or two of mindless TV. But the moment Loren swept through the door, I realized that was a dream that wouldn't come true. First, she cooks chicken cordon bleu, which is distracting as hell because she's wearing these tiny shorts and keeps checking the oven, which requires her to bend over.

I'm trying not to be a pervert so I'm not staring, but fuck me, do I want to.

Then, she offers me some, which is basically my love language.

To make matters worse, after dinner, she throws herself onto the couch next to me and she somehow still smells like peaches even after a long day of work.

The moment her ass hits the cushion, she's right back up like a fucking jack in the box, skipping over to the tv stand, and throwing open the cabinet doors.

For all she knows, I could have a bunch of old-school porn in there. That doesn't stop her. No, siree, boundaries are something Loren Piper has apparently never heard of.

And because I must've pissed someone off in a past life, she bends over right in front of me to root around. I force my head back against the cushion, staring at the ceiling fan instead of the way her hips are cocked at the perfect angle for—

"Holy crap! You have Scrabble?"

I roll my eyes at the box Loren pulls from beneath the TV. "I don't see why that's so shocking. It's a great game."

"It's shocking because you're not a seventy-five-year-old grandpa." The box shakes when she rights herself. "Let's play."

"No." Scrabble isn't mindless and if Loren finds out how competitive I am, there's a good chance this budding friendship will be over before it begins.

"Come on. Please? My parents and I always used to play Scrabble on weekends."

Mine too. It must be an only child thing.

She looks so damn excited and after everything that's happened to her, it feels like I don't have much of a choice. "Ugh. Fine." I clear my cup and plate off the coffee table, making room for Loren to set out the board.

It's funny that she mentioned grandparents, because the tiles are in a tube sock that used to belong to my grandpa. Weird, I know. But I can't bring myself to transfer them into something normal, like a baggie or whatever.

I sink back down on the couch covered in her ridiculous pillows. I wasn't a fan at first, but I must admit they're comfy when you're lounging, watching TV.

I grab my wooden rack and select seven tiles from the sock. "I have to warn you, I'm pretty good."

She grins down at her tiles as she places them on her own rack. "So am I."

We'll see about that.

With the TV playing a rerun of *Frasier* in the background, we start the game. Because I'm a gentleman, I let her go first. Wouldn't want to make this too unfair on her.

Don't get me wrong, I'm not going to let her win by any means, but it's the least I can do.

Tapping her lips, she moves her tiles around before playing her first word, "peasant," using every damn tile.

"Luck."

A smirk. "Skill."

After a few rounds, it's clear we're more evenly matched than I originally thought. Which is fucking amazing because the last time I played against August it was like that scene in *The Office* where the receptionist only plays words that have to do with cows, but instead of cows, August kept spelling food items. He claimed it was because he was hungry at the time, but I'm not buying it.

I throw down three tiles, then pick three more, finally getting the "K" I've been waiting for. Loren isn't paying me any attention, her focus solely on the board between us. Even so, I keep my eyes off that pink square just in case she catches me looking and decides to swoop in before I can.

She plays somewhere else, and I burst into laughter when I make my move.

DICK

"Fitting, since you are a dick," she mutters through flat lips, scribbling down my points on the notebook. Her gaze bounces between the board and her tiles while I sit back and select four new tiles.

When a smile splits across her face, I hold my breath as she steals the double word score right out from under me.

PUSSY

"I believe that's eighteen points. Oh, wait. Would you look at that? I used the double word score twice, so make that *twenty-seven* points, please."

So that's she's going to play it? "It is on."

When I throw down MOIST, she grimaces, then proceeds to use my "T" for CLIT.

"Dammit." I guess I'll have to find somewhere else for my next word.

Let's see...there is one place, but it feels like a throw-away since it won't get me very many points. Oh, wait. I can totally use her C for...

"Cunt? Really?"

My dick jumps when she says the word out loud. Good thing I have a pillow on my lap so she doesn't notice. *"Did you hear Elliott gets horny when playing Scrabble?"* This is not the sort of distraction I need. "What? It's a legitimate word, isn't it?"

She snorts and plays Q on my u. Add an I and a T and I am done for. I blew my chance of winning by lining up that damn word right next to a triple-word square.

"Shit."

"I believe you mean 'Quit' And that's probably what you should do. considering there are no letters left in your sock."

"I never quit."

"Oh, really?" The way she rolls the top of her beer bottle against her lips is downright pornographic. She's so busy gloating, I don't even know if she realizes what she's doing. But my dick does, which is damned inconvenient since this is the one girl I can't touch.

First: she's desperate for someone to love her, and I don't have the capacity for that anymore.

Second: she's vulnerable and this whole roommate situation we have going on can only end in disaster. I'm not going to take advantage of her just because she's hot and my hands are itching to get lost in that chaotic hair of hers.

Third: who the hell gets horny playing fucking Scrabble? I need to get laid so I can get Loren Piper off my mind.

She ends up winning, and while I'd like to blame my distraction for my poor score, she totally bested me.

"Winner cleans up," I say in my most cheerful voice so she doesn't realize how irritated I am.

"That's fair. You want to watch something on TV?"

There might as well be a red light flashing over her head: *Danger. Danger.*

I should say no, but the truth is, I do want to watch TV. And it's not fair of me to tell her that she needs to hole up in her room because I happen to find her attractive.

"Um... Yeah. Sure. Why not?"

"Woah, calm down, Elliott. There's no need to sound so excited."

This girl. She's funny. "You want another beer?" I ask, figuring it's safe enough to stand without my dick getting in the way.

"Sounds good. You have any popcorn?"

"No, but there might be some chips and salsa." I don't think I ate them all.

"Perfect."

We sit down to watch a movie, but as she flicks through our options, all I can focus on is Loren taking photos of the TV.

"What are you doing?"

She flushes. "I always forget what movies are on here and when I go to search for one, I can't find any of them." She shows me her screen. All romcoms.

"We can watch one now, if you want."

"Oh, we don't have to do that. I'm sure you'd rather choose something with murder."

"Why? Because I'm such a murderer?"

"No, I mean guys don't really like romances."

Good thing she's not living with August. He'd have her glued to this cushion for a romcom marathon if she even hinted that she'd be interested. That man has a thing for Kate Hudson.

She's pretty and all, but Meg Ryan is more my type.

I think it's the hair.

"They're not that bad," I say.

"Really?"

I nod.

"What's your favorite?"

"*The Notebook.*"

"You like *The Notebook?*"

"Rachel McAdams is hot."

"Okay, then. Let's watch *The Notebook.*"

So that's what we do. Or at least I watch *The Notebook.* Loren seems to be watching me more than the damn screen. "TV's that way." I nod toward the scene where Noah takes her out on that boat with all the birds. Animals with wings freak me out. It may look romantic, but can you imagine how much bird shit is in that water?

Loren's lips press into a flat line as she watches me watching the TV. "You're strange."

Okay...?

"I mean that in a good way," she adds. "I don't think I've ever met a guy who's willing to sit through a movie like this without an ulterior motive."

"Who says I don't have an ulterior motive?"

Her eyes narrow like she's trying to see into my mind. "Do you?"

"I've been really craving steak lately." Ever since she gave me a bit of her dinner that night in her apartment, to be exact.

"So you're offering companionship in exchange for food."

"I'm a simple man with simple needs."

Her laugh warms me like a sunny summer day, and she twists back toward the TV. The couple on screen are fighting when Loren's head falls to my shoulder. When her curls tickle my neck and cheek, I may or may not sniff her hair. I know how weird that is, but women always smell so damn good, and Loren is no exception.

I force my gaze back to the screen, watching in silence as Allie and Noah profess their love to each other. I know I'm supposed to be cheering for Noah, but I always feel bad for Allie's fiancé. He wasn't an asshole and didn't treat her badly. All he did was love her, and yet she ran off with someone else.

I pause the movie, listening to Loren's soft, even breathing until my own eyes drift closed. I really should get up and go to bed, but this couch and these pillows—and yeah, this woman—are all too damn comfortable.

When was the last time I had a woman over for more than just sex?

That makes me sound like a dick, but I'm not really in the market for a relationship. I work long ass hours, and my life is just fine the way it is.

At least it was.

Now that Loren is here, it's clear there's been something missing the last few years.

I'm just not sure I'm ready to acknowledge what that is.

6:45 AM

There's been a development!!

MEGALODON

!!!

"AND THEN, we fell asleep on the couch together." I still can't believe I woke up with Elliott's arms wrapped around me. I haven't fallen asleep with a guy like that since high school.

Meg swirls her fry in the ketchup on the corner of her plate, leaning forward as she listens intently to my story. "No way."

"Yes!"

"And then what happened?" Rebecca asks, stealing a fry for herself.

"Well, nothing. I had to pee and when I got back from the bathroom, he'd gone to his own room."

"Oh." Her fallen face matches my own.

"But it was so romantic."

Meg takes another fry, but this time foregoes the ketchup. "I don't know. Sexy Scrabble followed by *The Notebook* feels like it should lead to more than nothing."

"He could be wanting to take it slow." And slow is my jam. We can be snails for all I care as long as we end up at happily-ever-after.

Pins crash in the background and then a cheer erupts from the next lane over. Sounds like someone got a strike.

Rebecca bounces a little on the plastic chair. "Did he say that?"

"Well, no..."

"Loren." Meg takes me by the shoulders and turns me in my chair, our game forgotten in lieu of this very vital conversation. "You know I love you, right?"

Of course she loves me, and I love her right back.

I'm starting to love Rebecca too, but that's still new.

Meg's sigh floods my stomach with dread. "You do this though, don't you? You thought you and... *your ex* were more than you were."

Thank goodness she caught herself before saying Josh's name. That's a conversation I'm still not prepared to have with Rebecca.

"Is it possible that you're seeing what you want to see and not what's really there?" Meg asks.

I mean, yeah, it's possible. But Elliott was supposed to go out and he cancelled his plans to stay and hang out with me. That has to mean something, right?

Rebecca leans back in her own chair, the embroidered name on her shirt peeking from behind her folded arms. "Did you ask your roommate about it this morning?"

"He was already gone when I woke up."

Her lips purse. "That's not really the behavior of a doting suitor, is it?"

Dammit, she's right. If Elliott was actually interested in me, he would've at least stuck around for breakfast, right?

Meg gives my shoulders an encouraging squeeze before letting her hands fall. "I say this because I love you. But you deserve someone who chooses you, who makes it clear that you're his priority. Not another dipshit who makes you question everything."

Her words make sense even though I hate them. If I'm ever going to get out of this situationship slump, I've gotta stop jumping to conclusions and live in reality, no matter how much it sucks. "How did you become so wise?"

Grimacing, she stabs her fry into the ketchup. "Let's just say, I've dated a *lot* of dipshits."

———

Elliott isn't in the apartment when I get back from work.

So here I lay, sprawled on the couch, swiping away my misery on the latest dating app in search of someone who isn't a dipshit. I hear his keys in the door, and when he steps inside, I offer a polite hello, but don't bother looking up from my phone.

The girls and I have concluded that I fell victim to his hypnosis.

If I don't look him directly in the eye, he'll eventually lose power over me.

Elliott nods, then heads into the bathroom, coming out ten minutes later smelling like soap and fresh laundry. Meanwhile, I still haven't budged.

He putters around the kitchen, opening and closing the

fridge before meandering over to the living room with a bottle of water in hand. "Why are you panned out on the couch, staring at your phone like it holds the secrets to the universe?"

If only that were true. "I'm reminding myself there are other fish in the proverbial sea." After my chat with the girls tonight, it's clear I've been trying to squeeze my heroic roommate into a category where he most certainly does not fit.

It's time to get out of my own way and find someone who's actually interested in me.

Elliott catches me by the ankles, lifting my legs so he can plop down on the cushion. I probably should've forced myself to move. This is his couch, after all. But I'm wallowing.

It's not that I miss Josh. I miss the idea of Josh and mourn the loss of the beautiful life we could've built together.

Elliott settles my legs over his thighs and leans in close enough that the soap he used distracts me. What *is* that? It's plain and clean and I kinda want to lick his neck to see how it tastes. But I've tasted soap before—the one time I cursed in front of my mother—and it was terrible. So I imagine the taste won't live up to the smell.

"By trolling dating apps?" he scoffs.

That's right. Loren Piper is officially online. I don't even waste money on the subscriptions. I just lay here swiping and hope someone finds me.

"Let me see that." He snags my phone before I can stop him. "Seriously? This guy looks like a twat."

What is he, British now? "No, he doesn't. He looks nice." And he even has a puppy. Animal lovers make great boyfriends—or so I've read. Josh didn't have any pets.

Then again, neither does Elliott.

Elliott throws an arm over the back of the couch. "That's what I said: twat."

"Give me back my phone. Don't—"

It's too late. Elliot has already swiped the wrong way, eliminating my chances of ever finding love with William, 27, from Franklin.

Elliott snorts. "Oh yeah. Definitely a tool bag." *Swipe.* "Come on." He flashes me a photo of a guy in a black beanie with his nose and lip pierced. I've gotta admit, he's pretty hot in a dirty sort of way. Not dirty like he doesn't shower, but like he has a thing for having sex in public.

I've never had sex in public or kissed a guy with a lip ring. Could kill two birds with one—

"Toolbox," Elliot mutters, swiping to the next contender.

Okay. Guess that's a "no" on Mr. Lip Ring. "What's the difference between a tool bag and a toolbox?"

"You don't want to know. Oh, this guy. He looks okay."

"Really? Let me see." I sidle up closer, peering over his shoulder at my own screen. The man has pretty blue eyes and a nice smile. Although I would think the strip club in the background would be a red flag. Interesting that Elliott approves of him. It's hard to judge someone based on a photo. Maybe he doesn't realize it's a strip club. Or maybe they know each other.

"Just kidding. He's a ghoster for sure." Off he goes, swiping to the next man.

"Really funny." As entertaining as this game is, he obviously doesn't realize the point is to make a match and meet people. "Give me my phone."

Does he listen? No. Instead, he angles the screen toward me. "This guy definitely wants in your pants."

Swipe. Swipe. *Swipe.*

"If you keep going at this pace, there's going to be no one left!" I grab for my phone again, but he decides to be an ass and hold it above his head. I twist around, kneeling on the cushion next to him, flailing for my damn phone.

Elliott goes still.

This is when I realize that he is eye level with my boobs.

And he is *definitely* looking.

I chose today of all days to not wear a bra, which means my nipples are currently screaming, "HERE I AM! PUT ME IN YOUR HOT MOUTH."

While he is sufficiently distracted, I manage to retrieve my phone. He doesn't even try to fight, just lets the thing slip from his fingers.

When he speaks, his voice is three shades darker than before, as are his cheeks and ears. "Why don't you go out to a bar and talk to guys like a normal person?"

Oh, gee. Why didn't I think of that? "Because guys who pick up girls in bars are creepy."

"And guys who hide online are all pillars of virtue." He rolls his eyes and reaches for the remote as I settle back into my spot to keep searching for my soulmate.

Elliott doesn't even finish his sentence before I stumble across a discovery of epic proportions.

No freaking way. What a hypocrite. "I don't know. You look virtuous to me." I smirk down at my phone. Elliott smiles right back.

Not the real Elliott, mind you. That Elliott is scowling and clearly confused.

"Elliott Grant, thirty-two, lives in Mount Juliette." I steal a glance at his deepening scowl. "Likes dogs, mint chocolate chip ice cream, and texting late into the night."

His shoulder bumps against mine as he scoots so close our thighs press together, looking over my shoulder to see my screen. I could've shown him, but then I would've missed out on getting another good whiff of that soap.

Nothing is going to happen between us, but that doesn't mean I can't sniff the guy every now and again, does it?

"What the hell?" His hand comes over mine, angling the screen toward himself. I don't notice for the billionth time how big those hands actually are. Nope. Not at all.

"I've never been on a dating app in my life."

"This picture of you says otherwise. Oh, look! There's more." Swipity, swipe, swipe. "Uh, oh. Shirtless. *Big* red flag."

But also, can we take a second to appreciate exactly how many abs this man has? Right now, they probably smell like soap. Is there any non-creepy way to ask him if I can see them again?

No. Probably not.

Although we are living together so chances are I might be treated to another peek at some point.

One can only hope.

Elliott groans, dragging a hand over his face. "Fucking August. I sent that picture to show him what his dog did to me. Left a scar and everything."

As if he heard my internal struggle, the man—bless his generous soul—hikes up his shirt and sweet saints above, all I can see are ridges and the thinnest trail of dark hair disappearing into the waistband of his black basketball shorts.

When I saw his abs the last time, I didn't fully appreciate the perfection, but now...

I mean, anyone who looks at this man would know he's fit, but holy cow. Those abs are still there when he's hunched over on the couch. How is that even humanly possible?

"See?" he demands with righteous indignation.

Oh, I see, all right.

He taps his side.

Sure enough, a long silver scar runs down the length of his torso.

"I told him to get his damn dog's nails trimmed or I'd do it myself."

Mmmhmmm. Dogs. Nails. *Abs.*

So many abs.

I force my gaze back to my phone and swipe right for shits and gigs. "Oh, look! We matched!" A zesty little thrill tingles in my stomach.

His dark eyebrows slam down. Unfortunately, so does his shirt. "How is that possible?"

Okay, at first, I was skeptical, but now I genuinely think Elliott might not have been behind this dating profile. Am I disappointed? Sure. Not as disappointed as I am about the abs being gone. Wonder if he'd notice if I screen-shotted this picture...for posterity.

"Maybe August went through and liked everyone. I bet you have a ton of messages." If I came across his profile, I'd think he was too good to be true. Yeah, showing off the abs is a little douchey, but those abs would be worth at least a first date.

His gaze flies up to meet mine. "Really? Shit. How do I find out?"

The eyes, Loren! Don't look directly into his eyes! I drop my gaze back to my phone. "You'll need to log into the account."

Man, would I love to peek behind the curtain at what women send to men like Elliott. I mean, I know the kinds of messages *I* get (unsolicited dick pics are gross), but hopefully the fairer sex has a bit more class.

Elliott slides his phone from his pocket. "That fucker. I'm going to get him back for this."

Maybe it's because I've been duped recently, but I have to ask, "You really didn't make this profile?" Why would anyone go through the hassle of creating a fake profile, even as a joke, especially since Elliott had no idea it was even there?

He looks appalled. "Absolutely not. And mint chocolate chip? I fucking hate mint chocolate chip."

"You could probably press charges. I'm pretty sure making a fake profile is illegal."

"And make the holidays awkward? My mom would never forgive me. No, this calls for something better." The wicked curve of his lips sends my stomach into a nosedive. "*Revenge*."

CHAPTER 34

ELLIOTT

ONE OF THE main reasons I never considered finding a roommate was because I wanted to avoid awkward situations in my own home.

Now I've walked right into one of the most awkward situations of all.

Loren left her phone on the counter, and I happened to be walking by when her friend texted. It's not my fault she has no privacy settings in place so that any random pair of eyes can read whatever messages come in.

So here I am, standing in the middle of the kitchen, spoon of peanut butter in hand, not knowing what the hell to do with myself until she gets out of the shower.

Great. Now I'm imagining her in my shower. Naked. Water cascading down her—

Nope. Nope. *Nope.*

Let's see what I need to get from the grocery store. I shove the spoon into my mouth and throw open the fridge, scouring the groceries Loren bought earlier this week.

Still pretty stocked up, so this distraction was a bust.

Now her phone is lighting up again, and I'm not a saint, okay? I'm a man with flaws, and I need to know what it says. *Boom.* Another text from her friend Meg.

God, how does this woman have so many notifications? Don't those little red numbers drive her insane?

2,567 unread emails?

I am living with a psychopath.

The bathroom door finally opens, and Loren slips out in a fuzzy purple robe, reminding me of that dinosaur that used to be popular with kids way back when. Her head stays down, but when I call her name, she freezes.

Her hair is wrapped in a towel turban-style, up on top of her head. "Yes?"

I bet her hair smells like that peach-infused shampoo she uses. Yeah, I sniffed it in the shower. So what? Sue me.

"Your phone has been blowing up." I hand her the thing, and she tucks it into her pocket. "Aren't you going to check your messages?"

"I will when I get to my room."

Yeah, that's not going to cut it. I'm sick of waiting and these questions aren't going to answer themselves. "What is a sex bra?"

Her back stiffens, and she freezes mid-step. When she whirls, there's a fire in her eyes that I haven't seen before. "You went through my phone?"

"Of course not. It was on the counter and some messages popped up."

"That doesn't mean you're allowed to read them!"

Irrelevant details because I *did* read them.

"So...sex bra?" Obviously it's a bra, but the way those two words are combined have all sorts of dirty ideas running through my mind. Is it a bra specifically made for sex with like, the nipples cut out, or just a typo and her friend really meant "sexy" bra?

"No. You and I are not having this conversation," she says like she thinks shutting this down is going to keep me from bringing it up every chance I get. Eventually, she will break. When she does, I shall celebrate with one of those big chocolate chip cookie cakes they sell at the mall. I've always wanted to try them but have never pulled the trigger.

Loren doesn't seem like the type to wear a nipple-less bra. I guess there could be another option. "Is that the bra you wear when you want to get laid?" Her face flushes. "Holy shit. I'm right, aren't I? You have a lucky bra." It's like August's lucky underwear he used to throw on back in high school every time we had a soccer game, except way hotter.

"I do not. Go away."

"What color is it?" I bet it's red. Please, tell me it's red. "Can I see it?"

"I'm not showing you my bra, Elliott!" She sprints the rest of the way into her room, the hem of her robe flapping against her bare calves before she slams the door shut.

"You don't have to be wearing it," I call through the barrier. I mean, she could if she wanted to, but from the horrified look on her face when I brought it up, she doesn't seem into it. Which is absolutely for the best, especially if it's nipple-less.

"Come on, how else will I know when to avoid knocking on your door because you're knocking boots?"

There may be a door between us, but I can hear the smile in her voice when she says, "You're disgusting."

Yeah, yeah. "I'm not the one with a sex bra."

My cousin—the brother I never had—is about to understand the definition of wrath.

If murder wasn't illegal and if I didn't need him to help run the bar, he would be swimming at the bottom of the lake right now.

As it stands, my roommate has agreed to assist me in this most devious endeavor, along with her friend Meg.

When the leggy blonde walks into the bar next to Loren, the game is afoot.

August zeroes in on our new guests like a sniper. "Who's the stunner?"

I glance around at the few patrons already seated at the bar, pretending I don't know who he's talking about.

He takes either side of my head and points me toward the newcomers. "The one with your girl. She looks familiar. She was here before, right?"

Loren isn't my girl; she's my roommate. But saying that to August will only garner some stupid response like, "Methinks thou doth protesteth too much."

I shake him off. He knows how I feel about him touching me. "Yeah, she came in the night Loren dumped her ex." I twist around, catching Loren's gaze in the mirror behind the bottles. "Loren said you made quite the impression."

He steps closer, the toes of our shoes brushing. "Bullshit. Really?"

Why is this so easy? It's sad when you think about it. "I probably shouldn't be telling you this, but she was asking if you were single."

He peers over my shoulder at the women, who, thanks

to the mirror, I can see are now sitting at the bar, whispering and shooting not-so-subtle glances at us.

Like the idiot he is, he slicks a hand over his gelled hair. "Lucky for her I am very single."

Lucky for me, he means. Otherwise, this wouldn't have worked.

I twist and wave at Loren, and she returns the gesture. "I better go see what they want."

August presses a hand against my chest. "You finish the inventory. I'll help them out."

Hook, line, and fucking sinker.

My cousin strolls down to where the girls wait, leaning an elbow on the bar between them. He makes them two gin and tonics, then instead of coming back to help me count shit, he stays right where I want him.

I must admit, this plan of Loren's was ingenious.

As with all good pranks, I bide my time, taking care of the other customers and all the barback duties since it's Tuesday and we don't typically bring in extra help during the week. Loren whispers something to Meg and then brings her drink down to where I'm pretending not to watch Meg and August flirt. He looks like a giddy golden retriever, drooling and dancing around, waiting for someone to throw a ball.

Loren's lips, a glossy shade of plum, leave a mark on the end of her paper straw. "Hey."

"Hey." I nod toward our project. "How are the newlyweds?"

"Planning the honeymoon already."

Excellent. It should be only a matter of time before he makes his move.

Not even two minutes later, August brings Meg around the back of the bar to teach her how to pull a pint of

Guiness. There are lots of casual touching and crude jokes about head that girls laugh at whether they think it's funny or not.

"Man, you know him so well," Loren murmurs under her breath, poking at an ice cube with her straw.

"Too well." He really is like my brother. Any time he got annoyed with his crazy family, he'd hop the fence and come hang out with me. With six siblings, it happened a lot.

"Does it really work?"

"Almost every time."

Her cheeks hollow out as she sips, and I hate myself for where my mind goes. Let's just say it's not very gentlemanly. "I mean, I guess I get it," she says. "He's hot enough."

She did not just say that. "Gah." I stuff my fingers into my ears to keep those words from sinking in. "Please tell me you did not just call August hot."

Her lips tilt into a smirk behind her straw. "What? He is."

"Then I guess we didn't need Meg at all."

All she does is smile, which is more infuriating than the fact that she's attracted to August. "Yeah, why didn't you ask me to do it?"

Because my cousin never would've taken the bait. He believes I have a thing for Loren and that makes her off limits.

I'm starting to worry that he may be right.

Thankfully, I'm saved from responding when August whispers something into Meg's ear and the two of them slip away to the office.

So fucking predictable.

This is where the magic happens.

I drag out my phone, flick over to the camera, aim it toward the back, and wait.

An indignant yelp echoes down the hallway. Meg comes sprinting out, catching herself on the wall and doubling over with laughter. Damn, she's fast in those heels.

"What the fuck?" August stomps out, green globs dripping down his forehead.

He swipes a finger across his brow, his wide eyes meeting mine as I zoom in on his irritating face and say, "I hate mint fucking chip."

A startled laugh bursts out of him. "You're some bastard."

"Says the guy who put me on a dating app without permission "

"You're the one who said you wanted to get back out there after—"

I whip the sprayer from the sink and squirt him right in the face. The girls take off laughing again, and so do the other four people in the bar.

Now August looks like he's going to kill me. "What the fuck, Elliott?"

"Hey, I was just trying to help clean you off."

"Oh, it's on. You'd better watch your back. Don't fall asleep. Don't even fucking blink. And you two." He levels his finger at Loren and Meg. "You are both dead to me." He twists around and stomps back into the office, globs of melted mint chocolate chip ice cream dripping the entire way.

"Waste of perfectly good ice cream if you ask me," Meg mutters as she saunters past, returning to her gin.

Loren trails behind, swiping her own drink on her way. "Have I told you how amazing you are? I want to be you when I grow up."

Meg is amazing. And as a thank you, I think they could both use another drink. I throw some ice in two fish-bowl glasses, pour in a little extra gin, and add a little less tonic.

Meg drains what's left in her glass, then slides the thing over to me. "What can I say? I have a gift."

"And for using your 'gift' for evil, both of you drink for free tonight." I add two lime wedges and set them right in front of my new favorite women.

Meg accepts hers with a "thanks," but Loren stares down at her glass like I might have poisoned the thing. "Are you sure? I don't want you to get in trouble with the manager."

Manager? I mean, it's sweet of her to worry, but doesn't she know? "Chaos, I own the place."

CHAPTER 35
LOREN

WHEN I WALK into the living room, Elliott glances up from the bowl of chili he's shoveling into his mouth.

"Where are you off to?" he asks around the spoon.

"I have a date." As soon as I get this damn earring through my ear, I'll be leaving.

Men have it so easy. Take Elliott, for example. Should I wear this black T-shirt or that one? So annoying.

"What's his name?"

"You don't know him." I've been chatting with a few guys online but didn't really feel like meeting up with any of them. Enter: Paul, twenty-six, from Murfreesboro.

"How can you be so sure? I know lots of people."

Elliott seems like the kind of guy to claim he knows someone just to mess with me. I mean, he did go through with this big, elaborate plan to humiliate his cousin.

A grin stretches across his too-handsome face, and his spoon clinks against the edge of the bowl when he sets it on the counter. "It's Meg, isn't it? There's no need to be embarrassed, Loren. I think it's great that you and your friend hang out so much."

Says the man whose only friend seems to be his cousin.

"For your information, Meg is busy tonight. Her friend Karlo invited her to the movies."

"Friend. Okay."

"*Friend. Okay*," I mimic. "What does that mean?"

He scoops another spoonful of chili. "It means, guys and girls can't be friends."

"That's not true." I've had a bunch of guy friends through the years. Like Matthew and David all through elementary and middle school. And my friend Chris from the church we attended for a while.

Empty bowl in hand, Elliott stands to load his dish into the dishwasher. "Any straight guy who is willing to put effort into a 'platonic' relationship with a woman, secretly—or not so secretly—would absolutely jump her bones if given half a chance."

He can't be serious. Men and women can totally be friends. I mean, look at us. Elliott and I have known each other for months, and he has yet to try to "jump my bones." Who even says that, anyway? What is he, fifteen?

"We're friends though, aren't we?"

He turns and saunters down the hallway to his room, but not before I catch his smile tightening. "Yeah, Loren. We are."

He literally just said...

Wait.

He lifts a hand in a casual wave as he slinks into his room. "Have fun on your date tonight."

"Come back here. Elliot!"

Does he listen? Of course not.

I consider going after him and making him explain exactly what he meant by that cryptic little comment, but then I'll be late for my actual date and that wouldn't be fair to Paul.

Besides, like Meg has pointed out a thousand times, I shouldn't have to decipher cryptic man-messages. If Elliott wanted to be more than roommates, he would've made a move.

So I escape the apartment and head off to meet what could be the love of my life.

———

The date is a disaster with a capital "D." Not only is Paul twenty minutes late, he also doesn't even text to give me a heads-up. Tardiness notwithstanding, his eyes are so lifeless. He smiles with his mouth, but not his whole face. Which I admit is a stupid reason to discount someone, but here I am, judging everything about this guy who could very well be super sweet and just have a tiny issue with punctuality and smiling.

Not only am I judging him, but also I'm comparing him to my freaking roommate—a man who I have absolutely no business thinking about in any capacity other than that he lets me live in his spare room.

Why did Elliott have to make that damn comment about men and women being friends right before I left? Why couldn't he have said it tomorrow?

Or never?

Never would've been good.

It makes me wonder if maybe, just maybe, he thinks

about me as often as I think about him. And not in the platonic, he-lives-down-the-hall sort of way.

No, what I feel for Elliott is decidedly *not* platonic.

It's like I'm so desperate for love and affection that I think I see it in places that it cannot possibly exist. Like a mirage. A sexy, black-T-shirt-wearing mirage.

Which, unfortunately, means I need to move out as soon as I find a better place to live. It really sucks because I like living with Elliott. I was wary about the whole room-mate thing, but it's been nice having someone to hang out with in the evenings after work. Someone to talk to over breakfast.

And not just anyone.

Elliott Grant.

Loren Piper strikes again, romanticizing a relationship that has no right to be romanticized.

Now I'm offering to pay half of this dinner bill and brushing this guy off just so I can get home and yell at Elliott for ruining my night. He'll probably be on the couch sipping a beer, watching reruns of *Frasier* or *Friends*.

After the yelling is over, I should probably try to play nice since I don't want to live in a place filled with tension, so I'll grab a beer and sink down beside him. But I'm also kind of tired so I can totally see myself falling asleep.

The last time I did that, I woke up half in love with the guy.

It meant nothing, I know that now.

Tell that to my romance-loving heart. I mean, wouldn't this be the cutest story to tell our future children? How he swooped in and saved me from certain doom, how we did the whole "let's pretend to be friends" thing, stealing glances and partaking in sexy Scrabble before falling madly in love?

What is wrong with me?

Someone needs to give me a stern talking-to.

This relationship isn't going to end with a happily-ever-after. We're not even *in* a relationship.

An hour later, I pull back into a parking spot next to Elliott's truck and take my time climbing the stairs to our apartment. No need to rush. I'm going to simply go in, say hi, and then head to bed. Leave him wondering about my night. Be all mysterious and shit.

Guys like Elliott probably love mysterious women.

My keys jangle when I unlock the door. The only light comes from beneath the microwave, illuminating two half-empty glasses of wine on the counter.

Weird.

Elliott doesn't usually drink wine.

The TV is off, and the couch is empty. Also strange. Maybe he had to go into work or something. I slip out of my coat, hanging it on the back of the dining room chair before texting him.

When he doesn't answer right away, I'm not disappointed. Not really. If he's working, he's probably busy. It is Friday night, after all. There are drinks to be served and all that jazz.

I head into the bathroom to wash my face and brush my teeth, but the door at the end of the hallway catches my eye.

Not the door specifically, but the doorknob.

There's an *actual* sock hanging off it.

I've seen plenty of raunchy movies; I know exactly what that sock is supposed to mean.

I'm only shocked it's something people do in real life.

I can't believe I cut my date short because of this guy only to get home and have him bedding down with someone else.

I don't want someone who makes me second guess everything. Who makes me spend all night over-analyzing innocuous conversations.

I want a guy who says what he means straight out. No games.

I deserve that.

Not wanting to accidentally run into Elliott's mystery guest, I head straight into my room. My mouth is going to taste like hot trash in the morning if I don't brush my teeth, but right now, I don't care.

CHAPTER 36

LOREN

WHEN MY ALARM goes off the next morning, I don't leave my room until I hear the front door close. Expecting to emerge into an empty kitchen, I'm shocked to find Elliott standing next to the new Keurig cup-pot-combo I bought.

That's right, I paid for it all by myself.

If I were a petty woman, I'd tell him he wasn't allowed to use it.

He turns away from the coffee and throws open the fridge, the pair of dark shorts he's wearing slung dangerously low on those cut hips he wields like a weapon.

I'm pissed at him and don't feel like pretending otherwise. He's the one who told me to move in, so he gets to deal with my mood.

It's time he gets a peek behind the curtain. Time Elliott Grant experiences being the brunt of some good, old-fashioned feminine rage.

So yeah, I slam my door closed like a teenager throwing a tantrum. Guess what? It feels *good*.

He smiles at me like we're not fighting. He doesn't know I'm mad at him, but he's about to find out.

I swing open the cabinet door, but before I can lift onto my toes and grab a mug, Mr. Biceps does it for me.

Why is he so stupidly tall? He needs more obvious flaws so my traitorous mind doesn't keep glossing over them or making up stupid excuses for his terrible behavior that he doesn't even deserve.

He sets the mug down on the counter, but I don't thank him, not even when he holds out the coffee pot. I only let him fill my mug because I want to be waited on.

I wait for him to return to his room, but he doesn't. He eases himself against the edge of the counter and drinks his coffee, smirking in between sips.

Why isn't he talking? I guess it's up to me to start this conversation. "I think I need to move out."

That wipes the smartass look off his face. "Why?"

I don't owe him an explanation. I don't owe him anything.

He drags a hand down the back of his neck, looking sufficiently chastised. "Is this about sex bra? Look, I'm sorry I read your messages, but in my defense, the word 'sex' has a terrible habit of grabbing my attention."

I haven't given his little invasion of privacy a second thought. "This is about you crossing a line. We're supposed to be friends, and you went and screwed it all up with your..."

His lips twitch, and I despise him a little more.

"Your *mind* games." Damn hypnotist.

"Mind games? I see. Out of curiosity, what mind games have I been playing?"

"You said you wanted to sleep with me."

His brows arch beneath his stupidly adorable mop of dark hair. "Did I say that? Wow. That is so shitty of me. I should have lied and said I find you repulsive."

Wait. So he *does* want to sleep with me? Not that it matters when he literally had another woman in his bed last night. I'm not *that* desperate. "You shouldn't have said anything at all." Then I could still believe this attraction was blissfully one-sided and go about my days searching for Mr. Right instead of obsessing over Mr. Right Next Door.

This ends now.

I yank out my phone, open the first dating app I see, and start swiping. I don't care who they are. Living, breathing, and single are my only requirements. If they meet those three criteria, I'm going to date them.

"Really mature," Elliott mutters.

We passed mature the moment he put that damn sock on the damn doorknob.

He sets his mug on the counter. "You've made your point."

Swipe. Match. Swipe. Match.

"Loren. Stop."

Swipe. Swipe. Swipe. Match.

He takes the phone right out of my hands, eyes blazing when he clicks the thing off and sets it down on the counter. "What is wrong with you?"

I don't even know. I have no right to be annoyed but I am, so I'm just here stewing in it. "What's wrong with *you*?"

He takes a deep breath, then exhales through his nose.

Oh, is he annoyed too? Good. "I shouldn't have said what I did last night. We are friends. I find you repulsive. I wouldn't fuck you if you were wearing nothing but a sex bra and matching black panties." The corner of his lips twitch. "Blue panties? *Red* panties?"

"I'm not telling you what color sex bra is." He doesn't deserve to know.

His loud clap rattles my eardrums. "Ha! So the legends are true!"

"You're an asshole, and I'm leaving."

"Come *onnnn*. Don't abandon me. If I promise to behave from now on, will you stay?" He follows me down the hallway like a sulking puppy.

Why does he even care?

Maybe he's lonely too.

Ha! Look at that sock still hanging on the doorknob like a big old red flag. Elliott Grant isn't *lonely*. He can have "company" any time he chooses.

He seems to notice where I'm looking, and his brow furrows. "What the hell?" He stalks over and yanks the sock off the knob, holding it up as if I hadn't seen it already and been obsessing over it all freaking night. "Did you put this here?"

Yeah, like I put a sock on his doorknob. "Very funny."

"I'm serious."

"Yes, Elliott. I came home from my date and the first thing I wanted to do was put a sex sock on your doorknob."

"That sounds like a euphemism for something I might be up for."

Can't he take anything seriously?

"So, you didn't do it?" he asks.

"Of course not!"

He bunches the sock in his fist. "Fucking August."

"Are you saying your cousin did this?"

"He's the only other person who's been here."

I know I've been naïve, but that sounds a little too suspicious, even to me. "Maybe it was the girl you brought home last night." Okay, I did not mean that to come out so shrill, but there isn't anything I can do about it now.

"I didn't bring anyone home."

Yeah, right. "I heard her leave this morning."

"You heard me taking out the trash."

He didn't take out the—

Okay. The trash was taken out. But it's a little early for stomping down to the dumpsters, especially if he was drinking wine.

His eyes widen. "Is that why you've been biting my head off since the moment you stepped out of your room?"

There is no way I'm going to admit it. My pride is already shot after spending half the night tossing and turning, listening for the tell-tale thump of a headboard against the wall. From the silence, I assumed the deed had been done, but maybe he hadn't brought anyone home after all.

If that's the case, I feel like such an idiot. Time to go back to my room and hide for at least a year before showing my face again.

Elliott steps forward, his lips curving into a cocky grin. "You jealous, Chaos?"

"Don't call me that. And don't be stupid. Why on earth would I be jealous?"

"You tell me. You're the one who's jealous."

"I am not."

"*Mmmhmmm.* Keep telling yourself that."

Why are men so freaking infuriating? "You're the one who's jealous."

"Me?"

"How was the date, Loren? Did you give him a handy in the parking lot?"

"I didn't ask if you— Wait, *did* you give him a handy in the parking lot?"

Now, if I didn't know any better, I'd say his tone rings with jealousy. Which is crazy because I only threw that at him because I didn't want to admit *I* was the jealous one.

"And what if I did?"

Hold on. Did his left eye just twitch? Holy shit. It did! His left eye twitched, and that jaw isn't flexing because he's enjoying this conversation.

Could it be that Elliott really *is* jealous? I can think of one way to find out. "What if I told you I let him kiss me?"

His eyes darken. "I wouldn't mind at all." The bite in his tone undermines the words. "You're probably a shitty kisser anyway."

He did not just say that to me. What an asshole. "I haven't had any complaints." Guys love kissing me. If spin the bottle was a competitive sport, I'd totally take the gold medal.

"Maybe not to your face."

"Excuse me. I am a fantastic kisser."

He eases closer, assessing me, eyes scanning and brow furrowed. "*Mmm...* actually, maybe I'm wrong."

Elliott Grant admitted he was wrong. Write this date down on your calendar, folks; it might never happen again.

"Your lips are kinda full and not chapped or peeling." His eyes narrow on my mouth. "And you don't have any cold sores that I can see."

Cold sores? I'll give him a cold, sore, kick to the jaw if he doesn't back the hell up.

He leans back, his hip pressing into the counter. "I take it back. You have the makings of an average kisser."

Average? *Average?* "I am *not* average." I might be average in bed, but when it comes to making out, I deserve a freaking trophy.

He winks and says, "If you say so, fish lips."

The petty name-calling is the final straw and for unknown reasons that I'm sure to spend the foreseeable future trying to sort out, I grab him by the back of the neck and tug his mouth down to mine.

He hesitates for only a moment before leaning into me, his soft lips molding to mine like they were made just for me. He tastes like vanilla creamer, a hint of coffee, and shock.

It's an intoxicating blend of flavors I want to savor. I kiss him slowly and deeply, teasing his tongue with mine, just enough to leave us both clamoring for more.

This is how a first kiss is meant to feel.

Butterflies fluttering rapidly in stomach? Check.

Brain malfunctioning? Check.

Lady parts tingling? Double check.

What started out as a lesson to prove him wrong, starts to feel an awful lot like something else as his hands curl into my hair and he pulls me closer. It feels like maybe all those hours I spent daydreaming of exactly this weren't so crazy after all.

Elliott's tongue lashes greedily against mine, and when I pull away, the hottest curse I've ever heard falls from his swollen lips as he stares down at me, blinking slowly, his pupils blown out.

God bless my voice for remaining steady when I say, "Tell me I'm average, now, smartass."

"You were all right," he rasps.

The fact that he can barely get those words out proves

that I am more than all right. Still, his refusal to admit it really pisses me off.

Talk about a sore loser.

"Five out of ten," he adds.

"Five out of—are you nuts? That was at least an eight." The only reason it wasn't higher is because all our clothes are still on.

His smirk returns, the jealous man from only a few moments ago replaced by a smug asshole. "An eight for you, maybe."

Do I need to kiss him again to—

Wait.

WAIT.

Holy. Shit. "You tricked me into kissing you."

Elliott swipes a thumb over his lower lip, as if that sexy move can wipe away his smirk. "I goaded you into kissing me. There's a difference."

"They're the same thing."

"Actually, Loren, tricking implies that you didn't want to kiss me. Goading means you wanted to but needed that extra little nudge to get off your cute ass and do it."

It is way too early in the morning to be arguing over semantics. "I didn't want to—Did you just say I have a cute ass?"

His strong shoulders lift and lower in a casual shrug. "What? Am I not supposed to notice that either? Well, it's pretty fucking hard when you scamper around in those lacy things you call shorts."

"They *are* shorts! And I don't scamper."

"Please. You scamper like a fucking chipmunk."

"You're infuriating."

"So are you," he throws back.

"At least I didn't trick you into kissing me!"

His head snaps toward the hallway, his brow scrunching and eyes narrowing. "Hey! What's that over there?"

I twist to see what it is, finding nothing but his couch covered with fluffy pillows. When I turn back, his lips meet my cheek. Desire burns through my—

Nope. Not desire. Let's go with anger instead. *Anger* burns through my blood.

"See what I did there?" he says, his tone mocking. "*That's* me tricking you for a kiss."

Fine. Fair enough. He wins words for the day.

He stalks forward, corralling me into the corner of the kitchen, the cold edge of the counter pressing into my backside, his heat overwhelming my senses.

When he speaks, his voice is a dangerous growl, low and sensual, the voice of a man who knows how to get exactly what he wants. "You want me to kiss you again, Chaos? Give you a second chance to show me what that pretty mouth can do?" His thumb grazes my bottom lip, and my breath catches. "You think you can do better? I doubt it."

How the hell is this working? I am a grown woman, confident in her own skin. This childish game should not be making my knees weak or my heart flutter or my thighs press together.

"You're evil," I whisper.

For some reason, that makes him smile. "You still want to kiss me though."

"Do not."

He eases closer, the heat of his words fanning across my burning cheeks. "Liar."

Okay, fine. I want to kiss Elliott again. I want him to pin me against this counter and kiss me until neither of us can breathe. I want him to lift me up and fit his hips between my knees and grind himself against me so hard that I shatter.

My eyelids flutter closed and maybe...just maybe... my back arches and my chest thrusts forward and...

Nothing happens.

Not a damn thing.

When I open my eyes, all I see is Elliot's back as he walks away.

CHAPTER 37
ELLIOTT

SHIT.

CHAPTER 38

ELLIOTT

THE DOLLY'S SQUEAKY wheels are really starting to give me a headache as I drag yet another keg to the storage room. I set the thing next to the others and then head back for the next one. Usually, our delivery driver, Stan, carts everything in, but today I need to keep myself busy.

What the hell was I thinking, kissing Loren this morning?

I've spent every moment since plagued by the reality of that kiss. Not because it was incredible—and it was absolutely fan-fucking-tastic—but because a kiss is something you can't take back. Once you do it, that's it. Lines have been crossed and there is no way to revert to being "just roommates."

Unless I don't acknowledge what happened.

We gave into temptation, it was shit-hot, and now we know this spark between us could burn the whole fucking building down. Questions have been answered, flames have been stoked, and now it's time to let the coals turn to cold ash.

Eventually, we will both forget about it, and everything will go back to the way it was.

Unless Loren brings it up.

What am I going to do then?

August stalks into the storage room, clipboard in hand and a pencil tucked behind his ear. When he sees me, his mouth flattens. "You're a fucking idiot."

Did I forget to mention that I told August what happened, and he's been calling me names ever since?

Add it to my list of fuckups for the week. "You say that as if I don't already know."

I try to wheel around him, but he steps in my way like the irritation he is. "You have to do something."

"Like what?"

He slips the pencil from behind his ear, counting the kegs I've brought in so far and marking them down on the PO. "Like woo her, dumbass."

Woo her? Seriously? What is this, Pride and fucking Prejudice? "The shit you say makes me want to punch you so hard." Since I need him around, I decide against it. When the asshole decides not to get out of my way, I abandon the cart and head into the empty bar instead.

Even though the concrete floors have been scrubbed to a shine, the room still smells like stale alcohol. That smell never seems to go away.

August trails after me, clearly not getting the hint. "What's stopping you?"

"I'll give you one guess." A guess he won't even need because that was the stupidest question he has ever asked—and he once asked me if the moon followed me the way it followed him. Granted, we were high at the time, but still.

He practically chases me to the other side of the bar where the keg for one of the local beers needs changed. "It's been four years, Elliott. You need to move on."

"I have." I kneel down and unhook the kicked keg.

I've moved on many, many times.

"Sleeping with other women isn't moving on. It's fucking around. What are you waiting for?" He squats down next to me but doesn't offer to roll the empty keg out of the way.

What is he even doing here? Shouldn't he be moving something or taking stock? "I'm not waiting on anything."

"Look, I loved Alice too, but she's gone."

"You loved her too, did you?" He might as well have just punched me in the damn stomach.

"You know what I mean," he says with a wave of his hand. "She did a number on you, and you still haven't fully recovered. It's okay to admit you're lonely as hell and crave meaningful companionship."

Meaningful companionship? If I never hear those two words come out of his mouth ever again it'll still be too soon. "Thanks, Dr. Phil."

His hand falls to my shoulder, stilling my movements. "Stop making jokes for one damn minute, and you'll see I'm right."

So what if I'm lonely? Loren is too good to use simply to fill the void someone else left behind. She's looking for someone to sweep her off her feet or take her rowing through a bunch of fucking ducks or hang off a damn ferris wheel for her.

I am not Ryan Gosling.

I'm the loser Rachel McAdams left behind.

The longer August stares at me, the more his brow furrows.

You know what? Enough is enough. He can finish changing the keg himself. I'm not even supposed to be working right now. I only came in to keep myself occupied.

I stand and head for the door, grabbing my sweatshirt from the back of a stool on my way out.

"There's something else, isn't there?" he calls after me, coming to a stop by the end of the bar.

There's no point keeping the rest of my reservations a secret. He'll only annoy them out of me later.

I stop, take a deep breath, and turn around. "Loren moved down here for a guy."

August scratches his head with the tip of his pencil. "And you're afraid she wants to get back with him?"

"No." Loren has made it clear that she isn't pining over her ex, but the fact is, she's on the rebound. Not only that: "She doesn't seem to know what she wants."

Now she's wasting her time on a bunch of apps, hoping one of the assholes she meets there will treat her better than dickwad did, when I know for a fact that I can treat her better than all of them put together.

"A few weeks back, she was ready to cut and run without a second thought."

If I hadn't gone with her to that hovel she considered renting, there's no doubt in my mind she would've been on that highway heading north and I never would've seen or heard from her again.

She's still trying to figure her shit out, and I don't need

to fall for another girl who's going to leave me when she decides I'm not enough.

My idiot cousin tucks the pencil behind his ear. "Have you told her how you feel?"

What are we? Two girls at a slumber party? "No."

"And grandma thinks you're the smart one," August mutters, shaking his head. "Look. I might not know Loren very well, but from everything you've said about her and the few times we've hung out, I can tell you exactly what she's looking for."

Oh, look. August knows everything. Isn't that great? "What's that?"

"She's looking for a reason to stay."

Shit.

Shit.

His shoes squeak on the floor as he comes over to where I've frozen, my mind racing at a hundred miles an hour.

She's looking for a reason to stay.

"If you want to be that reason, you're going to have to peel back those oniony layers of yours and make yourself vulnerable."

I'd rather stab myself with one of the paring knives we keep under the counter. "You're a fucking onion."

"You're damn right I am. And when I find some lucky woman to settle down with, you'd better believe I'll be shedding my skin."

Despite his idiocy, August might have a point.

The problem is, being vulnerable requires a certain level of trust. And I refuse to take that step without being sure my insecurities aren't going to drive Loren right out the damn door.

CHAPTER 39
LOREN

OH NO.

The dreaded "we need to talk."

Did something else bad happen? I've been secretly double- and triple-checking all traffic and haven't found any errors. What if something slipped through the cracks?

Then again, Meg did tell me to meet her in the break room, not the conference room, so maybe this isn't dire.

Unfortunately, she's not here yet, so I'm left waiting and worrying and stewing in that worry until a squeal erupts from outside the break room that makes The Librarian nearly drop his entire bowl of noodles.

Meg bursts through the door, jazz hands high and a grin splitting her face. "Ahhhh! I got the house!"

I leap to my feet, a squeal of my own screeching through

my lips as we jump up and down for joy. This is huge! "Which one?"

"The one with the window!"

"That one's so cute!"

"I know, right?"

"Wait. I thought you didn't get that one."

"Turns out, the people who outbid me had issues with the mortgage and backed out before the papers were signed. I'm buying my own freaking house!"

Meg is still beaming as she retrieves our lunch from the fridge—two pepperoni rolls, courtesy of the new café that opened down the street.

"We should go out to celebrate." The offer isn't entirely selfless. If I don't get out of my apartment, I'm going to do something stupid like jump my roommate. Before I can explain all that, the Gray Ghost steps into the breakroom.

Meg claps her hands beneath her chin, startling the poor Ghost so bad he fumbles his gray coffee mug.

"Bowling?"

I shake my head. "I love The Alley, but I was actually thinking of something a little fancier."

"Ohhh.... You want to go out-out."

"That's right." Tonight, we're going out-out.

———

I stand in front of my mirrored closet, checking my new dress from all angles. The thong I'm wearing leaves underwear lines in the black silk. Men are so lucky they don't have to worry about stupid stuff like underwear lines. If I had my way, I'd be wearing a pair of cotton underwear that covers my whole ass, but no. Underwear lines are forbidden.

Women must be smooth and perfect at all times, from their faces to their asses.

All my other thongs are lacy and will show.

I should just go without.

Imagine me going out in public without underwear. Talk about scandalous.

You know what? I deserve a bit of scandal in my life. I'm going to do it. I slip off my thong and then turn around to check the back. Not a line in sight.

Perfect.

Since smooth is the new theme, I drag my forgotten straightener from one of the boxes I have yet to empty beside my bed. Thirty minutes later, my hair is as smooth and straight as my skirt. It's a fruitless exercise, really, because the moment my hair finds even a hint of humidity it'll be frizz city, but until then, I am sleek and svelte. Two words I would normally never use to describe myself.

When I step out of my room, I feel like a million bucks. The men of Nashville are in for a treat tonight. I'm not coming home until I have someone else's spit in my mouth.

Okay, that's gross. Let's try again.

I'm not setting foot back in this apartment until someone else's mouth has erased the feeling of Elliott's soft, perfect lips against mine.

Elliott is on the couch, his back to me, Ross and Rachel arguing on the TV screen. He has a glass of water in his hand instead of a beer. Interesting.

Not that I care about the change. He can drink whatever he wants just like I'm going to drink whatever I want.

"Hey," he says without turning around. "I was thinking about ordering pizza for dinner. Do you want some—" He throws a look over his shoulder and his question dies a slow, quiet death. His eyes widen, blazing a trail from the dress's square neckline to my red heels.

The answer to Elliott's unfinished question is an unequivocal *yes*. I do "want some." From the way his eyes darken, it looks like he does too. But since that's not going to happen, I shall get "some" elsewhere.

Slowly his gaze climbs, up, up, up, but his eyes never reach my face. Instead, they're very clearly stuck on my chest.

"Are you wearing what I think you're wearing?" he says in a reverent whisper.

"Maybe." I bite my lip to keep from adding, "And nothing else."

He lifts his glass to his mouth but never gets that sip because his lips flatten. "And you're wearing it tonight."

"That's right."

He adjusts his hold on the glass, his knuckles going white. "Is there any particular *reason* you're wearing it tonight?"

I wish he'd stop being such a coward and ask me straight out whatever question is in his head instead of dancing around it. But that isn't Elliott's style. He'd rather be all cryptic and shit.

Idiot.

I shrug as casually as I can. "I'm going out."

"On your own?"

"With Meg." Not that it's any of his business. I mean, if he wants to make it his business, I'd totally be open to negotiations. But since he tricked—sorry, *goaded*, me into kissing him two days ago, he hasn't brought it up once.

It's like it never even happened.

But it *did* happen, and my vibrator has been getting a serious workout these past few nights as a result. Like the wise Meg once said: If he wanted to be my boyfriend, he would have said so. If he wanted to date me properly or for us to be exclusive, he would have said so.

Instead, he chose to say nothing.

Which brings us to this moment.

"Is that okay with you?" I ask.

He finally takes that drink, a big gulp that makes his Adam's apple bob. Why is that so hot? It's just a lump in his throat, but for some reason, I have this crazy urge to lick his. I'd lick all of him if he'd let me.

"Why wouldn't it be?" he mutters.

Oh, I don't know. Maybe because we kissed each other's faces off and he hates the thought of me doing the same with someone else.

Men.

His loss.

Except as I hurry to answer the knock at the door, it feels a lot like my loss too.

Meg is smoking in a tight blue dress and a pair of nude stilettos.

"Damn." I whistle through my teeth. "My best friend is hot."

Her long layers fall over her shoulders when she laughs. "You're one to talk. Turn around and let me see your ass in that dress. Fabulous. Just fabulous. I need you to know that I am one hundred precent borrowing that next weekend."

With her boobs, she would absolutely slay in this dress. "Oh! I haven't even shown you the best part! It has pockets. See?" I don't know why it's a requirement to stuff your hands into the pockets and flap them around to prove the existence of said pockets, but it is.

"Convenient."

"So convenient." And they're big ones, too. Not like

those Thumbelina pockets in most women's clothing. I could fit both our phones in these things—not that I will since I'm trying to avoid unnecessary lumps.

Elliott is watching us from the couch with a scowl that would be scary if I cared about what he thought.

Meg glowers right back. "Oh, hey, idiot."

Elliott blinks at her, his scowl transforming into this confused little furrow between his brows. "Did you just call me an idiot?"

Meg's maniacal laughter makes me jump. "What? Of course not. I said Elliott."

I bite my lip to keep from bursting out laughing. "Bye, Elliott."

He twists back to the TV, telling me to have fun. I tell him that I will. And then I add, "Don't wait up," for good measure, kinda hoping he waits up anyway.

———

Meg said she wanted to come check out her new neighborhood. It's trendy and cute with tons of little bars and restaurants. Who would've thought that all of this existed right across the river from honky-tonk central?

We had the twenty-minute drive to gush over my kiss with Elliott and commiserate over her woeful love life. But ever since we stepped inside the bar, Meg and I have been reduced to communicating via hand signals. I like loud music as much as the next girl, but it's not conducive to conversations.

Maybe we should've just gone to The Alley.

As we push our way through the crowd, she curls her hand like she's holding an imaginary glass and tips it toward her mouth.

I nod. A drink is exactly what I need.

She grabs my hand so we don't lose each other and together we squeeze between everyone, snaking our way to the bar.

Five minutes later, Meg already has hearts in her eyes. When the dark-haired guy she's chatting with looks away, she glances over her shoulder at me, gesturing to her own toned arms and waggling her brows. She's an arm girl, and the guy she's snagged is cut. Since I didn't hear a word he said when he introduced himself to us, I've lovingly named him Timmy Triceps.

"You wanna dance?" someone shouts into my ear, rattling my eardrum.

I shake my head at the stranger in a pinstriped button down. He's left the top four buttons undone, exposing a very tanned, very toned chest. Unfortunately, he looks like he loves himself a little too much to entice me. Plus, I could never take a man seriously when his eyebrows are more groomed than mine. "No thanks." I need at least three more drinks before I feel like finding some lucky guy to grind up on.

A vision of Elliott in the kitchen flashes like a strobe light. If he were here, I wouldn't need any drinks at all.

Idiot is right.

While Meg works her magic on "Timmy," I sip my gin and tonic and pull out my phone.

My stomach flutters when I see a text from Elliott. He sent a screenshot of a red bra with a question mark.

I snort so hard, my drink goes right into my lungs.

9:15 PM

Not even close

Three dots pop up and another photo comes through. A silky brazier my grandma would have worn.

Warmer

What am I doing? I'm not supposed to be on my phone flirting with my roommate when I should be making eyes at someone who wants me as much as I want him.

I'm sick of being in one-sided situationships with guys who don't even deserve to have my number.

This time, when my phone buzzes, I ignore it.

Who is this new Loren and where did she get a backbone?

I think I love her.

Moving to Tennessee might not have worked out the way I hoped, but I'm still here, aren't I? I'm finally supporting myself; I have a job I enjoy, and one of the best girlfriends I could ever hope for.

All in all, it hasn't been so bad.

At least that's what I think until I look up and see Josh waltz through the door.

IDIOT

Can you at least give me a color?

WHAT THE HELL is Josh doing here? He never comes to the east side with the "hippies and shit." His words, not mine.

I don't want to be in the same state as that jerkwad, let alone the same room. Just looking at his face makes me want to puke. I need to leave. Now. But as I scan the bar for Meg, she's nowhere to be found. She wouldn't have left without me. We have a strict rule that if we want to go home with someone, we make sure to tell the other person first and get photographic evidence of the stranger so that he can be identified should one of us become a missing person.

She's probably on the dance floor with "Timmy," but I'm not going to stand up to look for her in case Josh sees me.

What is he doing here, anyway? This hole-in-the-wall is

the type of bar Mr. Fancy-Pants would never dream of setting foot in.

Then again, maybe I'm wrong. It's pretty damn obvious that I never knew him as well as I thought I did.

I grab my phone like a lifeline, opening my text thread with Elliott where he has sent a picture of nipple tassels.

Nope.

He texts right back.

Having a good night?

I was until dickwad showed up

All the way in East Nashville?

That's suspicious

Tell me about it

Hold on. I never told Elliott where we were either.

How do you know where we are?

Def not from stalking IG

I didn't post anything online. I open the app. Sure enough, Meg shared the pic we took outside the bar. Is Elliott following Meg?

Is that why Josh is here?

No. That's crazy. He hasn't tried to contact me in weeks. This is probably some terrible coincidence.

As if by magic, a bulbous glass appears in front of me. I glance up to find the bartender who served us earlier smiling down at me. Man, her eyeliner is on point. I wish I could do my makeup like that.

I return her smile as best I can as I slide the drink back across the bar. "I didn't order this."

She nods her pierced chin toward where Josh has found an empty stool at the end of the bar. Did that hurt? The piercing, not the nodding. "It's from your secret admirer," she says.

Would you look at that? Ratbag bought me a drink. I make a big production of handing it right back. I don't care if it's free. I would rather lick the floor than accept anything from him.

"You can tell my ex that he can drown in it."

The woman glances over at Josh, her eyes narrowing. "Done and done."

My pulse roars in my ears as I scowl down at my phone. You thirsty?

I text Elliott a photo of my half-empty glass.

The read receipt comes straight through, and three dots pop up. But then they disappear just as quickly, and I end up waiting way too long for a reply that never comes.

———

Why did I agree to this again? Oh, yeah. Meg. My best friend who is currently making out with Timmy by the DJ booth.

Good for her.

I glance over to Josh, who sits like a cockroach hiding in a dark corner. What did I ever see in him? Compared to Elliott, he's—

Nope.

Not going there.

"Excuse me?" I wave at the bartender with the piercing. "Can I get another one?"

The longer I'm here, the weirder this gets. I've had three glasses of gin, and Josh still hasn't moved. Does he think I'm going to go over and talk to him? HA! It'll take more than alcohol to get me to converse with a cockroach.

I pick up my phone. Still no messages.

Next time I drink, I'm leaving my phone at home.

I cannot believe I texted Elliott and practically begged him to come and save me.

Damsel much?

I can take care of myself. I don't need a guy to swoop to the rescue.

There shall be no swooping.

I'm going to save myself.

Because that's what strong, independent heroines do.

But first... I hold up a hand, calling one of the shot girls over.

"Which one do you want?" she shouts over the pulsing music, lowering the tray of colorful liquids so I can choose. Does it really matter which one I pick? If I drink enough of them, the end result will be the same.

A hand slips along my lower back, and my body goes stiff as a corpse. I turn, expecting to see Josh, but the hand doesn't belong to him.

Elliott is smiling down at me, his dark hair damp against his temples.

Elliott is leaning down to say against my ear: "Personally, I'm partial to the green ones."

Elliot Grant is *here*.

I throw my arms around his neck, breathing in the delicious cologne on his skin that smells even better than his soap. "You came."

Okay, that was a little exuberant. Chill out, Loren.

When Elliott pulls away, he doesn't look annoyed. If anything, he looks happy as he leans an elbow against the bar, blocking my view of Josh. "You asked if I was thirsty, and I am." From his pocket, he withdraws his wallet, paying for my shot and asking if the bartender could drop down a soda. "Where's Meg?"

"Dancing."

"Why aren't *you* dancing?" he asks, stepping closer, his strong arms caging me in.

My body melts from the heat of him. "I haven't found anyone I want to dance with."

"I'm sorry to hear that."

"No, you're not."

"No." A smirk. "I'm not. Where is he?"

"End of the bar."

"Fucking creep."

The bartender drops down our drinks and returns his card, along with a black checkbook.

Josh is a creep. And a ratbag. And a—

Elliot leans closer, his hand slipping to my hip. "I like this dress."

My roommate is touching me, and my brain is short circuiting, and holy crap his hands are so freaking large.

Your dress, Loren. He said he likes your dress.

"R-really?"

"Yes. Do you know what I like even more?" When I shake my head, his grip tightens. "The pockets." He slides one hand into my pocket. With my legs tucked beneath the bar, no one else seems to notice, but I do.

"What are you doing?" I whisper.

"Exploring these pockets you seemed so proud of earlier. Is that okay?" The silken lining is the only barrier between us as his fingertips skim where my hip meets my thigh.

Yes. Okay. More than okay. "My pockets are your pockets."

His fingers still. "Are you wearing panties?"

Heat blooms up my throat when I shake my head.

"Fuck." He resumes his exploration, more urgently than before, back and forth, dipping a little lower each time, until I feel like I'm going to spontaneously combust.

"I lied," he murmurs against the shell of my ear, sending tingles all the way down my spine. "I said I didn't care. The truth is, I care way more than I should. If you're going out, I want it to be with me."

I'm trying hard not to romanticize this. To keep my head above water. But each stroke of his fingers threatens to pull me under.

How easy it would be to drown in his touch.

I reach for my glass, desperate for something to do with my own useless hands. I should tell him to stop. But the truth is, stopping is the last thing on my mind. "What would we be doing right now if I'd come out with you instead?"

I feel his smile against my cheek. "Spread your legs, and I'll show you."

My mind is screaming so loudly, I'm surprised no one seems to be able to hear it. I can't believe this is happening.

Wait. *Is* it happening or am I dreaming?

Spread your legs, and I'll show you.

The lights flash red, as if the world is telling us to stop. From the end of the bar, I catch Josh glowering. "He's watching."

Elliott's nose grazes the column of my throat, the stubble on his jaw grazing my shoulder. "Good. Now, stop looking at him and look at me." He nips my earlobe, his teeth clicking against my earring. "Open up for me, Chaos. Let's show him how good I can make you feel."

My heart rate kicks up. Am I going to let this happen?

I've been fighting the hypnosis since the day we met.

I don't want to fight anymore.

Tonight, I want to give in.

I turn my head so I can stare into his deep blue eyes.

Yeah, I'm totally letting this happen.

I open my knees, making room for the hand still in my pocket to slide between my legs. The neckline of my dress tugs down a bit as he reaches a little further and those silk-lined fingers find my center. He begins massaging in slow, steady circles, teasing against my clit as the heat from his breath whispers down my throat to my collarbone, his soft, searing lips dotting hot kisses against my skin.

The strobes have nothing on the blinding lights flashing behind my eyes. The bass can't compare to my thundering heart.

The world around us turns to shadows. It's just Elliott and me and the steady pressure of his fingers.

Sounds grow muffled, all but our mingling breaths and my racing heartbeat. Pressure builds low in my stomach. Between my thighs. My head falls back against his shoulder, my chest rising and falling as I gasp, "Faster."

He obeys on command, fingertips working quicker than before. If he keeps that up, I'm going to—

Oh shit.

My glass slips, and we both shatter into a million pieces.

Elliott's Cheshire grin makes my stomach dip and twist tightly. "You were right. Those pockets are convenient."

Even from this far away, I can see Josh's jaw pulsing from the other end of the bar, like he knows exactly what just happened. But there's no way, right? The people closest to us don't seem to be paying any attention. How would he know?

Elliott stares into my eyes, his pupils blown wide and chest heaving, same as mine. "You want to get out of here?"

"Yes." But there's some reason I didn't leave the moment ratbag walked in and for the life of me, I can't remember— "Meg!" I can't leave without talking to Meg.

Elliott retrieves his card from the checkbook, leaves a generous tip, and then tells me to wait right here, as if I'd be able to stand up when my legs are still trembling.

"I'll find her and be right back." His hand slips from my pocket, and he cuts through the crowd to where Meg and Timmy Triceps are wrapped around each other.

Chills skate across my arms, as if someone jacked up the AC. When I look up again, Josh's infuriating face is only inches from mine. "Are you fucking kidding me, Loren? What the hell are you doing with *that* guy?"

Yeah, this isn't happening. "I don't want to talk to you." I try to slide off the stool, but he blocks me.

Thank goodness for these heels; I can almost look him in his sleazy, sleepy brown eyes. I can't believe I used to think he had puppy dog eyes. That's an insult to dogs everywhere.

"You want to talk? Fine? How about we talk about your *girlfriend*?"

He doesn't look the least bit repentant. If anything, the indignant fire in his eyes flares. "I was going to tell you about Rebecca."

"Yeah, well. You had plenty of chances, but you didn't." I'm not sad; I'm pissed off. But for some reason, my body thinks I need to start crying. Tears flood my eyes, and I hate every single one that rolls down my cheeks. Hate that he probably thinks they're for him.

They're not. They're for me. "I moved here for *you*." I left my home and my family for him—and he *let* me. All he had to do was tell me the truth, to say what we did was a mistake.

Instead, he chose to lie.

His gaze softens. "Can we go somewhere? Just you and me. At least let me explain."

What's there to explain? He cheats on his amazing girlfriend, makes me feel like shit, like I'm some dirty little secret, and he expects me to, what, forgive him? "No." The time for talking is long gone. Now's the time for leaving.

I grab my purse from the hook beneath the bar and shove past him.

"I should've known you were nothing but a slut with how fast you jumped on my dick." Josh speaks so loudly, the people around us all turn to stare.

Why can't he leave me the hell alone? I hate drama. I hate it with a fiery passion. But here I am, being gawked at by a bunch of nosey strangers in the middle of a bar.

I'm probably going to end up a meme by midnight.

If I'm going down, might as well go down in flames. "You barely have a dick to jump on, *Josh*."

He stumbles back as if I hit him. I really wish assault wasn't a crime, because right now, I want to smack his face so badly.

The vein in his forehead looks like it's ready to burst, and the shade of red painting his face does *not* look healthy.

Of course he doesn't leave me with the last word. That would be the gentlemanly thing to do, and ratbag is *not* a gentleman.

"How do you think your boss is going to feel when she finds out *you* came after *me*?" he growls like a rabid dog.

My confidence falters, leaking through the cracks in my bravado. "That isn't what happened."

His hand clamps around my wrist, forcing me closer. "Who do you think she's going to believe? Me or you?"

Rebecca is my friend. She won't believe him.

She dated Josh for years. Why wouldn't she?

"Let me go."

A hand lands on Josh's shoulder. "Back the fuck up, Joshy."

Elliott...

Thank God.

Josh jerks out of Elliott's grasp, his hand falling away in the process. "Fuck off."

Elliott inserts himself between us, giving Josh his back, an impenetrable wall of muscles between my ex and me. "You okay?"

I nod even as I blink back tears, hating that Josh's words are rolling around in my mind like a bunch of loose marbles.

No, not marbles. They're too colorful and fun. Josh's vicious promise is like cement in a mixer, growing heavier, thicker, harder to ignore.

I'm sick to my stomach and it has nothing to do with the drinks I had.

Elliott gently takes my hand, leading me toward the door.

"What did you say to Meg?" Thankfully, it's too loud for him to hear the tremble in my voice.

If only there was some way to hide my brittle smile.

Remember when folding fans were a thing? I could use one right about now.

"I told her that I'm stealing you for myself."

Cue stomach-flip. "What'd she say?"

"She told me it was about damn time."

CHAPTER 41

ELLIOTT

THE LOREN who climbs into my truck isn't the same confident, flirty woman from the bar. She fidgets and keeps tapping her phone screen, watching it light up and then letting it go dark again. Like she's expecting someone to text her.

Tell me it isn't her ex.

After what we just did, she shouldn't be wasting her time on him.

Was I wrong? Is she still hung up on that asshole? Is that why she was crying?

I told myself it was too soon, that she was still on the rebound after what he did to her, but did I really believe it? No.

I paced that damn apartment until it felt like the walls were closing in on me. Then Loren sent that text, asking if I was thirsty.

The moment that text came through, I made the decision I've been struggling with ever since we kissed.

To be her rebound if that's what she needs. To show her how she deserves to be treated, whether it lasts for a day or a decade.

And it's already coming back to bite me in the ass.

My hands strangle the wheel. "I thought you were over him."

She looks at me as if she doesn't have a clue what I'm talking about. Which, to be fair, is probably true considering I've been holding an entire conversation in my head.

"I am."

"Then why are you so upset?"

There she goes again, pressing the buttons on her damn phone. "He threatened me."

My hold on the steering wheel slips, and the truck weaves toward the shoulder. I correct quickly enough, but my mind isn't as quick to recover.

"He *what?*"

"He said he was going to lie to Rebecca, tell her I was the one coming on to him, that I knew he had a girlfriend. Make me look like the villain. And it's so shitty because she is honestly the nicest person."

And nice people are too forgiving. Narcissists like Josh know that, which is why they attach themselves to nice women like the leeches they are. Someone who will forgive all the bullshit they have to put up with.

It's fucking infuriating.

"What if she fires me?"

"She can't fire you for sleeping with her boyfriend."

Loren's head falls back as she mulls it over. "Maybe."

Not maybe. That's the law. They must have reasonable

cause to fire her, and something like that isn't it. Now, this Rebecca could certainly make Loren's life hell until Loren wants to quit, but if Rebecca is as "nice" as Loren claims, I doubt that will happen.

That doesn't mean Loren won't quit all by herself. I can see her giving up and running away instead of staying to fight. That isn't always a bad thing, but in this case, it would do more harm than good.

She loves her job—earned that promotion.

She doesn't deserve to pay for *his* shitty decisions.

Now I'm sorry I didn't hit her ex in his smug face.

I rack my brain for something to say that'll make this better, but all that does is make me want to turn this truck around.

Fifteen minutes later, we finally get back to our apartment complex. By the time I make my way to Loren's side of the vehicle, she still hasn't budged. I open the door for her and release the belt. I take her hand in mine, and she feels so small and fragile as she drifts along next to me, up the stairs to our front door.

Enough is enough. If there's anything I can do to resurrect her smile, I'm going to do it. "Do you want me to have August slash his tires?"

She blinks up at me, her eyes round as an owl's. "What?"

"If Josh is still at the bar. August would be more than happy to do it." My cousin loves a good misdemeanor.

Finally, a laugh. "I appreciate the thought, but I wouldn't want your cousin getting into trouble because of me."

August wouldn't get into trouble. Hell, even if a cop saw him commit the crime, he'd probably be able to convince the officer that Josh deserved it. "Fair enough, but if you change your mind, let me know. You want another drink?" Might help calm her nerves. Her hands are trembling.

"Sure." She shrugs out of her jacket, leaving it on the dining table instead of the hook beside the door. When August does that shit, it bugs me. When Loren does it, I find it endearing.

Don't get me wrong. I'm going to hang it up the moment I get a chance. But I appreciate her chaos.

I grab two beers from the fridge and set them on the counter.

She wraps her hands around her bottle but doesn't drink. "Thank you for coming tonight."

"Thank *you* for coming tonight."

Her blush is the prettiest shade of pink before she decides to hide it behind her hands. "I can't believe that actually happened."

"Why?"

"Look at you. You're like... a Nashville nine and I'm an Oakton seven."

I've never been to Oakton, but there is no town on earth where she is a seven. It kills me that she looks down on herself so much. "Only a nine, huh? Ouch."

"Oh, shut up. You know what I mean. A ten is perfection and nobody is perfect."

"That pocket of yours might disagree."

She drops her hands in favor of her beer, drinking until the bottle is half empty before setting it down to pick at the corner of the label. "Why did you come to the bar tonight?"

So many reasons. "August claims I have a hero complex. I see a woman in distress and must jump in to save her."

"Oh..."

Except tonight didn't have anything to do with that.

Tonight was about something else entirely.

It was about giving Loren Piper a reason to stay.

Being vulnerable terrifies me. When you bring a woman home for the night, the transaction ends the next morning. With Loren, she'll still be here tomorrow. And the next day. And the day after that.

Hopefully, anyway.

I've only ever been completely vulnerable with one other person, and that relationship crashed and burned.

But I think this is what she needs. She puts herself out there, consequences be damned. Heart on her sleeve and all that nonsense. From what I've gathered, the guys she's dated in the past haven't done the same for her.

We might not technically be dating, but I refuse to be lumped into the same category as everyone else.

"But August is an idiot. I think it's because I've had a crush on you since the moment you rocked up in those orthopedic shoes."

"They're not ortho—*wait. You* have a crush on *me?*"

"Contrary to popular belief, I don't slip my hands into just anyone's pockets."

A smile curves her lips. "I've had a crush on you ever since you gave me that beer on the balcony."

"While you were with Josh? Little devil."

"I won't tell him if you don't."

She sits in silence, sipping and scraping at the label while I watch a myriad of emotions play out on her face. After a solid five minutes, she nods to herself and our gazes connect once more. "So what do we do now?"

What a loaded question—one I'm not prepared to answer without a little more information. "What do you want to do?"

"What I want to do and what I should do are two very different things."

"Why don't you tell me what they are, and we can decide together?"

Her lips purse before she takes one final swig. "I should go to bed."

That's the opposite of what I think she should do, but I know when to keep my mouth shut.

Now isn't the time for games or goading. Loren is in charge tonight.

"But I really want to kiss you again."

"Why can't we do both?" I ease forward until our breaths mingle, waiting for her to close the distance. When she does, my heart goes into overdrive, pumping all my blood south. She tastes like sunshine and smiles, happiness and effervesce. I can't get enough, capturing her straightened hair while longing for the chaos of her curls, angling her head so my tongue can dive deeper between her parted lips.

She kisses with the same madness she embodies, the same unbridled passion.

"I need to go to bed," I murmur against her lips, "and you need to go to bed, and there's a bed right in there."

"True. But I'm not having sex with you tonight."

A small part of me leaps at the fact that she said "tonight" instead of saying we are never having sex.

"Damn. That sucks because weepy women are such a turn-on for me."

"Shut up." Chuckling, she links our hands together, leading us to her room.

I sink onto the end of her bed and wait while she scoops up her pajamas from the floor and vanishes into the bathroom.

She comes back a few minutes later, her long legs on display beneath the shortest shorts known to man. "You don't have to stay in here just for me if you don't want to. I'll be fine on my own."

"What makes you think this is just for you? Why can't it be for me too?" I *like* sleeping with a woman in my bed, whether we have sex or not. I miss the connection, knowing someone else is there.

She drops onto the other side of the bed. "Josh never wanted to sleep with me."

"I think we can both agree that guy is a shithead."

The smallest smile teases her lips. "True. I guess I assumed a guy like you wouldn't be big on snuggling."

"First, I'll have you know that I fucking love snuggling. Second, what do you mean a guy like me?"

"Commitment-phobes."

Shit.

Okay.

It's time.

I swallow the flippant answer I'd normally give and tell her the truth instead. "This room? It belonged to my ex. She'd sleep in here sometimes when she had to work nights at the hospital."

From the way her jaw drops, you'd swear I just admitted to being a serial arsonist. "Hold on. You had a girl-friend? How long were the two of you together?"

"Fifteen years."

She snorts but sobers almost as quickly. "Wait. Are you serious?"

"Yep. We met our first year of middle school."

"And you dated her until you were twenty-seven?"

Dated. Sure. We'll go with that. "Twenty-eight, actual-ly." She waited until the day after my birthday to end things. Really thoughtful of her, right?

"Wow. Okay. Now I feel like the shithead. I don't know

why I assumed you weren't the commitment type. I'm sorry."

"It's fine." Not like I gave her any reason to believe otherwise.

I know how to be in a relationship. What I don't know is how to be single. I fucked around for the last four years, but all I found was emptiness.

Loren doesn't make me feel empty.

She makes me feel so full I could burst.

We fall down next to each other, her head tucked into the crook of my neck and my arms wrapped around her, like this is the most natural thing in the world for us. Like we've been doing this our whole lives.

"Why did the two of you break up?"

Talk about killing the mood. It's like she just knocked me into one of those icy cold dunk tanks they have at my mom's fundraisers.

As much as I hate talking about the past, August was right. If I ever want to move on, I need to get used to being vulnerable again. This feels like as good a time as any to start.

Let's see. How do I explain what happened to Alice and me without telling her every single horrible detail? We stopped trying. In the end, neither of us had the energy or the inclination to stand our ground or meet each other halfway. We just kind of...evaporated.

"Let's just say, guys aren't the only ones who think the grass is always greener on the other side."

Her palms flatten over my chest. "Hold on. She broke up with you?"

"That's right."

"*She* broke up with *you?*" Loren repeats, slower this time.

She's so cute when she's indignant. "This is really doing wonders for my ego." If she keeps it up, I might never let her go.

"Seriously though. I don't understand why anyone would give you up."

She doesn't know how much I needed to hear that. I don't want to make Alice out to be the villain here. After everything that happened, we were both at fault. But Alice was the one who ultimately pulled the plug on us. Who decided that what we had wasn't worth fighting for.

That I wasn't worth fighting for.

I'm not saying that I'm a prize by any means, but I like to think I treated her well. That I loved her with all that I was.

"Alice and I were together since we were kids. I guess she just never got a chance to figure out what she wanted." Only that she didn't want me.

"Her loss."

I can't help but smile up at the ceiling. "Go to sleep, Loren."

"Will you kiss me first?"

"Chaos, I'll kiss you anytime you want."

When Loren eventually falls asleep in my arms, I breathe her in, letting her chaotic energy soften my calloused heart.

CHAPTER 42
LOREN

MEGALODON

Is it possible to fall in love with someone's arms but hate their personality?

Asking for a friend.

I WAKE up being poked in the back by Elliott's massive erection.

We're not talking regular morning wood. This thing is a two-by-four.

Since he is still very much asleep, I'm not sure exactly how to navigate this precarious situation. If we'd had sex last night, I'd let my itchy hands grab it. But since we snuggled and fell asleep in each other's arms, we're caught in a gray area.

And touching it without consent even though it is very much touching me feels wrong.

He stretches his arms over his head with a groan. "The longer you look at my dick, the harder it's going to get."

Guess he's not asleep after all.

Harder? How is that possible? That thing belongs with the other standing stones at Stonehenge. "Sorry."

A smirk. "No, you're not."

"No, I'm not. I mean, it's there. It's impossible not to look at."

"You keep giving me compliments like that, and I'll never let you leave."

It's not a compliment. It's a statement of fact. "So...this is awkward." Wonderful. Looks like I'm back to blurting, something I can't remember ever doing with Elliott.

"Doesn't have to be."

"How do you figure?"

He reaches down to adjust himself, which shouldn't be hot but totally is. At some point in the night, he kicked off his jeans, leaving him in a pair of black boxer briefs.

Loren approves.

"Strip out of those things you claim are shorts and I'll show you."

"That's a bad idea." At least that's what I tell myself. Because the list of reasons to avoid Elliott got a whole lot shorter last night.

Elliott Grant is absolutely the commitment type.

Not saying he's looking for a relationship with me, but at least it's not outside the realm of possibility like I originally thought. And he was respectful of my choice not to have sex with him. Didn't even try to push.

He showed me a side of himself even more irresistible than all the others: His insecurities.

"I disagree. As a matter of fact, I think it's the best damn idea I've had in a long time."

"So what? We have sex, get it out of our system, and then go about our lives as if nothing happened?"

His eyes narrow and his lips press flat. "Sure. If that's what you want to do."

"Really? Because you sound mad."

His biceps flex when he drags his hands down his face. Who knew frustration could be so sexy? "Yeah, well, being referred to as something to 'get out of your system' doesn't make me feel very appreciated."

After his girlfriend broke up with him because she thought other guys might be better, Elliott needs to be appreciated.

He showed his hand last night; it's only fair that I do the same today. I swallow past the sudden lump in my throat, bracing for the truth. "I don't know how to do this."

The way he scratches his chest draws my eyes to the trimmed hair covering his glorious pecs. "Do what?"

"Go from friends to whatever this is. If we hook up, does it mean we're dating?" At least he doesn't flinch when I ask. How mortifying would that be? "Are we just hanging out and hooking up? Friends with benefits and whatnot?" Who says whatnot? Me, apparently. "I'm just trying to figure out the rules before—"

"Loren?"

"What?"

"Shut up."

Excuse me? "Don't tell me to—"

His hand falls over my mouth, silencing my argument. "You're allowed two words: yes or no. Got it?"

Elliott Grant: Word police.

He wants one word answers? Fine.

"Do you want to fuck me or not?"

My face lights on fire.

Holy. Shit.

I cannot believe he just said that to me straight out. I am in so far over my head right now.

Is the answer to that question ever "no?" Look at the man.

From behind his hand I mumble, "I don't think that's a —" He presses a little harder.

"Yes or no, Chaos?"

I wait until he removes his hand to croak my one-word answer. "Yes."

"Good. Because this isn't how I normally wake up." He kicks the covers all the way off us, his black boxer briefs riding up muscular thighs sprinkled with dark hair. His large hand wraps around his length, stroking slowly, his eyes darkening to a stormy hue as they sweep from my disheveled hair to my shorts. "This is what happens when I have to spend the night with your ass pressed up against me, knowing I can't touch you."

His tongue sweeps across his lips, and that one simple move turns me into a sweaty, panting mess.

"Now, take off your shirt."

So many nervous words swell in my throat, but I swallow them down.

Yes or no. "No."

He quirks an eyebrow, his hand stilling on his massive erection. "No?"

Since I'm not allowed to say anything but yes or no, I sit and lift my arms, waiting for him to realize what I want. A grin finds its way to his lips, and he kneels before me, catching the hem and lifting it up and over my head. He sits back on his haunches, his dick pressing against his boxers as his gaze sweeps over my bare chest.

He holds out a hand, stopping a fraction of an inch away from my breast, and quirks a brow.

That's a big fat, "Yes." *Yes yes yes.*

His hands cup my breasts, holding and anchoring around them. He doesn't go for my nipples, just teases along the edges, deceptively soft and delicate for a man with such big hands. Even so, my nipples are straining for his touch.

He urges me back onto the bed and then settles over me, easing his head down and down, until I can feel his heated breath panting across my goose-bumped flesh. When his eyes rise to mine, I nearly expire as I pant out a desperate, "Yes."

I don't claim to be experienced in the art of lovemaking by any means, but Elliott Grant puts the three men I've been with to shame. Not only does he understand the meaning of foreplay, but also he is a master.

Every breathless, eager, "Yes" that falls from my lips leads to a new sensation. New pleasure. He doesn't seem to be in a rush at all, taking his time.

Back and forth, sucking, teasing, swirling his tongue over my nipples, even scraping with his teeth, until it feels like I ran through sprinklers in my underwear.

His hands glide down my ribs to my hips, gripping tightly before flattening against my thighs, spreading them wide enough to fit his hips between them. "You wet, Chaos?"

For some reason, this is harder for me to confess than any of the truths I've given him so far. "Yes."

"That's my girl." He guides himself against my underwear, notching between my folds, and pumps his hips forward, dragging against my clit. The overwhelming flood of sensations lifts me off the freaking mattress. "Look at you. Soaked all the way through." The way he holds my knees gives me a gloriously unobstructed view of those abs hard at work, flexing with each thrust of his hips. He seems entranced by the way our bodies slide together.

A dark lock of hair falls onto his forehead.

What was his ex-girlfriend thinking? She must cry herself to sleep every night remembering how she gave him up. Her loss is my gain—

He drops forward onto his elbows, dragging his tongue down my neck, kissing and sucking until he's back at my breasts once more. It's all too much. Every sensation. Every emotion.

I'm so close. Too close. Falling over the edge. *Flying*.

His eyes shoot to mine, pupils blown out. "Did you just come?"

"Yes?"

"Good girl." He doesn't stop there and stick it in. He keeps going, as if we have all the time in the world.

In one fell swoop, my shorts and underwear are gone. When my knees try to close, he pushes them apart once more. His palm flattens on my stomach, right above my pubic bone, his thumb casually stroking above my clit. It is infuriating and amazing at the same time. "Yes?" he rasps.

"*Yes*."

His thumb barely grazes over my slit, and I'm back to squirming all over again.

Each leisurely stroke brings me that much closer to the edge once more. He dips a finger inside, curling upwards. His thumb works in strokes, his other finger pumping in and out before he adds a second. "Look at all this just for me."

I can't take it anymore.

I grip him tightly. There's a wet patch on his black boxer briefs, from him or from me, it's impossible to tell. When I tug on his boxers, he removes them, then settles back into place. His thick tip glistens.

"Condom?"

He shakes his head. "One more first."

"One more wha—" He presses down with his thumb at the same time his finger curls and I'm on the edge again. My question ends with a whimper.

Now we need a condom.

"Drawer."

He grips the handle of the top drawer and arches a brow.

"Yes."

The random collection of items within slides to the front when he opens it. Chuckling darkly, he withdraws my neon pink vibrator. "Next time, we'll use this."

Next time.

If I wasn't so spent, I'd squeal with delight.

Elliott's frantic search comes up empty. I do have condoms, don't I?

I nudge him aside to search for myself. Damn, that's a lot of bobby pins. Where the hell is my freaking condom? I clamber off the bed, running out of the room to where I left my purse on the dining table. I dump the thing out, random items spilling across the table, lip gloss rolling onto the floor.

Elliott watches from the doorway to my room, one shoulder propped against the doorframe, his other hand gripping his dick that doesn't seem to mind the delay at all.

Receipts, a burger wrapper, those sunglasses I thought I lost... Wait! "I gave it to you."

His hooded eyes widen. "My room. Now."

He doesn't have to tell me twice. We fall into the room together, tangled up in each other's arms, my parts rubbing his parts and his parts rubbing my parts in a gloriously hedonistic frenzy as we drop onto his bed.

The air in here smells divine, and so do these sheets.

There will be plenty of time to talk about how clean it is later. Right now, all I care about is the fact that he is dragging a condom from the drawer.

The mattress dips as he kneels on the bed, tearing open the condom with his teeth before stretching it over his length. He catches my knees, spreading my legs once more. But then he stills, ocean eyes meeting mine. "You sure?"

That we've come all this way, and he is still asking if I want to do this means more than he will ever know. I have no doubt that if I told him I didn't want to have sex anymore, he wouldn't pressure me into it. But I am *not* backing out. Elliott Grant wants to fuck me, and there's no way in hell I'm telling him no. "Yes."

Inch by inch, he pushes inside, stretching my body with his until I can take no more. I can feel the panic start in my chest, tightening, making it difficult to inhale a full breath. He's given me two orgasms, and I can't even take all of him.

He drops a kiss to my forehead. "Relax, Chaos."

How is he so freaking sweet? "I think you're going to break me." I don't mean physically. Already, I can feel an Elliott-shaped hole in my heart.

"Nah. We'll make it work."

He stills, giving me time to breathe. I lift onto my elbows to kiss his bobbing throat, the stubble on his jaw.

"You feel so fucking good. If I didn't want to make this last, I could come right now." His words rasped against my ear melt me into a boneless pile of goo, making more room for him to ease his hips forward until he bottoms out.

I feel like giving him a high-five.

But since he's a little busy, I lay back and enjoy the ride.

And what a ride it is.

Elliott's fingers never stray far from my clit. I don't think it's ever had this much of a workout. It's like he's looking for a genie and I'm the magic lamp.

"You going to come for me again, Chaos? I hear third time's a charm."

"I don't think I can."

His eyes narrow. "Wrong answer."

I'm wrung out, no energy left, holding on for dear life. Then a tingling sensation that's becoming all too familiar gathers low in my stomach. Another orgasm rips through me, more intense than the others. His eyes seem to ignite when they lock with mine. He bucks his hips three more times, losing his tempo before collapsing with a muttered, "Holy shit," against my sweat-slickened temple.

Holy shit is right.

Elliott fucks like the world is ending.

He rolls onto his back, his chest heaving as he stares up at the chrome ceiling fan. His proud dick is still way too thick where it rests on his thigh.

Well, that was unexpected.

This man deserves a freaking medal.

His palm flattens against his heart, and he chuckles. With another muttered obscenity, he grabs a tissue from his bedside table and removes the condom, tossing both into the trash can.

I wait for the awkwardness to set in. For the blurting to start.

But then he pulls me into him, tucking my head beneath his chin and asks if I want him to make pancakes.

Not sure if we're still playing the game, but my answer to that will always be... "Yes."

CHAPTER 43

ELLIOTT

AUGUST HAS BEEN STARING at me for way longer than any person should. Seriously. It's starting to give me the creeps, but if I let him know, he'll only end up doing it more.

After a ridiculous amount of time, he adds the last two glasses to the dishwasher and closes the front to start the cycle. "You're smiling."

That's why he was staring? Here I thought maybe I'd gotten some of the teriyaki chicken I inhaled in the office in the middle of my shift on my face. "I'm always smiling."

"Yeah, but this one's different. This one oozes male

pride. You're like a peacock, strutting with his feathers all aflutter."

He is such a dumbass.

"You got laid, didn't you?"

Like I'm going to tell him. But he's right. I am smiling and I can't seem to stop. After pancakes, I spent all day in bed with Loren and it was one of the best days of my life. I was this close to calling in sick tonight but didn't want to let August down. So here I am. Working. Daydreaming about a girl waiting for me back at our apartment.

Our apartment. Feels weird to call it that, but that's what it is. Mine and hers. After what happened, I never thought I'd be happy sharing my space with another person again. But here I am. Happy.

So fucking happy.

A couple of regulars find their stools, but most of the Saturday night crowd are newcomers, people swinging by for a drink before heading into the city.

I make a couple of margaritas, a few simple whiskies on the rocks, and a couple of shots for a pair of bros with Greek letters printed on their sweatshirts even though they look way too old to be part of a fraternity. Maybe it's like an *Old School* thing?

Wonder what Loren is up to right now. I bet she's curled up on the corner of the couch, her hair piled in that sloppy bun, watching some romcom that makes her giggle.

That girl has a great laugh.

Something cold splashes against my fingers. When I glance down, I find the bottle of vodka tipped a little too far, spilling all over the counter.

"*Shit.*"

August whaps my arm on his way to finish slicing

lemons. "Get your head in the game before you pour all our money down the drain."

He's right. I'm at work and need to focus.

It's just so hard when all I can think about is Loren wrapped up in my sheets. I hope she's in my bed when I get back tonight. If she isn't, maybe I'll slip into hers.

Unless she doesn't want me to.

But she will, won't she?

Maybe I should text and ask, just in case.

After I rinse off my hand and clean up the spill, I pull out my phone, but before I can text my roommate, the front door swings open, and Loren steps into the bar.

My whole body comes alive, like opening the blinds on a sunny, summer morning. She waves, taking the barstool beside one-eyed Joe.

Don't worry. He has two eyes. It's just that the left one gets squinty when he's had a few too many drinks. That's when we know to stop serving him and call a ride share.

Damn, Loren looks good tonight. She's wearing a blue dress that I would like to see on my floor later. The heels though, those can stay on. They make her tanned legs look long enough to wrap around me twice.

August gives me a knowing smile and a not-so-discreet thumbs-up. If Loren notices, she doesn't show it as she hangs her giant purse on the hook under the bar.

"I hope it's okay that I came out tonight," she says, playing with the gold earrings dangling from her earlobes.

Is she kidding? "I'm fucking thrilled you're here." Now I don't have to be distracted wondering what she's up to.

"Really? I spent twenty minutes sitting in my car, second-guessing myself."

I hate that she's been in such shitty relationships that

she doesn't realize how great she is. That she doesn't realize the guy she's seeing should want her around.

If I had a choice between hanging out with anyone else in the world and hanging out with Loren, I'd choose her every time.

August waves me over to the register, and I tell Loren I'll be right back. Hopefully, it's not the cash drawer again. That thing has been giving us trouble all week. "What's up?"

August tucks a twenty into the slot and then tosses four ones onto the bar in front of some guy who ordered Jager shots.

The drawer slots back into place without catching once. Guess he didn't bring me over here to fix it after all.

He leans a hip against the bar and folds his arms, wearing a knowing smile. "You fucked Loren, didn't you?"

My teeth snap together. "Try again."

His grin grows. "You made sweet, sweet love to your very attractive roommate."

Still annoying, but at least saying it like that doesn't make it sound like what Loren and I did was seedy. Not that I will ever tell August any of this. "That is none of your business."

"And that is a yes. Good for you, man." He claps me on the back and then moves on to the next guy at the bar, a young man with a mustache and a beanie that's so small it doesn't even cover his ears.

Good for you...

I glance back to where Loren is scrolling on her phone.

Is it good for me? Or am I going to jump down her throat about being in a committed relationship too fast and scare her away?

————

It doesn't take long for the vultures to start circling. Two guys over by the pool table nudge each other, then nod toward Loren. If one of them gets up the balls to talk to her, I might have to ask him to leave.

One with a goatee takes the first step, and as much as I want to waylay him, that isn't fair to Loren. For all I know, she might want to go out with other guys.

And I might want to accidentally murder them.

When he props himself against the bar right next to her, she smiles, giving him the time of day. Then she says something, and he returns to his game of pool.

How do I ask what he wanted without sounding like a jealous asshole? I mean, I *am* a jealous asshole, but she doesn't need to know that yet, does she?

Loren has a few drinks, and I find myself drifting over to her whenever I can. August seems to be on board, because he really takes up my slack with the customers. Before I know it, he's flicking the lights, and everyone is settling their tabs before shuffling out the door.

August and I finish up in record time, and when he tells Loren goodnight, he insists I give him a fist-bump.

"He knows, doesn't he?" Loren says under her breath, her lips tilted into the sexiest smirk as she twists back and forth on the stool.

I don't know how I got so lucky, but I am one grateful S.O.B. What truly baffles me is how I ever resisted her in the first place. "Yeah. I hope that's okay? I didn't tell him, but he figured it out the moment you walked in."

Her brows lift. "How?"

"I got distracted staring at you."

Her hand folds over mine, tracing the veins on the back of my hand. "You got distracted, huh?"

"*Mmmhmm. Very* distracted."

"I guess it's okay that August knows...as long as you don't mind me telling Meg."

"Tell her whatever you want." As a matter of fact, I'd prefer it. That means she wants someone close to her to know she and I are...whatever we are.

"Good. Because I already did."

"Oh, yeah? What did you say?"

"That you're a sex god and all other men pale in comparison."

I laugh, but she doesn't. "Wait. Are you serious?"

"Yep."

Damn, this girl is good for my ego. "A sex god, huh? Has a nice ring to it. You're probably dying to jump my bones again, aren't you?"

She extends her foot, twisting from side to side, the low lights reflecting off the glossy black shoe. "Why else would I have braved a Saturday-night crowd in these heels?"

Why, indeed?

I catch her by the waist and nod at the bar. "Sit up there so I can get a better look at you." She lets me help her up, and I settle myself between her knees, making her skirt slip higher on her thighs. "This dress is something else."

Her white teeth dig into her lower lip. "You should see what's under it."

My stomach flips over itself. "Show me."

With her eyes locked on me, Loren slips the straps on the dress she's wearing down her shoulders, revealing a flesh-tone bra that is nothing short of transcendent. "Is that what I think it is?" I can't even find the right words because that scrap of lace makes my mouth water.

She holds her hands beneath her breasts the way Vana White used to back on old school Wheel of Fortune. "Elliott, meet sex bra. Plain and unassuming, but it makes my rack look phenomenal."

"It really does." Don't get me wrong, her rack *is* phenomenal so she doesn't need the help, but fuck me, I might. Someone throw me a buoy; I'm about to drown.

She hooks a finger through the beltloop on my jeans, dragging me against her. "Well? Are you just going to keep standing there or are you going to touch me?"

Loren doesn't have to ask me twice. I can't get enough. My hands are itching for her skin, my throat is dry, and there's only one thing that's going to quench my thirst.

I grip her knees, urging them wider. "Open up, Chaos. Let me see what else you're wearing under that fine dress." She spreads her legs, revealing a lace thong that matches the fabled sex bra.

I grab the closest stool, dragging it so I can sit down in front of her and throw her long legs right over my shoulders. She lets out a shocked laugh, her smile wide and eyes hooded as I catch her hips and urge her closer, until her ass rests on the edge of the bar.

Only then do I look up, wanting to be sure she's comfortable with where this is about to go. "Yes or no?" I nod toward her panties, the patch covering her center darker from where she's soaked through the delicate material.

Her teeth scrape across her bottom lip. "If you want."

"I want." I *really* fucking want. "But do *you* want?"

Still biting her lip, she nods.

I hook my finger beneath the damp material, tugging it aside, exposing her glistening flesh. "Look at all this." My fingers sweep through her wetness, opening her wider, searching for her clit. The moment I find it, she lets out a ragged gasp. "Right there? That's the spot, isn't it?" I press the pad of my thumb flat against her, rubbing in slow circles, not needing the confirmation but wanting it all the same.

Her legs quiver where they're draped over my shoulders. "Yes. Right there."

I ease forward, breathe her in, and replace my fingers with my tongue, lapping at that spot until she's tearing my hair from its roots and grinding against my face.

I know plenty of guys who hate going down on a woman, but I think that's only because they don't know what the fuck they're doing. I flick her clit with my tongue, spelling out my name like a subliminal message, letting her pussy know who it belongs to now.

The harder she grinds, the harder I work, and when I suck her clit into my mouth, holding the suction for as long as I can, she screams my name. I slip two fingers into her tight little slit, working her into a frenzy until she's pulsing around my fingers, drenching me and the bar.

"I... I can't..." Her head falls back, and after one final squeeze, she lets go of my head, staring down at me with fire in her eyes. "You are..."

"Amazing. Epic. Phenomenal."

Her huffed laugh hits me right in the heart. "Full of yourself."

"No, Chaos." I bring my hand to my lips and lick her from my fingers, one by one. "I'm full of you."

I should probably grab the bleach and give this place a good scrub before we head home.

Home.

I might have been living in that apartment for the last twelve years, but it hasn't been home in a long time. Now it's a place I'm looking forward to going back to every night, knowing she's there.

I help Loren fix her dress back over that spectacular bra and then offer her a hand down off the bar. She does this adorable little shimmy as she tugs her skirt back into place.

Her hungry eyes fall to my very obvious erection, a coy smile tilting her lips. "What about you?"

I slide a hand down, cupping the globe of her ass and whisper, "Chaos, that was *all* for me."

ELLIOTT

> How many pancakes are too many pancakes?

I USED to love watching TV with Elliott. Now all I can do as I snuggle beneath his arm is think. It's like my brain can't let me just be happy. It has to be all, "Are you sure he really likes you"? and stuff.

It's all Josh's fault. What did I ever see in that jerk?

Elliott plays with my curls, tugging a strand, then letting it spring back into place. He doesn't complain about how it tickles his face or how he wishes I would straighten it more often. He seems to accept me as I am.

If that's really the case, then he will still like me if I interrupt this very interesting rerun of *NCIS* to ask some of the questions hanging on the tip of my tongue.

I smile up at him. Man, he's good-looking. How did I ever get so lucky to land someone with a jawline like that?

Are you sure you actually landed him?

He must feel me ogling him, because he snatches the remote from the arm of the couch and pauses the show. His head twists, a smile already on his lips even before our eyes meet.

"Hey," I say.

"Hey," he says back.

There's no sense wasting time pretending to be happy when I'm driving myself crazy thinking we're one thing when he's thinking something else entirely. I've read way too many romance novels to know that is how conflicts arise.

I trace the collar on his white T-shirt, stopping to dip my finger into the hollow at his throat. "Are we a couple?"

His smile climbs higher. "Yeah, Chaos. We're a couple."

He says it like the answer should be obvious. Like he can't think of anything he wants more than to be with me.

"Just like that?" A few mind-blowing kisses and a couple rounds in the bedroom and we're a pair?

Seems too good to be true.

"Just like that," he confirms with a kiss to my forehead.

This mind of mine, sometimes I hate it. Because even though Elliott has established that we are, in fact, a couple, what does that *mean*, exactly?

This isn't like back in my parents' day when you went steady with a boy. Nowadays, there are so many different definitions for dating with a thousand different connotations. "So we're committed to each other, then? Like, you're not going to be sleeping with other women while you're sleeping with me?"

His smile falls. Not in an "I'm irritated" sort of way. More like an "it should be obvious, but I know why it isn't" way.

"You're the only one I'll be sleeping with, Loren."

Not that either of us have gotten much sleep since this thing between us started. Elliott is a sex machine, and I'm a big old ball of lust. I can't even be in the same room as him without wanting some part of me plastered up against some part of him.

Case in point: we're both sitting on the same cushion on the couch. There are two more cushions there, but I'd rather be wrapped around him.

"You hungry?" he asks with another kiss.

"Kinda." That salad I had for dinner didn't really fill me up.

"What do you want?"

"Pancakes?" It might be eight o'clock at night, but pancakes transcend time and they also happen to be the only food Elliott knows how to cook.

"Pancakes it is." He kisses me once more, then stands and straightens the top of his sweatpants on his way into the kitchen. That ass of his is something else.

Instead of staying on the couch, I follow him into the kitchen.

Turns out I'm part lost puppy. Who knew?

If it wasn't way too soon and it wouldn't terrify the poor man, I'd say I loved him. He is quite literally everything I have ever wanted in a guy. If you would have asked me five years ago to describe my dream man, he would have been Elliott Grant.

This feels too good to be true. And like that one time I bought "Birkenstocks" for $20 online, I'm worried it might be.

I lean a hip against the counter, watching him swing open the fridge door, illuminating the dark room in blue-white light. "What's wrong with you?"

He takes out the eggs and buttermilk and sets them

beside the tin of flour before glancing over his shoulder at me, his brows coming together. "Excuse me?"

"Tell me something awful about yourself."

Out comes the mixing bowl from the middle cabinet. "Like what?"

"I don't know. Maybe you kick puppies or you're a secret peeping Tom." I scoot the pepper and salt shakers to the side so I can sit on the counter and watch him work. Elliott is a damn good pancake chef. Even the first pancake always comes out perfectly golden and fluffy, which is *not* an easy feat to accomplish.

He picks up the shakers and moves them back on his way to the utensil drawer where we keep the whisk. *Interesting.* "I hate to disappoint, but I love puppies and prefer any woman I look at to know I'm there."

I nudge the shakers when he isn't looking, then smile innocently when he does. His brow furrows as he pushes them back into place.

I think I've found Elliott's flaw. Little neat freak. I'm so relieved, I could kiss him.

You know what? Now that we're dating, I'm *going* to kiss him.

I catch his shirt and twist. He stumbles forward, knocking his hip against the edge of the counter. When I press my lips to his, my heart leaps and my stomach flutters and my lady parts sing.

"What was that for?" The heat of his whispered words dances across my lips.

"You're not perfect."

"No one is perfect."

True. But for a while there it was too close for comfort.

I only let him go because, as much as I want him, I want pancakes too. He cracks the eggs, but before he can add the other ingredients, I suddenly remember: "We don't have any syrup."

I meant to pick some up yesterday, but then work ran late and I wanted to get home before Elliott had to leave for the bar and it completely slipped my mind.

I slide off the counter. Now to find my purse. "You bake, and I'll go to the store." The pancakes won't be nearly as good by the time I get back, but it's a sacrifice I'm willing to make since it was my turn to do the grocery shopping.

"How about we both go to the store?" He turns off the stove and swipes his keys from the hook beside the door.

"Are you sure you're ready for that level of commitment?" Sure, we've been banging left, right, and center, but we have yet to leave the house together as a couple.

He arches a brow. "Are you?"

Please. I was born for this.

I lace my fingers with his and tug him toward the door.

This is going to be fun.

———

Elliott's hand slides off the gearshift to poke my thigh. "Why are you smiling like you just watched someone kick your ex in the balls?"

Man, that would be some great entertainment. "Just thinking."

"About what?"

I'm not entirely sure I should tell him but not telling him would be lying by omission, and I don't want to start this relationship on a lie. "I was thinking that, normally, my first dates are to the movies or a nice restaurant, not a grocery store."

His lips press into a flat line as he flicks the blinker,

changing lanes to overtake a minivan crawling down the road. "This isn't our first date."

"Yes, it is."

"No, it isn't."

Is this his second flaw? Having a terrible memory? "Fine. When was our first date?"

"New Year's."

"Oh, you mean when you made out with someone else in front of me?"

"You made out with her too."

I can't help but laugh.

"Okay, maybe not New Year's." His thumbs tap the steering wheel as he considers. "How about the night I gave you steak sauce?"

"That doesn't count because I bought my own dinner, and you didn't even stick around for dessert." Not saying a woman can't pay her own way on a first date, but I wouldn't want to brag about that if anyone were to ask.

"Fine. The night I picked you up at the bar."

"I don't think fingering me through my pockets is a very good story to tell our grandkids."

He chokes on a laugh, then sobers. We hit the traffic lights, and instead of turning left to the store, he hangs a right.

"Um, hello? The store's that way."

"We're not going to the store."

He drives to a little ice cream parlor right on the edge of the moonlit lake. The gravel crunches beneath his shoes as he runs around the front of the truck to open my door for me. He buys me a peanut butter milkshake, and I make fun of him for his plain vanilla ice cream.

Elliot insists vanilla is the building block of all the best sundaes and shakes, so I eventually let him have this win.

His shoulder bumps mine as he crunches his cone. "How was that for a first date?"

"Best first date I've ever been on."

"It's not over yet."

"No?"

The strands at the front of his hair fall across his brow when he shakes his head. "Not at all."

Our next stop is the grocery store.

Elliott insists I stand on the end of the cart like a little kid while he steers me up and down the aisles. This is the first time I've been here and not been worried about money, which means I throw in a giant, family-sized package of extra quilted toilet paper and colorful boxes of high fructose everything.

Elliott plucks them right back out to read the labels.

Another flaw. Thank goodness.

He returns the boxes to the shelves, trading them for bland tan boxes with the word "organic" stamped across the front. "These are healthier."

I guess I now understand how he got those abs of his—not that I'm complaining. I drop the red box back into the cart. "But these taste better."

"How do you know? Have you tried these?" He gives his own box a shake.

"No, but..."

"But nothing."

But everything. I gesture to his box. "Those are four times the price." I don't care how good they taste—and that has yet to be decided. I can guarantee you that they aren't four times as yummy.

"And?"

"And I don't really feel like spending a thousand dollars on groceries for the week." Is this our first fight?

He drops both boxes into the cart, his jaw pulsing. "You're not spending anything on groceries."

"I'm not with you so you'll buy me fancy food."

"I know." He steps closer, sandwiching me between the cold metal cart and his hard, hot chest. "You're with me because I have a big dick and can make you come anytime you want." He stamps a kiss to my cheek. "But I'm not letting my girlfriend foot the grocery bill."

He takes a few steps back to wrap his fingers around the red handle, pushing the cart down toward the frozen food.

All I can do is stare at him.

Holy shit. Holy shit. Holy shit.

He's almost to the end of the aisle before he realizes I've stalled in my tracks. "Loren?"

"You just called me your girlfriend."

He leaves the cart, coming back to where I stand and propping his hands on his hips like he's about to scold me. "Did we not already have this discussion back home?"

"Yeah, but you never used the words 'boyfriend' or 'girlfriend.'"

He looks genuinely confused. "What did you think 'dating' meant?"

I have to remind myself that this guy was with the same woman for over a decade. He's been single for a few years but apparently hasn't entered the dating pool, more like dipped his toes in it. Meaning he clearly doesn't understand our generation's aversion to labels.

Giddiness wells up inside me, like I drank a bunch of celebratory champagne and it's all bubbling to the surface. "I have a hot boyfriend with a massive dick," I whisper from behind my hands with a giggle.

Mischief sparks in his sea-blue eyes. "And I have a sexy

girlfriend with the sweetest pussy I ever tasted," he says loud enough that anyone could hear.

"Elliott!"

"What?"

Who does he think he's fooling with that innocent blink? "We're in the middle of a grocery store." There are two old ladies picking up frozen dinners right over there.

He arches an arrogant brow. "And? Too bad there aren't any pockets in those yoga pants."

I think I need to climb into one of those freezers because I am on *fire*.

Elliott takes my hand like he's been doing it his whole life, and grins. "Good first date?"

Like I told him before: "The best first date I've ever been on."

MOM

Will you be at the reunion or not?

IT'S BEEN A MONTH, and I can't get enough of Loren. She is a whirlwind from the moment she steps through the door to the moment she falls asleep in my bed. We are in the thrall of the honeymoon stage of a relationship, and damn does it feel good to finally be here.

Well, not *here*, here. Because *here* is in my parents' living room, staring down the barrel of a loaded gun, my mother on the other end with her finger on the trigger.

Not a real gun, mind you, but from the way she wields her words, it might as well be. She's already asked about work in her usual sneery way, but her opinion doesn't sting as much as it used to.

I'm proud of what I do, and that's become enough.

"You're coming next weekend," she drawls, making it clear that this isn't a suggestion or question, but an edict. The pleats on her forest-green skirt are perfectly straight where they drape across her knees, and her ankles are crossed like she's a queen on her floral throne.

It's not that I've forgotten about the family reunion.

I've completely blocked it from my mind.

As far as I'm concerned, this year's event has been canceled due to...bad weather?

That's right. It's been too sunny and warm lately. No one wants to be out in that.

Maybe I could lie and say I have plans.

Except I don't have plans, and my mother has a built-in lie detector.

She knows something is up, has already pointed out how little I've been here over the last few weeks. How I never want to have dinner with them anymore.

I can't come right out and tell her that Loren's dinners are better. (And her desserts too, if you catch my drift.)

To be honest, I've been hesitant to tell her anything about Loren because we're in this romantic little bubble and my mother is like a porcupine.

Maybe if she sees how happy we are together, she'll find a way to be happy for me.

My mother smooths a nonexistent wrinkle from her white silk blouse. She looks like she's about to head off to the church for a bazaar, not spend the next hour in the kitchen cooking for Dad.

"Nobody knows how long they have left with the ones they love," she goes on. "For all we know, your grandmother could drop dead in the morning."

My hand clenches around the glass of sweet tea she forced into it the moment I set foot inside. "Is grandma sick?" Hopefully, she didn't catch something on that cruise she went on a few weeks ago. My grandmother travels more than anyone I've ever met.

Mom's lips pinch. "No, but she could *get* sick."

So could I but turning the argument back on my mother will only end in tears. I wouldn't want to be the cause of her mascara getting smeared.

Like most of our conversations, we both know where this is headed. I don't like disappointing her, but I also don't like being told where to go, what time to be there, and what to wear.

Her eyes glisten, tears poised, waiting for her command to fall.

If there's one thing I hate more than the aforementioned things, it's a crying woman.

Shit. Shit. Shit.

With a deep inhale, I swallow my protest and say, "I'll be there."

Her face brightens, like she wasn't just on the verge of tears a split second ago. This woman really missed her calling as an actress. "You will?"

"Sure." Maybe it won't be so bad to hang out with my aunts and uncles and many cousins, assuming they don't ask any probing questions. My grandparents are getting up there in age as well. By up there, I mean they're in their late sixties. The joys of being part of a family where everyone is married with children well before they hit twenty.

Almost everyone.

Maybe I could convince my girlfriend to come along.

That still feels so weird to say after all this time. *Girlfriend.* To be honest, the term sounds childish when Loren is so much more. But calling her "my obsession" makes me sound like I need to be institutionalized, "my lover" makes it sound like we're in the midst of an illicit affair, and "my everything" would make her turn tail and run right back to Maryland.

So she's my girlfriend, and as such, she should be by my side when I face the firing squad. Who knows, maybe my family will be so focused on her that they won't even notice me.

———

When I get back home, I find my *girlfriend* on the couch, surrounded by blankets and with that box of too-sweet cereal she loves so much and a bowl of milk that has turned green from the dehydrated marshmallows sitting on the coffee table.

She smiles up at me, pausing the TV and tossing the remote next to her discarded spoon. "How's your mom?"

"Same as every other time I see her." I drop my keys into the bowl and remove my shoes, setting them beside the pair of heels Loren wore the other night. The heels and nothing else.

The memory makes my dick swell. But there will be plenty of time for that later. First: "We need to talk."

Loren throws her hands up to her face, hiding behind her palms. "It's the new shower curtain, isn't it? I knew you'd hate it. I'm sorry. I'll take it down right now."

The neon yellow curtain she bought two days ago makes me feel like I'm showering inside a lemon, but it's sunny and bright like Loren, so how can I complain? "It's not the shower curtain."

She peers at me between her fingers the same way she does at the stressful parts in movies. "Is it the coasters? I can never find one when I need it."

That's because she keeps putting them "away" when

she cleans up, only she never puts them in the same place twice.

It's fine, though. That coffee table is as old as the hills, so I don't care if her bowls of milk leave stains. I've been meaning to get a new one anyway.

I gather her pile of blankets and slide beneath them. "Sorry, I shouldn't have started the conversation like that. This isn't bad news." Unless she has no desire to meet my family. Then we need to have a whole different conversation. "At least I don't think it is."

"Tell me before I die."

Always so dramatic. My mom is going to love her. "My family reunion is next weekend, and I was wondering if you'd be my date."

She gasps softly. "You want me to meet your family?"

Oh shit. Are those tears in her eyes? Did I move too fast?

Dammit. I moved too fast. I catch her hands so she doesn't go back to hiding again, holding them between mine. "You don't have to if you don't want to. I know we've only been dating for a few weeks."

Her curls tumble over her shoulders when she shakes her head. "I want to. I really, really want to."

"Really?" When she nods, some of the tightness in my chest eases. "I have to warn you, they're...a lot. If my mom corners you, she'll probably grill you about our relationship and may or may not cry when she finds out we're living together." On second thought... "Maybe this isn't a good idea."

"I'll be fine."

She doesn't know what she's in for. But I do. Just in case, I'll ask August to stick close. He'll be more than happy for a reason to avoid his own mother.

I haven't been to a reunion in four years, so I already know I won't be as lucky.

"My family is insane."

She slides onto my lap, her knees falling to either side of my hips and her smiling lips grazing mine. "Then it's a good thing I'm a bit of chaos on my own."

CHAOS

What kind of cookies do you like?

Your cookies

Weirdo

MY GREAT AUNT and uncle's cabin sits on a slight incline, overlooking the lake. Now, I use the term "cabin" in the loosest sense of the word considering the wood-clad monstrosity boasts eight bedrooms and more glass than any one of the high-rises downtown. It wasn't always like this. Back when I was little, the cabin was a cottage made of stone, with an A-frame roof and a bunch of single-beds in a loft.

Then my uncle bought a winning lottery ticket, and the old cabin was replaced with this one.

A rhododendron-lined drive snakes down toward the lake's dark-blue water. Brick paths and patios lead to brick stairs, all the way to the lapping shore. Colorful sailboats bob lazily on the horizon, skirted by the occasional motorboat blaring music and leaving a trail of white-capped waves in its wake. The smell of meat on the grill fills the air. Towering oaks block out most of the sun, shading the mossy grass below.

Loren and I arrive twenty minutes late, which means we're stuck parking right next to the bushes. I offer to let Loren out before I park, but she insists she's okay with climbing over the center console and getting out through my door. With that little white sundress she's wearing, the whole process is quite entertaining. When I catch a flash of the lacy white thong she has on underneath, I seriously consider hopping right back into the truck and driving home.

The dinner is a potluck, and she baked a bunch of sugar cookies so soft your teeth sink right into the gooey vanilla goodness. I may or may not have already consumed three. Since she moved in, I've eaten like a king. If I don't stop, I'm not going to be able to see my toes come Christmas.

The moment Loren's strappy sandals hit the pavement, her eyes go wide as saucers. "Holy crap, that's a lot of kids."

Holy crap is right because there are children *everywhere.*

We're talking in between the bushes, hanging out on the balcony, screaming through the lawn, splashing in the water, and passed out on loungers next to the picnic tables.

My mother is the only one of her five sisters and two brothers to have one child. August is one of six. My aunt Verna had ten children. *Ten.* Like, do they not have a television in their house or what? To make things even more insane, each of their children have at least three kids.

The yard looks like a damn day care center.

A woman in one of those shapeless dresses that looks like a pillowcase waddles up to us, smiling and waving with a tiny shovel in her hand. "Hey, Elliott. Long time, no see."

Would you look at that? My cousin Kelly is pregnant... *again.* "Hey, Kelly. Is that number three or four?" I ask, nodding at her swollen stomach.

Her belly shakes when she laughs, just like I imagine Santa's is supposed to. "Five, actually." Her eyes track to Loren, and she gestures at her with that shovel. "Who is this?"

I throw an arm around Loren's stiff shoulders, pulling her closer. "This is my girlfriend, Loren Piper."

Kelly's grin stretches even wider. "He must really love you to subject you to this madhouse."

Loren's smile tightens. *Shit.* She's uncomfortable already. This was a bad idea. As soon as Kelly moves on, I'll ask Loren if she wants to leave.

As if on cue, a little kid who looks like Kelly's carbon copy starts screaming down by the slide.

Kelly whirls, pressing a hand to her forehead. "Oh, sugar. That's little Kelsey."

"Oh, sugar?"

"Yeah, well, we figured it was time to stop cursing when our youngest told his pre-school teacher she was a fucking disaster. I'll talk to you in a bit. Sign-up sheet is on the door. Nice to meet you, Loren."

"You too," Loren says, then turns to me to add, "She seems fun."

"She used to be." We all used to sneak away from the mayhem and smoke weed up in the rhododendrons. Now she has her own fucking basketball team. I step in front of Loren, waiting for her to look up. "Are you sure you want to do this?"

"Positive. But first, explain this sign-up sheet."

It's hard to tell if she's saying that because she wants to be here or if she's only being nice out of respect for me. Either way, I'm not going to push her. The second she looks like she wants to bolt, we're gone.

"All the adults take turns playing lifeguard. You sign up for a thirty-minute slot and have to watch the water to make sure the kids don't accidentally drown." I gesture to the homemade lifeguard's chair, painted hot pink, sitting smack-dab in the middle of the lowest patio, right at the edge of the water.

The lake must be freezing right now, but the kids don't seem to mind.

"That's really smart."

"Yeah, well, when there are this many people, you learn to mitigate the mayhem." After a close call when we were kids, we had to step up our game. As long as one person is on duty, everyone else can relax. We all take the responsibility very seriously. No distractions, no phones allowed, that sort of thing.

Loren and I make our way down the brick path to where someone has taped a piece of paper onto the screen door. Names fill each of the lines, but there's a gap around noon.

I sign us up for that slot, figuring we'll both need a break from my family by then. Plus, most of the kids will be out of the water eating burgers and hot dogs, so it won't be as hectic.

Inside the house, it's like an airport gate, with people running this way and that. Except, instead of suitcases, they're hauling colorful beach towels or condiments or sand toys. I take Loren's cookies and set them beside the pies and cakes and weird cool-whipped concoctions our grandmother and her sisters make. Inside the kitchen is a scene straight out of the 1950's, with women bustling around in printed aprons while men stand outside on the deck talking shit. Three of my cousins with tiny babies sit in a circle in the living room, all breastfeeding their kids.

I feel like an outsider, so I can only imagine how awkward Loren must feel. A few people nod to me, but I'm saved from having to engage in conversation until Loren leaves me for the bathroom.

That's when everyone descends, asking about business. Who the girl I'm with is. Where I'm living now. How I've been.

Coming from big families, they're all used to this sort of mayhem, but most of my life it was just me, my mom, and my dad, so it's hard to cope with all the commotion and conversations taking place at the same time.

The noise at the bar rarely gets to me because it's not directed at me.

Today, I can't get away from it.

Speaking of my parents, where are they?

From across the room, Uncle Arnie makes a beeline for me. He brews his own beer and has been trying for years to convince me to stock it at the bar. I've tried explaining about the laws regarding that sort of stuff, and that he would need to obtain a license and pass safety inspections and all that, but he doesn't seem to get it.

I glance back down the hallway where Loren disappeared. I hate to leave her but cannot handle a conversation with Uncle Arnie unless I've had at least three or four drinks, so I head outside and sink onto one of the Adirondack chairs near the grill. Arnie's head swings right and left, no doubt searching for me, but I keep my head down until he's out of sight.

Loren steps out onto the deck, her gaze finding mine like a homing beacon. The scalloped hem of her sundress sways along her tanned legs as she crosses over to me. I jolt to my feet, offering an apologetic smile. "Sorry. I was hiding from someone."

"Hopefully, not from me."

"Never."

My dad climbs the stairs, beer in one hand and a plate of hot wings in the other. When he sees me, he comes straight over.

This is it. One of the two moments I've been dreading. Not that I don't want Loren to meet him. More like I'm afraid of what he's going to say or do when he does meet her. I still remember when Alice and I were getting prom pictures taken and he came out of his room wearing Mom's fuzzy robe and hot-pink shower cap.

At least he's wearing clothes today. "Loren, this is my dad, Ernest Grant. Dad, this is my girlfriend, Loren."

Dad's brow furrows as he looks Loren up and down, his sauce-stained lips pressing flat with disapproval. "You never told us you had a girlfriend."

Loren's head falls, her cheeks flaming pink. "That's because he's ashamed of me."

Hold on. She thinks I'm *what?* "I am not ashamed of you." I'm proud to call her mine. Have I not made that clear?

Dad sets his beer on the railing and swirls one of his wings through the blue cheese dressing glob on the side of his paper plate. "We raised him better than that, I assure you, Lily."

Of all the scenarios I worried about, my dad acting like an asshole was not one of them. Doesn't he know that's mom's job? "Her name is Loren, Dad. *Loren.*"

Loren's shoulders start to shake. Great. He made her cry. I'm never going to forgive him for this. I step in front of my dad, blocking his view. "I'm sorry, Loren. Please don't cry. We can go home right now." Screw everyone here.

Her head lifts, and while there *are* tears in her eyes, she's also smiling. Laughter bursts from her lips, and she starts cackling. Behind me, my dad sputters, his deep chuckle even more confusing.

Loren runs a finger under her eyes, still laughing. "You should see your face right now."

"What is happening?"

Dad steps around me, offering Loren his plate. "Do you want to tell him, sweetheart, or should I?"

Loren steals one of his wings, gives it a little dip into the sauce, and takes a bite. "I had the pleasure of meeting your dad when I asked him where the bathroom was."

So what she's saying is that they colluded to pull one over on me. Loren really should know better after what we did to August. But if she wants to make me her enemy, then so be it. I will make her pay in the most delicious ways.

Dad hip-checks me. "You have yourself a keeper."

I think so too. I grab them some napkins held in place beneath a concrete frog. One down, one to go. "Where's Mom?"

Dad swings a wing toward the water. "Guarding lives down by the lake."

One of my great-uncles calls my dad's name, lifting two fishing poles over his head. Dad launches his plate of bones into the trash bag tied to one of the balustrades. "It was lovely to meet you, Loren. Hopefully, my son won't be too ashamed to bring you by the house sometime."

She beams. "One can only hope."

I fold my arms across my chest, waiting for her to finish

cleaning her fingers. The longer she takes, the redder her cheeks get. When she finally looks up at me, her eyes sparkle with sunlight and happiness.

"You were gone for five minutes."

She shrugs. "What can I say? People like me."

People do like her—and for good reason. She is the sunniest, warmest, and most welcoming woman I've ever met. "Because you're amazing."

"You say this as if I don't already know."

———

August waves when he sees us and carefully extricates himself from the grandma table where he's probably been hiding since he arrived. He shoves his lime-green sunglasses onto his forehead. Between those and the salmon-colored polo shirt, he looks like a frat bro from the nineties. "Hey. You're late."

"Traffic."

"Liar," he snorts, opening his arms for a hug. Not from me, that'd be weird. But Loren steps right up and hugs him back. "You're a brave woman, Loren Piper."

She draws away, catching her hair and throwing it over her shoulders. "I don't see what the two of you were so worried about. Everyone has been lovely."

August's brows rise as he shoots a glance my way. "Has she met your mother yet?"

"Not yet."

"You'll get it soon enough," he says to her before nodding at me. "Did you see Kelly?"

"Sure did."

"Knocked up *again*. You may want to avoid the punch, Loren. I hear it's catching."

She laughs into her glass, not realizing that for once, August isn't joking. Couples *do* have a habit of getting pregnant after the family reunion, but I think that has more to do with how much they drink, not what's in the punch.

Then again, my grandma refuses to tell anyone her secret recipe, so maybe there is some truth to it.

Turning his head slightly, August talks out of the corner of his mouth like a creep. "So, weird question, but is that our cousin over there in the green bikini?" He tilts his chin at a woman with dark hair braided down her back.

She looks familiar, but it isn't until I see the woman with gray threaded through her hair sitting on a lawn chair next to her that I realize why. "I'm pretty sure that's Leah Norton's daughter."

"Damn."

"Why?"

"No reason." His throat bobs with his gulp of beer.

Hold on... "Tell me you're not scoping out women at our family fucking reunion. That's incest, August."

Loren chokes on her drink; red drops spill down her chin that she quickly swipes away before they can stain her dress.

August tilts his beer at me. "It's not incest if they're someone's stepdaughter or related to us by marriage, now, is it?"

"You're disgusting."

"It's this fucking place, man. Seeing all these pregnant women messes with your mind. Drives your testosterone through the roof. My dick is like: *Must. Make. Babies. Fucking Nolan genes,"* he mutters with a shake of his head.

Fucking Nolan genes is right.

Although I laugh into my beer, I take a good, long look at Loren, wondering if she's ever thought about having kids.

Probably not the sort of conversation to have after only dating for a month, but still...I wonder.

I immediately stop wondering the moment I see my mother climbing those brick stairs, her hair perfect as ever. She zeroes in on me and smiles. Then her head swings toward Loren and her eyes narrow.

This is it. The moment I've been dreading.

I'm *not* ashamed of Loren. I just need to get to my mom *before* she gets to my girlfriend. Lay a few ground rules.

"Hey, August." I clap him on the shoulder. "Do you mind showing Loren the treehouse we used to play in? I'll just be a second."

He seems to realize the situation I'm trying to avoid and casually steers Loren up the hill. "Come on, Loren." Quieter, he adds, "If anyone asks, pretend you're my girlfriend, okay?"

"Not a fucking chance, dickhead," I bark.

He grins over his shoulder at me. "Hey, it was worth a shot."

Time to face the most terrifying woman I know.

Mom comes to a stop by a hollowed-out stump that my aunt has turned into a flowerpot, but she's too busy watching August rescue Loren to spare me a glance. When she looks back at me, the only thing that gives away her irritation is the slight twitch in her right eye. "Elliott. So good of you to finally show up."

Would you look at that? It didn't even take her a minute to throw in a subtle dig. This is going to be fun. "Nice to see you too, Mom."

CHAPTER 47

LOREN

I ASSUME the woman who cornered Elliott is his mother since he is her carbon copy—minus the blonde hair. If she's anything like his dad, I have nothing to worry about. When I bumped into Ernest Grant while trying to find my way through that maze of a house, I knew immediately who he was. Elliott might look like his mother, but the dark hair and blue eyes came from his father. It was like running into future Elliott, and let me tell you, the future looks bright.

Not for the first time, I wonder what the heck Elliott's ex was thinking, giving him up. If anyone tried to take him from me, I'd cut them.

That's right. I'm talking straight up shivving.

As long as that man wants me, I'm his, and he is all mine.

"That's Elliott's mom, right?" I whisper to August, not wanting everyone else here to realize I haven't met Elliott's parents yet. Not that I'm going to lie if asked; I just don't see the point in broadcasting the fact that this relationship is brand new.

All I get is a nod of confirmation.

I guess any information I'm going to glean will have to be from the woman herself.

"Oh, shit." August twists, burying his face in his beer. Whatever color was in his cheeks drains away completely.

I take a beat before glancing over my shoulder to where he was looking only a second ago. All I can see is a woman with glossy red hair in a pair of heels I'd kill to get my hands on. Literally, because there is no way I would ever be able to afford them otherwise.

"Don't look!" he snaps, snatching my wrist and tugging me closer.

August has always seemed a little nuts, but this is weird, even for him. "What's wrong?"

He darts a look over my shoulder, then curses again. "Alice is here."

Alice? I know I've heard that name before but—

Holy shit.

"Alice, Alice? As in, Elliott's ex-girlfriend Alice?"

August looks at me as if I'm the one who's nuts. "Ex-girlfriend? You mean his ex-wife."

Yeah, okay. This is one of August's jokes. This guy really needs to give it a break. Elliott doesn't have an ex-wife. He would've told me if he did.

Wouldn't he?

From the way my boyfriend continues to chat casually with his mother, he clearly has yet to notice the newcomer.

As if Elliott knows I'm silently begging him for some sort of explanation, his head lifts, gaze catching mine. At first, he smiles, but that smile quickly fades as his eyes shift to August. My companion tilts his chin toward the driveway. I watch Elliot's brow furrow. Then I watch him turn and his shoulders go stiff when he sees *her*.

Ex-girlfriend, ex-wife, there really shouldn't be a difference because both are past tense, but there *is* a difference.

That woman shared not only his heart and his bed, but also his last freaking name.

What's worse, she could be Rebecca's twin. I bet she's nice too, which makes me hate her even more. And here Elliott assured me Rebecca "wasn't his type." I knew he was lying, didn't I? Clearly Rebecca is *exactly* his type.

He told me this family reunion was a casual affair, so why the heck does she look like she just glided off a runway? At least if I'd worn something with a heel, I wouldn't feel so dowdy, standing here in my sundress like a child on Easter Sunday.

Elliott whips back around and starts for me.

I can't talk to him in front of all these people. This is his family, and I'm the outsider. When I make a scene in front of them, they'll never forgive me. Because a scene is about to be made. I head off toward Elliott's truck. At least in the parking lot, we may be afforded some privacy. These tears aren't going to stay put for long.

"Loren, wait," he calls.

Yeah, okay. Like I'm going to listen to him.

"Loren, please."

Oh, look. There are those southern manners. Maybe his mother should've taught him about the importance of telling the freaking truth.

I can see the truck. It's right there, parked up against a massive wall of rhododendrons.

Two more steps.

One more step.

I reach for the handle like a lifeline only to find it locked.

I'm going to breathe through this, swallow my tears, and drive away like the composed, mature woman I am. "Give me the keys, Elliott."

His hand flies to his pocket, as if I'm about to dig around in there and find them myself. "No."

"I would like to leave."

"I didn't know she was coming."

That's all well and good, and do you know what? I believe him. Mostly because, if he'd known, he probably wouldn't have invited me. "Did you know she was your *wife*?"

His jaw begins to pulse. "Loren..."

What is that wince supposed to do? Make me feel bad for him? I don't. "You know how important honesty is to me."

His fingers rake through his hair, his searching eyes looking as lost as I feel. "I'm sorry. I didn't think it would matter. We haven't been together for four years."

How do I even know if that's true? "Then why is she here?"

"I don't fucking know."

Maybe. Maybe not.

"Tell me everything," I say, giving him one more chance.

"You already know—"

"*Everything*."

His hands fall to his sides, and he stuffs them into his

pockets. "We grew up neighbors. Started dating in middle school. Got married our sophomore year of college."

"Why did you break up—oh, wait. I'm sorry. I mean why did you get a divorce?" Hold on. "You *are* divorced, right?"

"Yes, we are divorced. And I already told you. She thought the grass was greener on the other side."

"Oh, really?"

"Yes, *really*. We were together for so long, I guess she thought she'd missed out on living, on dating around and the whole rebellious phase."

"That's all?"

His jaw works.

"Elliott, please... I'm giving you one more chance to tell me the truth. All of it."

"She was pregnant."

My heart doesn't just stop. It falls completely out of my chest. "You have a *kid*?"

His head shakes slowly. "We lost the baby."

Holy shit.

Now the fact that he lives alone in a two-bedroom apartment makes complete sense. He had a wife and a baby on the way. After she left him, he never moved out. That isn't just because of rent controls or whatever other crap he told me. That's good old-fashioned grief.

Growing up in a funeral home, you see plenty of people holding onto whatever they can because moving on means having to let go.

Elliott still hasn't let go.

If he had, he would've told me about his ex-wife.

His throat bobs with each rapid swallow. "When we... when it happened, it was like she realized she never got to live, that she never got to experience dating or going out or just being single."

Too bad I hadn't met her back then. I could've told her that being single sucks.

Then again, if I'd done that, maybe she and Elliott never would've broken up, and he and I might never have met.

It's all shit, isn't it?

That he and his wife had to suffer such a tragedy. That their relationship didn't last. Everything about his story sucks. "I'm sorry that happened to you. I can't imagine how difficult that must've been. But you should've told me. I deserved that much."

His head falls, and he nudges a leaf with the toe of his shoe. "I know. Fuck. I'm so sorry."

I can't say it's fine because it's not. I thought our relationship had been built on trust and honesty. Instead, it's been built on a foundation of lies. Why didn't he just tell me the truth? Does he not trust me? Am I just someone to fill the gap she left behind? Now that she's back, is he going to want to be with her instead? They have *years* of history together. Why wouldn't he?

I just...

I need a moment to think without him staring at me.

I hold out my hand. "I would like your keys, please."

"Why?"

"Because I want to leave."

"You don't have to—"

"I do."

His keys jangle as he withdraws them from his pocket. "Let me drive you."

I don't want him to drive me. Right now, I don't want him near me. "I'd like to be alone. Besides, you have lifeguard duty, remember?" At least that will give me some time to sort my shit out, because standing this close to him, seeing the remorse in his eyes, makes it impossible to think straight. "I assume you can get a ride to the apartment?"

He drops the keys into my palm with a sorrowful nod. "I'm sorry, Loren."

"I know you are." But that doesn't make the lie hurt any less.

CHAOS

Weirdo.

12:26 PM

Please call me back

I'm so sorry

I DON'T EVEN HAVE the stomach to watch Loren drive away. Today was going so well, and then *this* happened. I stalk down the hill to where Mom and Dad are whispering, no doubt conspiring with each other over this.

They must hear me coming, because both of them look up at the same time, matching frowns on their faces.

"What the hell, Mom?"

Dad stands up taller, stepping between us with his eyes narrowed. "Language, son."

My language should be the least of their worries, right now. "Why the hell did you invite Alice?" Because I know in my gut that this is *her* fault. Mom never got over our choice to separate, and she's been trying to get us back together ever since.

"It's not your mother's fault, Elliott," a woman says from behind me, her smooth, silken tone making the hair at the back of my neck stand on end. "I asked her if it would be all right to come."

Of course, my ex-wife would be right behind me.

Just when I thought this day couldn't possibly get any worse. I turn to face the woman I loved for so long. She's still as beautiful as ever, but when I look at her, all I feel is disappointment. In myself for not being what she needed, but also in her, for being so quick to give us up.

We were supposed to spend our whole lives together, and now, I don't even know where she lives.

My mother offers her former daughter-in-law a tight smile. "You've always been part of our family, Alice. You are welcome any time."

The thing is, Alice *isn't* part of our family, not anymore. She gave up on them the same day she gave up on me.

I blow out a breath, but it doesn't do shit for the anger spreading through my chest. "I would've appreciated a heads-up."

And then what? Would I have told Loren the whole truth? I really don't know. I definitely wouldn't have come here today, that's for damn sure.

Mom's eyes soften. "You never told me you were dating someone."

"Can you blame me?" Who in their right mind would want to be subjected to this shit?

"Elliott..." My father's tone holds a warning.

This is bullshit.

I never should have let Loren leave without me. Now

she has my truck, and I'm stuck here until someone decides to leave.

You know what? No.

I'm not stuck. I'll walk home if I have to. Whatever it takes to put distance between me and these traitors who are supposed to have *my* back. To take *my* side.

Instead, they've been colluding with *her*.

I'm done

So fucking done.

I leave the three of them without another word, searching for August among the sea of faces swimming in front of me. When I catch a glimpse of him near the grill, that's where I go. He sees me coming and meets me in the middle of the lawn.

"Did you know?"

His chin jerks back as if I just decked him. If he had anything to do with this, I might.

"I know I'm an asshole most of the time, but if I'd known your ex-wife was going to show up to our family reunion, I would've one hundred percent told you. That's fucked up."

He may be an asshole, but at least he is an honest one.

Unlike me.

I hope Loren can find it in her heart to forgive me, even though I don't deserve it.

I'm no better than Josh. Yeah, I didn't cheat on her, but I sure as hell lied by omission. I wouldn't blame her for wanting nothing to do with me anymore.

Shit. I've gotta get home to make things right before it's too late. She's probably packing up her things right now.

"I need you to take me home."

"Why can't you take yourself?"

"She took my truck."

August sets down his plate of potato salad and drags out his keys. "No problem, man. But my Jeep's blocked in, so it'll take me a few minutes to get it out."

Of course it is. The only thing that could make this worse is if—

"Elliott, can we go somewhere to talk?"

That. That's what could make this worse. Apparently, my ex-wife didn't get the hint when I walked away. "I have nothing to say to you."

Alice still bites her lip the way she always used to when she was nervous. I hate that I remember that about her. I hate that I remember anything.

"I know you don't owe me anything after what I did, but I owe you. Please. Hear me out and then you'll never have to see me again."

That's not really true because her mom and dad still live next door to my parents. But pointing that out doesn't feel very helpful right now.

Nothing she says can make this any better, and now the only woman I want to speak to is gone. But since August has disappeared to free his car, it's either be a complete asshole or hear her out.

"Fine."

Her shoulders rise and fall with the soft breath that pushes through her rosy lips. "I'm sorry. I know I said that before, but I am sorrier than you'll ever know. I shouldn't have run away. I should've stuck it out. You deserved better than that."

All those things are true, but I'm not sure what she thinks saying them now is going to do.

Her lips lift into a soft smile as she spins the wedding ring I gave her around her ring finger.

What the fuck is she doing still wearing it?

"I had this idea in my head that I was missing out on so much," she goes on, still spinning, spinning, *spinning*. "Every time I went online, I saw all my friends going out to clubs, dating a different guy every other weekend, living life to its fullest." Her hands fall, and her eyes lift, glittering. "What I didn't realize was that they were all searching for something I'd already found with you."

I told her that, didn't I? So did everyone else.

She didn't listen.

"So, what? All it took was a dickhead or two treating you like shit for you to realize I wasn't such a mistake after all?"

A single, solitary tear trails down her perfectly sculpted cheek. "I never said you were a mistake."

No, she didn't. She just made me *feel* like one. That feeling of inadequacy lived in my bones until the day Loren Piper moved into my apartment and into my heart.

"What do you want from me, Alice?"

Her soft, hopeful smile makes me want to turn and run in the opposite direction. "I came here hoping for a second chance."

How long did I wait by the phone, hoping and praying to hear those words?

Too damn long.

Now that she's said them, I feel nothing but sadness. Because as much as I loved this woman, she has become a stranger to me.

"But when I arrived, I saw you with someone else. You looked so happy." Her words tremble, and more tears fall.

I am happy. Or, at least, I *was* until all of this went to shit.

Alice smiles, revealing the dimple in her right cheek. "Your girlfriend is a very lucky woman."

I don't know about that, but hearing her say it, seeing the sincerity in her tear-filled eyes makes me feel like it might just be true. If only I hadn't fucked it up by lying. "I'm the lucky one." Loren brought me back to life.

August beeps from the driveway, waving a hand at me.

"I'm sorry, Alice. I have to go." If she says anything else, I don't hear her. I'm already running toward my future.

But then my cousin Kelly steps out of the house with a neon sun hat and a whistle and shouts, "Your turn to guard the fort, Elliott!"

Shit.

I completely forgot about signing up to play lifeguard. August leaps out of his Jeep and jogs down the hill to snag the whistle. "I'll take his shift."

"You sure?"

"Yeah, man. Go get your girl."

I take off running toward his running vehicle.

I only hope Loren is still there when I get back home.

BOYFRIEND

I'm so sorry

I FIGHT with myself the whole way home. This whole situation is such a conundrum, isn't it? On one hand, I understand why Elliott lied: To protect himself. On the other, if he truly trusted and cared for me, he would've respected me enough to tell me the whole truth. It's the least I deserved.

He told you the whole truth eventually.

Did he though? How do I know that in six months' time he won't come to me with another monumental secret that shakes the foundation of our relationship?

The problem is, I *want* to forgive Elliott, so I'll end up twisting the story in his favor and offering excuses he might not deserve. Look at what happened with Josh.

Except Josh was a ratbag.

And even though Elliott lied, I don't think he's a ratbag.

I still think he's the most wonderful man I've ever met.

But as I sit in the parking lot, staring up at the windows of our apartment, I'm not sure I can go inside because all I'll end up doing is thinking about *him*.

Is he only with me because it's convenient? Because he can mosey down the hallway to my room any time he wants? Is this whole relationship solely based on proximity?

I reverse out of the space and call my best friend. Meg, the angel that she is, answers on the first ring. "Hey, babe. How's the reunion?"

"I don't know. I left."

"What? Why?"

"Because I just met Elliott's ex-wife."

"Holy shit. Elliott was married?"

"Yup. Can I come over? I need to talk to someone."

"I'm just headed over to the house to meet the inspector. I'll send you the address and meet you there."

———

Ten minutes later, I'm pulling in behind Meg's tiny hatchback. "So this is the place." It's smaller than in the pictures, but still one of the cutest houses I've ever seen. With a coat of fresh paint, the blue-gray paneling on the craftsman home will look brand-spanking-new. And there are even window boxes. Man, I love window boxes.

Her long ponytail swings when she twists back toward the house. "This is the place. Three bedrooms all to myself...Unless you have any interest in moving in."

It would be super convenient being this close to work, but the thought of moving out makes me sick to my stomach. I wouldn't do that to Elliott. He's already been through enough trauma with his ex-girlfriend—I mean ex-*wife*.

"If I ever need a place, I'll let you know." At least I have options now. Who knows? Maybe Elliott will come back from the reunion and tell me he's fallen for his wife again.

Oh, no.

I think I might puke.

"Meg?" a familiar voice calls from the house.

"Is that Rebecca?" I whisper.

Meg winces. "Sorry. I forgot to tell you she was coming."

"Why are you sorry? It's fine."

Rebecca beams at us from the porch, one hand over her eyes, shielding them from the sun. "Hey, Loren. I didn't know you were coming. How was the reunion?"

Meg squeezes my arm for moral support.

"Hey, Rebecca. The reunion was fine." That's all I want to say about that. As much as I like Rebecca, she has her own relationship woes to worry about without adding mine to the pile.

Determined to distract myself so I don't fall to pieces, I ask Meg for the grand tour. The house is small but cute, and all the updates to the kitchen make it feel more modern. Meg will put her own stamp on it in no time. I'm so happy she has this for herself, especially since she's been looking for so long.

Rebecca's shoe taps against the refurbished hardwood floor as she studies the living room. "Do you know what would look great in here? A green couch."

"I love green couches," Meg agrees.

My head is too wrapped up in everything that's happened to even think about couches or anything else.

A phone rings, and we all rush over to where we discarded our purses on the kitchen island to see which one of us is getting a call. Turns out, it's Rebecca. Her lips purse as she frowns down at the screen, and I'm close enough to see Josh's face smiling back at me from beneath a Vanderbilt hat.

What the hell is he doing still calling her? "Is that your ex?"

She nods. "Yeah. He keeps wanting to meet up for coffee."

Meg folds her arms over her chest as she scowls at Rebecca's phone like it's covered in worms. "You're not thinking of going, are you?"

Rebecca tucks her phone into her back pocket without answering the call. "I don't know. I mean, we dated for so long, the least I can do is hear him out."

Josh doesn't deserve more chances to lie. He doesn't even deserve to breathe the same air as Rebecca James.

And I can think of one way to keep him away forever.

You always hear about the bro-code. *Don't snitch. Always have your bro's back.* Blah blah blah. What about us women? Why don't we have some catchy name for our relationships?

I'll tell you why: Because the world wants to pit us against each other. They want us squabbling and fighting and tearing each other down instead of building each other up. We're all "competing" against each other, hoping a guy will choose us, when we should be the ones choosing ourselves.

Rebecca needs to hear the truth, just like I did.

She's my friend and she deserves total honesty.

I don't know how this is going to impact my job, but I can't let Rebecca make the biggest mistake of her life. If she still chooses Josh after she knows everything, then that's on her.

But if I continue to keep this terrible secret, that's on me.

"He doesn't deserve it."

Rebecca glances at me, her brow furrowed. "What do you mean?"

Just rip the band-aid off. Keep it short and sweet. "Josh is a lying, cheating ratbag. He wasn't just cheating on you. He was cheating on you with me."

Rebecca goes as still as the weird concrete owl perched on the corner of the railing.

"I swear I didn't know he had a girlfriend," I say, my voice catching. "We met at his great aunt's funeral back in Maryland. He's the reason I moved to Nashville. The moment I found out, I broke things off. Told him to tell you or I would." If only I'd been strong enough back then. "But I chickened out and had Elliott do it instead. I should've told you as soon as I found out, but I was too afraid to lose my job. I understand if you never want to look at me again. I'm so sorry, Rebecca. I hope someday you can forgive me." I turn on my heel and run for the door, shame washing over me like a shower of ice.

All I want is to curl up in Elliott's arms and cry on his big, strong shoulder.

Elliott.

How can I be angry with him for keeping his shame hidden when I've been doing the same thing since I found out about Josh?

If he feels half as shitty as I do right now, then he's going to need some consoling too.

"Loren, wait!"

I freeze, almost too afraid to turn around. When I finally drum up the courage, I see Rebecca standing behind me, mascara streaks painted across her perfectly sculpted cheekbones.

She swipes at her eyes, but still the tears continue to fall. "Thank you for telling me the truth."

My vision blurs as I blink back my own tears. "I'm so sorry."

She throws her arms around my shoulders, pulling me in for a hug. "This isn't your fault. It's *his*."

All of this is Josh's fault. But I've gotta say, part of me is grateful to the ratbag because he brought me here, to this moment, to these amazing people.

When we finally let go and say our goodbyes, I drive away from Meg's new house feeling lighter than ever before, no longer hiding or running away from a terrible lie.

Today, I'm running toward someone.

When you find love, you chase after it, no questions asked.

If you don't, you'll be living in a perpetual third act breakup instead of finding the happily-ever-after you deserve.

And I've found one of my own.

CHAPTER 50
ELLIOTT

LOREN ISN'T HERE.

I know in my heart it's true before I even get a chance to search the parking lot. She'll have to come back eventually—she is driving my truck, after all—but there's no telling when that will be. A day? A week? A month?

What if she comes back while I'm at work? What if she packs up all her stuff and leaves before I get back and I never see her again?

I climb out of the Jeep, but the thought of going back into the apartment seeing that Loren isn't there—or worse, finding all her shit packed up and gone—makes my chest feel like it's collapsing in on itself.

Rationally, I know she wouldn't have had the time to pack everything up, but we're past being rational.

Instead, I sit on the bottom stair and wait.

Why didn't I just tell her the truth from the beginning? It seems like such a stupid thing to hide now. She probably wouldn't have even batted an eye.

But here's the thing with secrets: the longer you keep them, the bigger they grow, until they feel insurmountable.

My eyes sink closed, and I tip my face up to the blazing sun, contemplating every single thing I've done wrong. And let me tell you, that list is *long*.

If there's one good thing to come from this, it's that my mom actually texted to apologize for meddling in my affairs, saying she only wanted to see me happy.

I told her I was happy—happier than I've been in a long time.

Thanks to this lie, that's all over.

I hear the familiar rumble of my truck before I see it. When Loren pulls into a parking spot way down the lot with no cars nearby, I smile.

Then she climbs out, and my heart starts to ache.

She doesn't walk, she runs, straight across the pavement. I push unsteadily to my feet and catch her in my arms, getting a mouthful of curls in the process. I don't even care if she chokes me so long as she never lets go.

"I thought you weren't coming back," I confess with a broken sigh, my eyes starting to burn.

Her arms squeeze me a little tighter, her words muffled from her face still being buried in my chest. "What kind of monster would I be to leave a man with abandonment issues?"

"I don't have—"

She peers up at me, her eyes hidden behind the golden lenses on her sunglasses. Even so, I can see the smile twitching on her lips. "Fine. I have abandonment issues as big as the Grand Canyon." Now she knows and she isn't running away. She's still holding onto me as tightly as I'm clinging to her. "I kept thinking about coming home and finding all your stuff packed up." My forehead falls to hers, knocking her sunglasses askew. "I don't want you to leave. I never want you to leave."

"I'm not going anywhere, Elliott. That's not what you do when you love someone."

Love. She said love.

"You love me?"

"Yes, you big idiot." She balls up her fist and punches my shoulder hard enough to make me wince. "But we're fighting so we can talk about it later."

I'd rather talk about it now, because...*holy shit.* Loren loves me.

Loren shoves her glasses onto her forehead, pushing back her curls as well. Seeing her red-rimmed eyes wipes the dopey smile from my face. "I get why you didn't tell me and I'm sorry she left you, but I'm not her."

"No. You're not." Thank God for that.

"But I do think I deserve an explanation."

At this point, I'll give her anything she wants as long as she lets me be her reason to stay.

We sink onto the step, and I tell her the extended version of my story, sparing no details. When I finish, we're both fighting back tears. I don't miss Alice, and it's clear now that we weren't meant for forever, but what we went through really sucks. Saying it out loud is like reliving the shit all over again.

"When we separated, I thought maybe she'd change her mind and come back," I explain. "So I sort of just existed for the first year. Then, when it was clear that she wanted nothing to do with me, I thought I'd try to make up for lost time by sleeping with anyone who was interested. All that was fine, but the moment you get off, that's it. There's no connection, nothing deeper." I enjoy sex, but I'm not just looking for sex. I want more. I've always wanted more. "But I thought..."

Loren squeezes my arm, encouraging me to continue.

"I thought that maybe Alice wasn't satisfied with our sex life. I thought if I had some more experience, I'd get better and then if she ever came back to me, she'd realize I could be what she was looking for."

"But she never came back."

"Not until a few months ago."

Loren's soft gasp hits me straight in the heart, but I soldier on. There can be no more secrets between us. No more barriers. "She showed up to my parents' house when I was supposed to stop by. I didn't go in, but I saw her car parked outside. She texted me a couple of times, wishing me Happy New Year, asking if we could talk."

"Weren't you curious about what she wanted?"

I shake my head. Maybe a few years ago I would've been, but now? "I didn't care because I was more curious about what *you* wanted."

Although a smile plays at the corner of her lips, she looks impossibly sad. "If you still love her—"

"I don't. Seeing her today only confirmed that. The whole time she was standing there, talking to me, all I could think about was coming to find you. I'm sorry I didn't tell you before, but I didn't want to scare you off." Saying it out loud sounds so silly now. "You thought I had an aversion to commitment when it's just the opposite. I don't need to know if the grass is greener in anyone else's pants." My lips twitch when I repeat Loren's words from what feels like forever ago back to her. "I have no desire to go looking for something I've already found."

Her head tips back, the sun glistening off her dark curls as her smile slowly blooms into a beautiful grin. "And what is that?"

"A woman I love."

"You're not just saying that to make up for your lie?"

My head shakes as I gather her closer, until her body melts against mine. "I'm saying that because I mean it. Fight with me all you want, Chaos, but love me while you do it."

Her soft lips find mine and she murmurs, "If you insist."

ACKNOWLEDGMENTS

To all my readers who took a chance on this book and fell in love with my unhinged FMC, I'd like to thank you from the bottom of my heart. Without you, these characters in my head would have stayed there.

To my editor, Meg Dailey, thank you for being so flexible and for loving these characters and encouraging me to tell their story to the best of my ability.

To my cover designer Lils, I was SO excited when you agreed to work with me and truly cannot imagine this book with any other cover. Thank you so much for lending your talent to this project. Shall we do it again?

To my amazing beta reader Meg, thank you for hyping this story before anyone else.

To my PA Kelsy, thank you for reading between momming and for helping me behind the scenes to get this book in front of readers.

To every author who agreed to read an unedited version and loved the story enough to offer early praise, it's an honor to be part of this community with you.

Finally, to my husband, thank you for supporting me and believing in me even when this was "just a hobby."

Jenny has been a lover of love stories ever since she picked up her first romance novel one summer vacation with the family. She enjoys breaking readers' hearts and sewing them up by "the end." See that smile on her face? She's secretly plotting her next heartbreaking fantasy romance or romcom that will make you swoon.

ALSO BY JENNY

CONTEMPORARY ROMANCE

(Co-written with Natalie Murray)

STILL SPRINGS

Hating the Best Man

Loving the Worst Man

INNER SHORES

A Shore Thing (2026)

FANTASY ROMANCE

(Written as Jenny Hickman)

BOUND AND FREED

(*Adult Fantasy Romance*)

Bound by Gravity

Freed from Gravity

WILLOWHAVEN ROMANCE

(*Cozy Adult Fantasy Romance*)

For Ever

All Ways

THE MYTHS OF AIRREN

(*Adult Fantasy Romance*)

A Cursed Kiss

A Cursed Heart

A Cursed Love

Prince of Seduction

Prince of Deception

THE PAN TRILOGY

(*YA Sci-Fi Romance with a Peter Pan Twist*)

The PAN

The HOOK

The CROC

www.ingramcontent.com/pod-product-compliance
Lightning Source LLC
Chambersburg PA
CBHW030742310726
48969CB00005B/1291
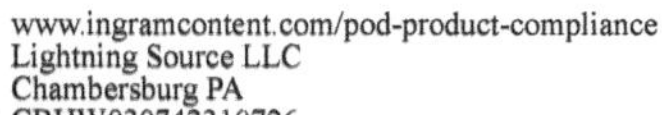